STORIA is a major new antholo
short stories by women that will a
the Spring and Autumn. We will b
best short stories from well-know
writers from Britain and around
dip into at your leisure.

STORIA has a pioneering quality to it too, for alongside brand new stories by major well-known writers, you will find original and innovative work of the highest quality by women who are just embarking on their writing careers. In this first edition we are particularly proud to be publishing two remarkable works of fiction by previously unpublished women writers. Ann Ziety's scrapbook of poems, jokes and stories that form 'The Collected Experiences of Suzi Dishcloth' is hilarious and vividly describes the way that everyday traumas can turn into uncontrollable monsters, while Anne McManus's 'Man of '68' tells the story of an encounter at Rotherham bus station. There is a sensuous, undulating rhythm to her poetry that will haunt you long after you have finished reading it.

Everything published in STORIA is and will be new work – well almost. Daphne du Maurier's 'Happy Christmas' and Janet Frame's 'The Reservoir' have been included because they are simply wonderful stories that are as fresh now as they were when they were written. Read and enjoy.

Kate Figes
Editor

STORIA
1

PANDORA

London
UNWIN HYMAN
Sydney Wellington

First published in Great Britain by Pandora Press in 1988

PANDORA PRESS
Unwin Hyman Limited
15–17 Broadwick Street, London W1V 1FP

Allen and Unwin Australia Pty Ltd
8 Napier Street, North Sydney, NSW 2060, Australia

Allen and Unwin New Zealand Pty Ltd with the Port Nicholson Press
60 Cambridge Terrace, Wellington, New Zealand

British Library Cataloguing in Publication Data

Storia. – 1–
1. Short stories in English.
Women writers, 1945– – Anthologies
823′.01′089287 [FS]
ISBN 0-04-440276-7

Printed in Finland by
Werner Söderström Oy

Contents

STORIA
1

A Daughter Never Forgets

DYAN SHELDON

Dyan Sheldon was born in the USA and now lives in London. She is the author of two novels, *Victim of Love* which was published by Heinemann in 1982 and by Penguin in 1984, and *Dreams of an Average Man* which was published by Heinemann in 1985 and by Penguin in 1986. Her short stories have been included in various anthologies, such as FIREBIRD, LONDON TALES, and WINTER CRIMES.

Helen is leaning against the freezer, at about the point where the Black Forest gâteau meets the onion rings, wondering if some sorbet might not go well with the ginger cake for Sunday lunch. The nice thing about shopping late on a Friday night is that the supermarket is almost empty, its aisles free of whining children, always getting in the way, and old ladies with their trolleys, always sticking packets of chicken in your face, 'Excuse me, love, but can you read the price? I can't see with my eyes.' Although it is also true that it is sometimes difficult to get chicken wings or soured cream on a Friday night, this small inconvenience is more than made up for by the fact that you can be in and out in the time it takes to wait on a Saturday morning queue. Helen, whose life is a busy one, doesn't like to waste time, doesn't like to make trivial tasks the focus of an entire day. She is not a housewife, after all.

She has just ticked off the words 'dessert Sunday?' on her list and is about to reach for the tub of orange sorbet when a voice directly behind her says, 'Don't you think those chocolate eclairs look good? They were always my favourite. Remember?' Helen prides herself on being a calm, in-control person. She is a woman who does not scream when spiders suddenly swing into her hair, who does not sit up all night clutching the garden spade because she heard a strange noise in the kitchen, who does not blanch or turn to tears when shouted at by angry men. Nonetheless, the sudden proximity of another person when she thought she was alone makes her jump. She turns around, prepared to smile and make a little joke, you certainly startled me, hahaha – but there is no one there. Instead, Helen's mother stands at the other end of the cart, stretching for something at the back of the freezer. She looks as though she is about to dive in. She is wearing a grey skirt, a light pink blouse and, because it is a cool evening, a handknitted grey cardigan with mother-of-pearl buttons and a grey tweed jacket, Marks and Spencers. No one ever accused Helen's mother of not being a neat dresser.

The smile sets on Helen's lips. Trying not to show her confusion, she looks around. Further down the aisle two young men unpack boxes of toilet roll and kitchen towelling; on the other side of the freezer, their backs to her, a young couple nuzzle each other as they select a salad dressing. Slowly, slowly, Helen begins to ease the cart along, sidling past the Oriental Style Vegetables and the minted peas, reminding herself what a long day she's had. By the time she has rounded the corner where the jam roly polys and the puff pastry lie, she is feeling confident enough to look back. Of course there is no old woman with curls as tight as rosebuds, support stockings and practical shoes rising triumphant from the arctic depths of the freezer with a packet of eclairs in her hand. There is no one there at all. Although there are still three things on Helen's list that are unticked – Dijon mustard, coffee beans and honey – she skips the last two aisles and walks snappily past the drinks and wines and straight to checkout number one. She glances back once as she unloads her basket, but there is no ghost charging around the corner by the pasta, calling her name.

Helen has already put the groceries in the boot and is slipping into the driver's seat when she realizes that her mother is in the car. The old lady's arms are folded across her chest, her head rests against the window, as though she's been dozing. 'Took you long enough,' she says as Helen, unable to think of anything else to do, shuts the door and presses down the lock. 'You always were a dawdler, though.

Remember how long it used to take you just to clear the table or to get home from school?'

Helen snaps her seat belt in place. If she doesn't look at her mother it is almost the same as though she isn't there. Helen's father ignored her for most of the twenty-seven years of their marriage and it worked well enough for him. 'You have to strap up,' Helen says sharply, slipping the key into the ignition. 'It's the law now.'

Mrs Eliot touches the black rayon harness as though it is a bull whip. 'Put this on?' she asks, a woman who never went out without her girdle, who made her twelve-year-old daughter wear a back brace for her posture, who was often heard in loud support of law and order. 'Lock myself in? Tie myself down?'

The engine rumbles. 'It's the law,' Helen repeats, her voice conjuring up dungeons and stiff fines, rubber truncheons and handcuffs.

'Don't be ridiculous,' says Helen's mother, never one to ask a question because she intended to listen to the answer. 'They wouldn't put me in jail for something like that.'

'Suit yourself,' says Helen, and they pull into traffic.

'Did you signal?' asks her mother, bracing her feet against the floor of the car, the way she always did. 'Do you know what the speed limit is? Did you remember to turn on the lights?'

When Helen was little she and her mother were always together. Helen's mother would wheel the heavy, stand-up hoover through the house, and Helen would follow with her Little Miss carpet sweeper, going vroom vroom vroom. Helen's mother would kneel at the edge of the garden, digging and clipping and wrenching out of the earth, and Helen would kneel beside her with her tin pail and shovel, not allowed to do anything lest she do the wrong thing. In the afternoon they would go to the park, where Helen's mother never sat in a herd with the other mothers and Helen almost always played by herself. She held her mother's hand as they walked down the street and cried when her mother yelled at her for doing anything wrong. It was Helen's mother who bathed her, who washed her hair, who took splinters out of her fingers, who put iodine on her wounds, who taught her right from wrong, who explained the world. Sometimes Helen's mother would tell her stories about the family. Helen would sit on the red step-stool in the kitchen, her hands folded in her lap if she wasn't doing something useful like shelling peas, and her mother would talk as she sliced or stuffed or stripped or dried the glasses till they shone like bubbles. Helen's grandfather, Bill, appeared frequently in these stories, handsome but unreliable, adventurous but a wastrel, a lover of children and stray animals but a bad husband; famous for the time he got drunk and fell down the hill with the doll's house from Germany, even more famous for the time he got drunk and set the flat on fire. But the central character of most of the stories was Helen's grandmother, the beautiful and doomed Victoria, who turned down proposals the way other girls turned down the collars on their coats, who could have married into money and position, but who, instead, married badly and for love. 'Oh, she was in love with him all right,' Helen's mother would say, running her cloth over the top of the stove, no spots or spills permitted to linger in her home. 'He was older than her, of course. He'd been married before, but she died. It was then he took to the drink.'

'And was he in love with her?'

'Of course he was,' Helen's mother would say, ringing the cloth in detergent and warm water and hanging it to dry as soon as she was done with it. 'All the men were in love with her. She had the face of an angel. Once an artist wanted to paint her. But she wasn't that type of woman, of course.'

'And were they happy?'

'Happy?' Helen's mother would ask, as though puzzled by the word. 'Well, I guess they were as happy as most.'

Helen turns the car into her street. The sight of the neat rows of two-storey houses with their tiny front gardens and tiled entranceways nearly makes her dizzy with relief. She parks between the blue Ford of the publisher next door and the dented orange Mini of the clockmaker down the street.

'Well,' says her mother, 'and how much does a place like this cost nowadays?'

In Helen's garden the shrubs are thick and green and the lobelia is in bloom. Over Helen's front door the house number shines pearly white amid flowers of coloured glass. In Helen's front window a fat ginger cat squats between potted plants, its eyes like tiny lights of welcome. Helen's heartbeat begins to slow down. She is home – and she is safe. Nothing has changed. The street has not changed, she has not changed, her home has not changed, time itself has stayed in place.

'Wait a minute,' says Helen's mother as Helen slams out of the car and trots around to get the shopping out of the back. 'Wait a minute, Helen. I can't get this thing unfastened.'

But Helen doesn't care. All the way home, while her mother directed her driving and chatted on about people and places Helen has long forgotten, Helen kept telling herself that the old woman was no more than a hullucination. Brought on by stress. Brought on by the beginning of term pressures; by the return of the doctoral student who had been so upset by her criticisms of his draft thesis that he broke the glass in the door of her office, banging it behind him; by, perhaps, the recent news, told to her by chance, 'Oh, Helen, of course I thought you must've heard,' that Will's new girlfriend has not only left her husband and moved in with him but that she is pregnant as well. And all the way home Helen's mother periodically interrupted herself to say, 'I'm sure I could do with a nice cup of tea after this,' fervently clutching the seat belt Helen had finally fastened for her as they took the turns a little sharply, swerved around parked cars and obstacles in their path just a little too severely.

Helen swings the carrier bags out of the boot, shuts and locks the door, and heads for the house. Once inside everything will be all right. She is a mature and intelligent adult person, a free agent. She does not have to unsnap her mother from the car, does not have to take her into the house and make her tea, does not have to fix her a bed on the convertible sofa. Helen's mother, dead now for over fifteen years, was an unloving, unpleasant and hateful bitch when she was alive, cold and unsympathetic, owed nothing. Even if she has forgotten that fact, Helen has not. Helen is not about to start taking responsibility for the old bag now.

Helen's mother bangs on the window as she rushes past. 'Helen, Helen. Helen, aren't you going to help me out?'

Helen turns at the gate. The small, pale face, pressed against the window of the car, stares back at her. Helen's neighbour, coming down the pavement with his dog, gives them both a curious look. Helen relents. She goes back to the car, opens the door, unfastens the faulty belt, and hauls the old lady out by her arms.

'Thank you, dear,' says Helen's mother, holding on to her for just a second. 'You know I was never any good at mechanical things. And now, of course, I don't have the strength in my hands. You remember about my arthritis, don't you?'

Helen picks up her bags in silence.

'Would you like me to help you with those, dear, if they're not too heavy?' asks her mother, following her through the small iron gate and up the concrete path. 'Shall I hold them while you get your keys out?'

'No,' shouts Helen, her voice enormous in the domestic quiet of the night. 'Just leave me alone, will you? Just leave me in peace.'

The door opens, the light goes on, and Helen steps into the living room – followed closely by her mother.

Helen's mother has never seen Helen's flat before. Helen used part of the proceeds from the sale of her parents' house for the down payment, the rest she spent on travel. From the time of her widowhood until her own death, one of Helen's mother's favourite topics of conversation was 'How Much My Possessions Are Worth' – the silver, the good dishes, the heavy, old-fashioned furniture, the crystal, her fur coat and her collection of china birds. She would call once a week to advise Helen on how to proceed after her death. 'You will remember that that punch bowl has been in the family for three generations, won't you, Helen?' 'You will remember what I taught you about caring for the furniture, won't you? They don't make pieces like that any more.' 'Things things things!' Helen would shout down the receiver. 'That's all you ever think about – things!' When Helen's mother died, there was a ten-page letter, written by hand, itemizing every object in the house, its history, maintenance and probable value.

'Well,' says the old lady, looking around. Helen's flat is small but busy. There are plants in baskets and pottery containers, books along the walls, prints, hangings, photographs and mirrors covering every available inch of space, wooden parrots peeking through the foliage and hand-woven rugs on the floors. 'Well, I guess you didn't have much room for my things.'

Helen takes the groceries through to the kitchen. She sold everything in her mother's house to the nearest dealer, keeping only the photo albums, personal papers and the four Chinese bowls, never used, that she herself had given her mother one Christmas. She certainly hadn't wanted anyone to think that her mother's taste was hers, that inside Helen, sophisticated, respected and successful professional woman, lurked any shades of Viola Eliot, rigid, frigid and provincial philistine.

'Well,' says her mother, searching through the open shelves of brightly painted bowls and cups and plates for her own mother's rose bowl and the crystal vases, 'you certainly have some very colourful things. Most unusual.'

Helen opens the refrigerator, puts away the milk and the yoghurt, the butter and a wedge of low-fat cheese. 'I travel a lot,' she says.

'Oh, do you,' says her mother, staring up at the woven baskets on the top shelf. 'Isn't that nice. I always wanted to travel, you know, but of course it wasn't possible. I had too many responsibilities. First your grandmother, and then your father and you. You can't gad about the world when you've got a family.'

Helen stacks the cat food under the sink with a grunt. The only places her mother ever showed any interest in visiting were the local church, the local beauty salon and the local cinema, infrequently. Once Helen's parents went to Paris for a weekend, but they came back a day early, disgusted by the lack of decent food and the preponderance of foreigners. Her mother distrusted the world outside, with its sin and its unpleasant details, its diseases and its disasters, that place where anything could happen and almost certainly would. Helen stands up, kicking the cabinet door shut with a sigh. 'Well, you're making up for it now,' she says.

Helen's parents had no friends, no clubs, no hobbies, no outside interests like boat racing or foreign films to lure them from their home, but every Sunday they went for a drive after dinner, weather permitting. Helen's parents would sit in the front seat of the car, her father with his elbow out of the window, whistling to himself, her mother beside him with her folded hands and her purse on her lap, complaining about the heat or the cold, the distance or the condition of the road, the speed or her husband's inability to control the behaviour of other drivers. Helen would sit in the back, her eyes on the gentle monotony of the passing landscape, forbidden to move around or make any loud noises in case she distracted her father and they ended up in a ditch. She often wondered what other families did for fun. Where had they gone on all those drives, her father mumbling about the price of petrol and her mother grumbling about the state of public toilets? What had they done when they got there? Helen's mother had strict rules for conduct outside of the house as well as in. One was not allowed to do anything that might get one dirty or sweaty, one was not allowed to talk to strangers, one was not allowed to eat on the street, one was not allowed to sit on toilet seats, one was not allowed to order anything in a restaurant that could be heated up, one was not allowed to waste money on nonsense, on junk. If one was Helen's father there were additional rules to be followed: no smoking in the car, no driving too fast, no sneaking off to buy your daughter some forbidden sweet or to put her on some dangerous ride while her mother's back was turned, no drinking so much as half a pint of lager while in charge of an instrument of death. Given all that, there were not many places they could go, little they could do when they'd arrived. Helen can remember once going to some seaside town on a chill winter afternoon, standing against the railing between her parents. Her father, silent and distant, stared out across the water and puffed on his cigar. Her mother, bundled in her sheared beaver coat, talked against the squawking of the gulls about some man she'd read about in the paper who ran off to Brighton with his secretary, his wife's body wrapped up in plastic bags in one of the pieces of his matching luggage. 'It's much better to visit those places at this time of the year than in the summer when they're so crowded,' said Helen's mother on the way home. 'What with all those germs and the sand and everybody undressing. We wouldn't want Helen catching polio or something like that, would we?'

Helen always gets up at nine o'clock on Saturday mornings. She doesn't like to waste the day. She has come a long way from her parents' life – from their immaculate rooms and good manners and predictable expectations – but not by lying in bed till noon. There have been times, of course, when there was a man around, when she did lie in bed until an indecent hour – but there is no man around now. No one to say, oh, Helen, come back to bed, oh, honey, just one more hug, oh, baby, have a heart, we don't have to get up yet. No one to disrupt her schedule, demand or expect things from her, tell her what to do. She has known too many women who acquired boyfriends or husbands lose touch with their friends, retire from their own lives; become mothers and vanish from the earth, surfacing every once in a while bearing nappy bags, stained blankets, changes of tiny T-shirts and overalls and carrier bags of food, not on an afternoon's visit but on a pilgrimage, having nothing to talk about but child development and visually interesting toys, the wonders of the world narrowed down to a querulous creature that cries all the time and pukes on the rug.

On this Saturday morning, Helen wakes slowly, crawling out from a bad dream. She puts on her dressing gown and slippers, as she always does, folds the duvet away and covers the bed with its patchwork spread, as she always does, opens the blind and looks out on her back garden, as she always does. Lying in a patch of sunlight on the grass, the cat stretches. For a few minutes it is possible for Helen to believe that last night never happened.

When Helen enters the kitchen she goes straight to the sink to fill the kettle, turning her back on the old woman in the fluffy pink dressing gown who stares after her, blinking like a toad in the friendly morning light.

'I couldn't find any tea bags,' says her mother, humbly, tentatively, as though afraid of being shouted at. 'And I would have fixed myself a piece of toast, but I couldn't find the toaster.'

Helen's mother was always one for labour-saving devices. Laziness, Helen's father called it, telling of his own mother's constant cleaning and cooking for her husband and her six sons, with narry a complaint or anything more helpful than a broom or a rolling pin. Practicality, Helen's mother called it, filling her kitchen with pressure cookers, toasters, electric knives and mixers and skillets, the first on her street to champion frozen food. Keeping up with the neighbours, Helen called it, conspicuous consumption, cheap distractions for an empty mind. Helen bakes her own bread, bones her own chicken, owns two woks and a clay oven and a samovar but no toaster, no electric chip fryer, no convenience foods.

'I don't use tea bags,' says Helen, her voice not rising above the running water. 'And I don't have a toaster. You have to use the grill.' Though normally the most considerate of hostesses, she does not offer to make a pot of tea or a plate of toast. She turns off the tap and puts the kettle on the stove. There is no sound but the striking of the match, the fizzle as the flames hit the water at the bottom of the kettle, the beating of Helen's own steady heart. When she turns around at last, her mother is still at the table, her watery blue eyes upon Helen, a childish, hopeful smile making her mouth look unnatural, as though she has borrowed it from someone else. The expression on Helen's face is a groan. 'I suppose you'd like some breakfast,' she says, looking at something behind her mother's head.

'That would be lovely, dear.'

'I only have brown sugar and low fat milk,' warns Helen.

'That's fine, dear,' says her mother, for all the world as though she has always been reasonable, always been just. 'All I want is a nice cup of tea. And maybe just a slice of toast.'

Helen's cupboard holds camomile, Lapsang Soushang, jasmine, Earl Grey, Keemun, orange and green teas, each in its own attractive, air-tight tin.

'Don't you have any regular tea?' asks Helen's mother, still smiling. 'Just plain old tea?'

Helen's bread bin holds two loaves, wholemeal with seeds and nuts and extra wheatgerm and sourdough, heavy as bricks.

'Don't you have any regular bread?' asks Helen's mother. 'My teeth aren't what they once were, you know.'

Helen slaps the slices on to the grill tray, slams the Earl Grey down on the counter. Was there ever a time when her mother wasn't trying to make her feel guilty about something, wasn't trying to make her feel that she was a disappointment, short of the mark? Helen's mother had blamed her for being born and causing her pain, for not appreciating all the sacrifices she had made for Helen and causing her pain, for not being the person she had wanted her to be and causing her yet more pain, for never marrying the man of Viola Eliot's dreams and therefore breaking her heart. When her parents flew home from their aborted weekend in Paris Helen was even made to feel guilty for not picking them up at the airport. 'But I don't have a car,' Helen had argued. 'I don't know how to drive.' Her mother had been less than forgiving; a good daughter would have learned.

'You don't have to have anything if you don't want it,' says Helen. 'But don't take it if you're only going to waste it.'

'Oh, no, dear,' says her mother hastily. 'That'll be fine.'

Helen turns the toast.

Helen pours hot water into the pot, swishes it around, pours it into the sink.

Helen's mother takes the top off the sugar bowl, puts it back on.

'I don't suppose you have any preserves, do you dear? Black-currant or cherry?'

'Oh, for God's sake,' snaps Helen. 'I can't do everything at once, you know.'

'Remember that plum jam we always used to get in the summer when we went to visit your Aunt Laura?' asks Helen's mother, her voice so soft and intimate she might be trying to sell Helen something. 'They always had their church fair that week and I'd buy half a dozen jars, all homemade. Remember? Remember how delicious it was? We always used up the first three jars in no time at all and then we'd have to make the rest last till the next summer. Remember? You used to love it spread on digestives for tea.'

Helen fairly bounces three small jars on to the table. What she remembers from those weeks with her aunt – the only holidays they ever took, her father too busy to come along – was the two sisters whispering in corners, their eyes always on her, their fingers always pointing at her, stand up, go out, don't do that, don't wear that in public, watch what you say, worrying together about what the neighbours might be thinking every minute of the day.

'Didn't we have good times then? Remember how we used to play that game in the evenings, what was it called, the one where you make up words. . . .'

And sometimes on those holidays, late at night, Helen would hear the sound of crying down the hall, her aunt still weeping for the husband tortured to death by the Japanese all those years before. Her mother was never known to cry.

'Scrabble,' says Helen, and slams the teapot down on to the table.

'That's it,' says her mother happily. 'Scrabble. I really enjoyed that, didn't you?'

Helen flips over the toast, pours water over the coffee in the filter, unhooks two mugs from the rack on the wall. How she had hated those games. She can see the three of them seated around the old folding card table so vividly that they might still be there – Laura and Viola, their brows furrowed in competitive concentration, their hands poised to whip open the dictionary at any suspect word, counting their scores up like misers counting up coins, smiling their kindly little smiles, oh, too bad Helen, you almost reached that triple word score, oh, good try, Helen, but you can't spell 'surprise' with a z, hahaha; Helen scowling, sitting hunched over her tray, slipping vowels into her socks in the hopes that it might hurry up the play. 'It's only a game,' her mother would say whenever Helen lost. But on the rare occasions when she herself didn't win she would throw the pieces back into the box, her smile as hard as the Rock of Gibraltar, 'Well, of course you won, Laura, I had nothing but consonants, did I?' When they weren't playing Scrabble they were playing cards or Chinese checkers or Mah Johng, the sisters slapping down their tiles so quickly and so urgently that it sounded less like the happy hopping of sparrows than the murderous marching of troops. As far as Helen is concerned, her mother never enjoyed anything except making everyone else miserable.

'Yes,' says Helen, her voice as personal as a time tone. 'It was fun.'

'I was always after your father to play,' says Helen's mother, almost wistfully, 'but he didn't like games, not word games at least. I used to look so forward to those two weeks with Laura.'

The cat pads into the room, ready for breakfast.

'Oh, look,' says Helen's mother, 'a cat,' and leans over to scoop it up on to her lap. 'What a beautiful puss,' she coos, rubbing behind its ears. 'And whose lovely cat are you?' The cat closes its eyes, lifts its chin and begins to purr.

Helen plonks the plate of toast on the table. As a child she was never allowed a pet. Birds carried diseases, fish died too easily, cats shed all the time and ruined the furniture, dogs had fleas and might suddenly turn.

'I thought you didn't like cats,' says Helen.

'I don't know what ever gave you that idea,' says Helen's mother. 'I've always loved animals. I always used to bring home the strays when I was a girl. It was your father who didn't want pets. He had all those allergies. Don't you remember?'

Helen stares across the table at the sweet old woman and the happy cat. What she remembers about her father is that he was always busy, but that when he was around he never yelled at her about her grades or her manners or her poor complexion or for breaking some hidden rule. As distant, as preoccupied, as he always was, there was an alliance between them, a bond. They had private jokes, secret looks, unspoken understandings – Helen's mother knew they all concerned her.

'No,' says Helen, raising her coffee mug to her lips. 'No, I don't remember that at all.'

Helen's mother's eyes are on the cat, now sprawled across her warm pink robe. 'That doesn't surprise me,' she says. 'You always did have a selective memory.'

The only times Helen remembers seeing her parents kiss or embrace was on occasions such as Christmas and her mother's birthday. Then her father would solemnly hand Viola his present (a nightgown, a slip, or a handbag) and lean over to give her a peck on the cheek. Aside from that, they never touched – unless by accident, the brushing of an arm against an arm as her mother put the dinner on the table or her father helped her on with her coat. There were no quick hugs or touches in the Eliot home, no kisses sticky with lipstick or scented by her father's small cigars, not even for the tiny Helen, whose hand was only held when crossing streets or when she was liable to get lost in a crowd. Helen never heard the squeaking of springs or the whispers of intimates coming from her parents' ice-white room, never saw them so much as dance together, doesn't remember ever being held in their arms. Helen often heard her father laughing with a customer over some joke or anecdote in the shop, but he never laughed with Helen's mother. He never told her stories or winked at her the way he winked at his female customers, they giggling back, oh, Mr Eliot, you are a one – the way he sometimes winked at Helen. It was Helen's mother who kept the books for the shop, who wrote the letters that Helen's father signed. 'My silent partner,' he would call her, and throw Helen a wink. 'My silent partner. Only she's never that silent.' 'You two think you're funny,'

Helen's mother would say, catching the look that flashed between them, the stifled grins. 'But you'll be laughing out of the other side of your faces some day. Life is a serious matter. It's not a joke.' After Helen's father died, Helen's mother talked about him all the time, bringing him into every conversation. 'Your father always liked his salmon fresh,' 'Your father never approved of those explicit movies,' 'Your father wouldn't have liked all these new gadgets,' 'Your father never could stand that Tony Benn.' 'For God's sake,' Helen would shout, 'the man is dead. Can't you leave him in peace?' 'You don't wipe out nearly thirty years of marriage just like that,' Helen's mother would snap back. 'You don't forget somebody just because they're dead.'

On Saturday night, Helen goes to a party at a friend's house. The friend teaches at the college with Helen, the husband is a psychotherapist. There are a lot of academics, psychologists and psychiatric social workers at the party, as well as a scattering of actors, writers and painters, most of whom Helen guesses to be clients of the psychologists and social workers.

Helen hates parties. She is shy in social situations, awkward in groups of strangers unless they're students. When she was younger she went to parties partly in a spirit of hope – perhaps she would make a friend, meet a man, strike up an acquaintance with someone who might be useful to her career – and partly because she wanted to have a good time, to be like the girls at school who never had to eat alone, or go to a film alone, or holiday by themselves, to be popular, 'Oh, don't forget to invite Helen.' Now she goes because if she stops going people will stop inviting her – and then she will turn into her mother, friendless and isolated, uninteresting to everybody but herself.

Helen spends an hour or two wandering from one genial cluster to another, her wine glass in her hand and a pleasant, interested expression on her face. Every time she catches one of the psychotherapists looking at her, even if it is clear that she or he wants Helen to pass the crudités and cheese dip, she wonders if something about her has been noticed, if she has given some sign that she may be losing her mind. When she isn't worried about that, she is worried about what her mother is doing back home. She has no trouble imagining the old lady climbing up to the top shelves of the cupboard, searching through the bureaus and the desk, running her finger along the door sills, holding a glass or a dish up to the light. Helen is listening to a conversation on schizophrenic behaviour and its societal roots when she has such a clear image of her mother diving into the dresser in her bedroom and coming up with a stack of photograph albums, old letters and Helen's diaphragm, joy and horror making her face shine, that she stands up suddenly and fairly bolts from the room.

Helen jumps two red lights and narrowly misses hitting a dog on the drive home; parks the car and races down the street as though she's being pursued. When she finally reaches her house, she drops her key twice and accidentally rings the upstairs bell before she manages to get inside.

Her mother is sitting in the living room, watching some old movie on the television, the cat asleep beside her, its head on her lap. Her hair is up in metal curlers and covered with a pink snood. A cup of tea and a plate of custard creams that couldn't have come from Helen's kitchen sit on the coffee table, on top of three back issues of *Daedalus* and a new novel Helen is reviewing for a university journal. She is shrieking with laughter as Helen enters the room. 'I saw this film with Tommy Savage right before the war,' she gasps, wiping the tears from her eyes. 'We laughed ourselves silly.'

Helen knows that her mother rarely went to the cinema – foolishness, she always called it, a waste of money and time. Just as she knows that her mother never sat in the back row with some cocky young man, her head on his shoulder and exuberance in her heart. 'Tommy who?' asks Helen.

'Savage,' says her mother, leaning forward to take up her cup. 'Tommy Savage,' and smiles so sweetly that she might almost be a girl again, full of romance and dreams.

Helen watches her sip her weak and milky drink. For some reason, it never occurred to her before that her mother might have dated anyone but her father. They were so unsuited for each other that it seemed impossible that it could have been a matter of choice. She was so obsessed with the details of domesticity that it seemed impossible that she had ever thought of love – a woman who irons her sheets is unlikely to be all that passionate when lying on them.

'What happened to him, then, this Tommy?' asks Helen, her eyes on the monochrome screen. 'Was he killed in the war or something?'

'Oh, he was something, Tommy Savage,' says her mother, watching the same scene Helen is watching, the brash, spunky young heroine leaning down from the branches of a tree to hear what the villains are plotting. 'He was as handsome as they come. He drank too much, though, and he had a wife in Cornwall. My mother didn't approve. Because of my father, you see. You couldn't blame her. But he was a charmer, Tommy Savage. A real charmer.' She breaks a biscuit in half, scattering crumbs. 'Look at how young they all look, Helen. Why, you'd think it was only yesterday.'

'Would you have married him if he hadn't been killed?' Helen persists, still standing in the doorway, her jacket on, her bag dangling from her hand.

'Oh, he wasn't killed,' says her mother, dunking her half a biscuit into her tea. 'My mother sent him away. She didn't want me to go through what she'd gone through, you know, so she sent him away.'

Helen stares at her, transfixed. In the twenty-five years she knew her mother, she never once dunked a biscuit into her tea. She never once set her own hair. She watched television only for educational programmes and what she considered historic broadcasts. She certainly never mentioned other men. 'Why didn't you go with him?' Helen asks in a whisper. 'If you loved him, why did you listen to her?'

'Oh, I couldn't go with him,' says Helen's mother. 'My mother was all alone. She depended on me. I couldn't have gone against her, not when she was acting for my own good. And anyway,' she adds, her mouth hidden behind her cup, 'if I'd gone with Tommy Savage I'd never have met your father.'

'But—' begins Helen.

'And what about you?' asks her mother, wiping her mouth on the sleeve of her dressing gown. 'Why didn't you get married? Didn't you want a family? Were you too good for them all?'

Helen's mother always impressed on her that the worst thing a woman could be was common. Common people laughed at crude jokes, talked too loudly, discussed their private lives in public, wore curlers in the house and wiped their mouths on their sleeves after dunking biscuits in their tea. 'You've been snooping through my things!' Helen screams, forgetting that only common women lose their tempers, talk back to their mothers. 'I knew it! I knew I couldn't leave you alone! You've been going through my things! You've been prying into my life!'

Helen's mother is as calm as water in a bathtub. 'You still haven't answered my question,' she says. 'Didn't you want any children? Did you want to be all on your own?'

On the screen, the undauntable heroine speeds through the night in a murderous storm to rescue the hard-bitten reporter she loves. Helen's purse drops to the floor.

'Sometimes when I was young,' her mother continues, 'I used to imagine being a career girl, you know. Sharing a flat with two or three other girls and working in an office and doing what I pleased. There were always girls like that in the movies, especially in America. They always seemed to have such a good time. Of course, by the end of the film they'd always found someone to love. You know, someone handsome and considerate and with a good sense of humour. Someone like Clark Gable or Spencer Tracy. They never ended up all by themselves. Or married with a broken heart.'

The last time Helen's mother saw her cry was when Helen was seven and the neighbour's dog tried to rip off her upper lip. 'Why don't you leave me alone?' Helen sobs. 'I'm happy, for God's sake. Can't you see that I'm happy? You lived your life the way you wanted. Let me live mine the way I want.'

'That's it,' says her mother, her voice as gentle as a caress. 'You cry. It's always the best thing. I used to cry all the time. I cried for years.'

'No you didn't,' sobs Helen. 'No you didn't, you never cried, you unfeeling bitch. You never cried at all.'

The cat opens one eye to stare at Helen for a second, then closes it again. 'That just shows how much you know,' says Helen's mother, 'you with all your brains.'

Every now and then Helen's father would take her with him on one of his business trips, out of the neat predictability of the suburbs and into the cramped unrest of the city. The journeys themselves were not exciting – Helen was left for hours in the car on her own, eating crisps and reading *The Beano*, staring out at the backs of warehouses or the fronts of shabby homes – but being away from her mother for an afternoon was. Sometimes, on the way home, he would take her to a café for tea, buying her cream buns and orange squash and ice cream with whipped cream and strawberry sauce, winking at her as she scooped a spoonful into her mouth. 'This will just be our little secret, love. No need to get your mother all upset.' Once, in the summer, he took her to a pub for lunch, and they sat outside at a picnic table eating sausages and chips. Instead of orange, her father ordered her ginger ale with a cherry, just like one of those American cocktails. The barmaid brought it out to her herself, carrying it in front of her on a tray, laughing with Helen's father, 'She's got something of you around the eyes, Art.' Several men came over to talk with her father, clapping him on the shoulder as though they were war buddies, slipping her a coin or a sweetie or a packet of crisps. That evening, just as her mother opened the door to greet them, Helen threw up on the rhododendrons, her mother screaming, 'What have you been feeding that child? What have you been up to?', shaking Helen by her shoulders, 'You tell me the truth. What have you been doing all afternoon?', Helen and her father saying together, 'It's nothing. Just carsickness,' nothing at all. He never took her with him again. 'It's just as well,' said Helen's mother. 'London's no place for a child. Especially a girl.'

While Helen, wearing an old shirt and a pair of jeans, mops the floors of the kitchen and the halls and the bathroom, her mother sits in the living room, the radio on, reading a glossy magazine that has suddenly appeared among the serious periodicals. Today Helen's mother, despite her age and the wintery rain that falls outside, is wearing peddle pushers and a short-sleeved shirt in bold, bright stripes. In one of the old photo albums in the dresser in Helen's room there is a picture of her mother wearing just this outfit, sitting in a row boat with a smile on her face and someone's shadow falling across her arm. Helen doesn't know where the picture was taken, or what her mother was doing there, but now she wonders if the shadow belonged to her father, as she always assumed, or if it belonged to someone else.

Helen is having people over for dinner, a date made weeks ago and with difficulty, impossible to change. As Helen works her way around the flat with her cleaners, her cloths, her broom and her hoover, her mother talks, holding on to her with a string of words. 'What do you think of this?' she asks. '"A university-educated woman of forty or over who is still single has more chance of being killed by a terrorist than of finding a husband." What do you think of that?'

Helen backs in from the hallway, her shoes clamped under her arm, her hands full with the mop and the pail. 'Don't put your feet on the couch,' she scolds. 'And why don't you do something to help me for a change instead of sitting around reading that garbage?'

'Do you know there's even a test in here to see whether or not you're good at living alone,' says Helen's mother, neither moving her feet nor offering to peel the potatoes. 'Maybe you should take it.'

'You've moved the magazines,' says Helen, who only finished with the living room half an hour ago. 'I thought I told you not to move anything. Look what happened when you moved the waste basket in the bathroom,' one soap wrapper, one clump of hair and one tampon wrapper loose on the floor.

'Maybe it's just as well that you never had any children,' says Helen's mother. 'I don't think you have the patience for it.'

'Now look what you've done,' snaps Helen as dirty water sloshes all over the rug.

'Don't shout at me,' says Helen's mother, vanishing behind the magazine. On the cover a young woman with flawless skin and a sunshine smile winks at Helen, confident that everything the world has to offer will be hers.

'I'm not shouting,' shouts Helen, and lifting the pail in her arm breaks through the louvre doors and into the kitchen. When she turns around from throwing the dirty water out of the back door her mother is sitting at the kitchen table, still reading her magazine.

'There's also a quiz you can take to see if you and your boyfriend are compatible,' she says. 'Were you and what's his name compatible?'

'Who?' asks Helen. 'What's whose name?'

'You know who I mean,' says Helen's mother, who had wasted no time finding out who put up the shelves in the living room, who fitted the shower in the bathroom, who gave Helen the charcoal sketch of embracing lovers that hangs in the hall. 'Were you compatible?'

'We had a lot in common,' says Helen evenly, though it is difficult now to imagine what all that was. When she thinks of Will she remembers his socks on the floor of the bedroom, his hairs on the soap, his lousy time-keeping, his fondness for red wine, his ex-wife's hysteria, his lack of discipline about money, his tiresome need for affection, his waking her up in the middle of the night, drunk and weeping, repeating and repeating, 'But I want to be a father again, I want to settle down.'

'What about love?' asks Helen's mother. 'Did you love him? Did he love you?'

'What about you and my father?' asks Helen sweetly. 'Did you love him? Did he love you?'

'Don't be impertinent,' says Helen's mother, turning a page. 'You weren't raised on the street.'

When Helen's father died, her mother called her, her voice firm and strong, no tears. 'You have to stand beside me now,' she shouted into the telephone. 'That's what children are for.' So Helen went home and stood, dressed in a black skirt and a grey blouse, crying gently for the two of them. Her mother made all the phone calls, made all the arrangements, talked to the lawyer, chose the suit and the shirt and the tie and the shoes to bury him in, sorted through his things as though cleaning out the closets in the spring. Helen was surprised at how many people turned up at the funeral parlour to pay their respects, at how gently they spoke to her mother, as though she were bravely hiding her grief. 'Look at all the flowers,' said Helen's mother. 'Look at all the cards.' At the funeral itself there were several people Helen had never seen before, standing to one side, sombre but unfamiliar, dark mourners who might have been there by mistake. 'Who are they?' she asked her mother. Her mother barely allowed them a glance. 'I'm sure I don't know,' she said shortly. 'Your father had a lot of friends I didn't know.' Eventually, Helen's mother sold the car, gave away his suits and his coats and his well-made shoes. But the twin beds in their room were still covered with matching spreads, the wedding picture stayed on the mantel, the ashtray remained on the coffee table, his umbrella was left in the stand. If you didn't look in the driveway or check in the closets there was no way of telling that he wasn't coming back; no way of being sure that he had ever been there at all.

When Helen's mother died, the solicitor arranged everything over the phone. The only other person at the funeral was the next-door neighbour of over twenty years, a woman whose sense of Christian duty had always been strong.

Neither she nor Helen cried. 'She was always proud of you,' said the neighbour, throwing a flower on top of the coffin. 'Because you've done so well, you know. It's a sad business, life.' Yes, life is, thought Helen, finally released from the past by a spadeful of earth – but not death; death had set her free. That night, back at the house in which she'd grown up, she turned on all the lights, left dishes in the sink, emptied whole drawers on to the carpets, ran naked through the rooms, screaming. She'd never felt happier, reborn, whole and unencumbered, at twenty-five. The next morning the neighbour invited her over for a cup of tea. 'Remember when you and your mother and me used to go to the matinées on a Saturday? Remember when you came third in the fancy dress contest?' 'No,' said Helen, looking out of the window over the sink at the window over the sink next door. 'No, I don't remember that at all.'

Helen's mother has dressed for dinner in a neat navy blue dress and a string of cultured pearls. She is anxious about meeting Helen's friends – a professor of English literature, a Russian translator, and a film maker. 'You've never introduced me to your friends before,' she says, standing in Helen's light as she bends to check the meat for doneness. 'I always thought you were ashamed of me.' From somewhere she has got a cigarette, blowing smoke towards Helen's head.

'You never smoked,' snaps Helen. 'Put that damn thing out.'

'It can't hurt me now,' says her mother, shaking ash on to the immaculate floor. 'I need something to steady my nerves.'

Helen is so nervous herself that she has already had a glass of wine. When she was a child she was only rarely allowed to bring friends home, and then for only controlled periods, and only children who had been approved. No friend of hers was ever allowed to stay to supper or to spend the night. When she was older, of course, it was she who never allowed her friends into her parents' home. They were part of her secret self – like the books she read, the music she loved, the dreams she dreamed – part of the real Helen Eliot, the soaring young woman who was no relation to that ice matron Viola with her dusters and her doillies and the arctic in her heart. Once Helen had left home and no longer had to explain her comings and goings to her parents she never mentioned her private life again. Likewise, she never mentioned them to her friends, let everyone assume they were dead and gone long before they were. If hell is a different thing to each of us, then Helen's hell would have been to have her mother suddenly appear at a faculty dinner, her lips as bright as a stop light and her glasses hanging around her neck on a shiny chain, talking about how things used to be in her day, when England still belonged to the English and no one took drugs, or sold women, or abused children, or had sex before marriage, or stole anything from anyone else. Now it looks as though hell has moved in with her.

'What'll I say to these people?' asks Helen's mother, moving out of Helen's light and into Helen's way as she straightens up from the oven. 'I've never been very good at this sort of thing, you know. I've always been rather shy.' She stumbles backwards and treads on the cat. 'I never even finished school. You know that.'

'Sit down,' orders Helen. 'Sit down and shell the peas.'

When the doorbell rings, they both jump. 'I'll get it,' says Helen. 'You just stay where you are.'

But of course Helen's mother doesn't stay where she was. When Helen leads the first arrivals – Barbara, the professor of English, and her husband, Jonathan, the film maker – into the living room her mother is positioned on the sofa by the window, sitting up straight with her hands on her lap and a show-willing smile on her lips, looking as though she's about to meet her bank manager.

'Why, you must be Helen's mother,' says Barbara before introductions can be made. 'I'd recognize you anywhere. What a nice surprise.'

'Let me take your things,' says Helen, tugging at the sleeve of Barbara's jacket.

'Have you come far, then?' asks Jonathan, settling himself on the other couch.

'Not too far,' says Helen's mother.

'White wine or red?' asks Helen, shoving a bowl of taco chips into Jonathan's hands.

Barbara sits down next to the older woman. 'We had no idea you were visiting,' she says. 'Helen should have told us. We could have come another time.'

'Or maybe you'd prefer a gin and tonic or a whisky,' suggests Helen, her smile as bright as a polar ice cap. 'I may even have some sherry.'

'I'd love a sherry,' says Helen's mother.

'Of course,' laughs Helen, turning to Barbara, 'I haven't been able to touch sherry since we saw that Ayckbourn together. Remember?'

'We always used to get a bottle of sherry in for Christmas,' says Helen's mother. 'I always think of it as something special. And of course there's trifle. I liked to make it with peaches and black cherry jelly. But of course it was a long time after the war before we had real cream again.'

Helen tries to steer the conversation towards Jonathan's coming trip to Nicaragua, Barbara's forthcoming book on structuralism, and the seminar she herself has been invited to run on contemporary North and South American fiction in the spring. But when she mentions Central America, her mother brings up Carmen Miranda and Colombian coffee, too strong for her taste. When Helen mentions French literature her mother comments that she personally never liked foreign films because of all those subtitles, and doesn't Barbara agree that the French are rather rude? When Helen mentions fiction, her mother says that she never could understand how people found the time to read made-up stories, don't they have enough to occupy them with real life? what about getting on in the world? what about truth? Helen already has a headache. She can hear that her own voice sounds loud and rushed; that her laughter is about as elastic as steel.

'I don't suppose you two have a family,' Helen's mother says to Barbara, doing some steering of her own. She knocks back her second sherry like a pro. 'Not with you both working, and him gadding all over the world.'

Barbara, who only last night was discussing her biological clock with Jonathan, shoots her husband a clearly significant look and then stares into her wine glass, empty for the second time. 'I always thought I'd like to have children,' she says at last. 'It's funny how things turn out.'

'I know just what you mean,' says Helen's mother. 'I never thought at all about having a family when I was a girl. I'd seen what it did to my mother, you see. All I was interested in was having some fun.'

'It's not that I'm against having kids,' says Jonathan, who isn't; whose two sons live with their mother in Paris and call him Jon. 'But Barbara and I still have time. We don't have to rush into anything.'

'Make hay while the sun shines,' says Helen's mother, her smile a little wobbly, holding out her glass for a refill.

'You shouldn't drink too much on an empty stomach,' warns Helen. 'You were never one for alcohol, you know.'

'Oh leave her be,' says Barbara, filling up her own glass. 'We're having a good time, aren't we Viola?'

While they wait for Ulli, the Russian translator, Jonathan analyses American foreign policy in Central and South America since the nineteenth century for Helen, and Barbara and Helen's mother discuss the rigorous demands of motherhood, the pros and cons of day care centres for young children, the recent upsurge in interesting patterns now available for the home knitter. Helen is less interested in Jonathan's indictment of the United Fruit Company than in monitoring everything her mother says or does or might be thinking. 'Oh, mother,' she says, overhearing her mother say something about 'those feminists'. 'For heaven's sake, mother,' she says, catching the end of a statement on single parenting. 'Mother, please . . .' she hisses, realizing that her mother is wondering out loud why a single woman would want a double bed.

Helen can't understand how Barbara can talk to her mother as though she is a normal, reasonable woman, a person just like everyone else. Barbara herself is intelligent, sophisticated, has taught at Harvard – how can she be interested in Viola's opinion of Winston Churchill? Helen can't understand how Jonathan can let her mother interrupt his important conversation with her remarks about the laziness of people from hot climates and her questions about how often he sees his children, answering her politely and earnestly – as though she is not making a fool of herself, as though what she thinks could possibly matter to him.

By the time Ulli arrives, Helen is almost too drunk to care. 'So this is your mother,' says Ulli, not realizing that Viola has never liked being touched, enfolding her in a generous hug. 'You look quite alike, don't you? It's there, around the eyes.'

'Helen always favoured my side of the family,' says Helen's mother. 'Although, of course, I was much thinner when I was her age. Because of the war.'

Everyone compliments Helen on the excellent meal – the spicy chicken, the aromatic pilau, the tangy salad. 'Of course I never used to use too many seasonings myself,' says Helen's mother, scraping the sauce from her chicken and picking the bits of onion from her rice. 'Because of Helen's father, you know. He had a delicate stomach. Isn't that right, Helen?'

Helen says, 'Um.'

'But I always let Helen help me in the kitchen when she was little. She loved to cook, just like me. Remember, Helen? You always wanted to make apple pie. We even had matching aprons. Remember that? My husband used to say he could hardly tell us apart.'

'Maybe you'd like to pass Jon the salad,' says Helen. 'If you're not going to eat your chicken, then save it for the cat.'

When Helen hears her mother ask Ulli if she has translated what's his name, that man who wrote that Communist book, the one that's like their bible, from Russian into English, she laughs so much she starts to choke. 'Pat her on the back,' commands Viola. 'Lean her forward and pat her on the back.' Jonathan leans Helen forward and pats her on the back. 'You always did rush at your food,' says Helen's mother once Helen has recovered. 'That's why I never let you have fish.'

Over the cognac, Jonathan, perhaps having run out of amusing anecdotes about being robbed in Africa or entertained in Japan or mistaken for a CIA agent in Guatemala, turns to Helen's mother and says, 'You must be very proud of Helen, Mrs Eliot. She's certainly a credit to you.'

Helen can't believe her ears.

Metamorphosis

MIRIAM TLALI

Miriam Tlali was born in Doornfontein in Johannesburg and grew up in Sophiatown. She enrolled as a BA student at the University of the Witwatersrand just before blacks were barred from entering the university and studied African Administration, Psychology, Sociology, History of Art, Zoology and Bantu Languages. She now lives and writes in Soweto. Her first novel *Muriel at Metropolitan* has recently been reissued by Longman in their African Classics series. Her novel *Amandla* was banned in South Africa within six weeks of its publication in 1982. This ban has recently been lifted. She has also written short stories and two plays. 'Metamorphosis' comes from a new collection of short stories, *Soweto Stories*, which is to be published by Pandora in the Spring of 1989.

The narrow street tapered even more towards the west where the sunken sun had left a beautiful golden glow barely visible in the grey smog. Velani noticed the crimson ardour only because he – out of impulse – had decided to remain seated in his Volkswagen Golf. One never really noticed the setting sun's beauty in Soweto. He shut his eyes and tried to listen to the music from the car radio.

He was waiting. He looked around. His car was parked near the gate of house no. 2249. In this township of Mapetla there were no numbers on the doors. They had been erased with white paint. The houses were 'faceless', 'mute' match-boxes, Velani thought smiling. The 'comrades' had done a perfect job of it. It was amazing how these youths thought of everything to befuddle the system. If he had been a stranger and did not know his uncle's house, he would have been completely at a loss as to which one of the rows of similar match-boxes on either side of the dusty road it was. His wife, Mavis, a district nurse, had often spoken of developments in and around the townships but he had never really taken everything seriously. All she said had been just a lot of 'woman-talk'. Even at the spot which he frequented, 'Suzzie's Haunt', people had alluded casually to 'incidents' but he always thought there were more serious matters a man could think of. He recalled that Mavis had once said that it was important for the struggle that 'we be one thing – no one should be labelled "good" or "bad" by the authorities,' that injury to the one must be injury to the next. '"After-all," they say, "we are all black; we all belong to the soil. Besides, we are all oppressed. An attack on the one must be an attack on all."'

Velani tried to listen to the music but the kids in the street were excited. They were frolicking around, jumping and chasing one another. He looked through the window and clicked his tongue loudly. He shut the window and closed his eyes. It was becoming dark and he was sitting there waiting for his mother – affectionately known as Aunt Tilly (for Matilda) – and his sister Tembi. He spoke to himself:

'Waiting . . . "Ngisalindile namanje" I'm still waiting even now. You always have to wait for "abantu bes fazane" you always have to wait for womenfolk. They never seem to get over what they are doing. It doesn't matter whether it's talking, washing their faces, exchanging greetings, even praying. . . . I bet they're on their knees right now, praying "Nkulunkul'olungile-e-e-eyo . . . Nkulunkul' olungile-e-eyo!" ("merciful God . . . merciful God!".') He shook his head vigorously. And this was Friday mind you, he thought regretfully; Friday, the day on which he and the 'MaGents' would normally be 'in conference', enjoying good music, chatting the night away over a c–o–o–l beer.

It was his own fault, Velani thought regretfully. What on earth had made him go via his mother's house anyway? Somehow his dear mother never seemed to hesitate to send him off on one errand or another. On this day, he had tried to dissuade her. He had emphasized, 'You know Ma that I never refuse to drive you "U-Malume", ("Uncle's place"). But *today* . . . it's not safe to drive to Deep Soweto, surely you *know* that Ma. Moreover, travelling there with two "abantubes' fazane" . . . If you were *men*, yes: but "abantubes' fazane"' . . . he shook his head. . . . '"hayi, hayi, hayi."' To which his mother replied,

'But Veli, you rarely ever come except in the late hours. In fact, this time you're early. And you *know* that unless you drive me to U-Malume's place I can never hope to see him. Besides, I don't think I can have a good night's sleep when a message came this morning that your Uncle Bafana is very ill indeed. Who knows what can happen? Even *he* would rush here if he received news that I was on the brink of. . . .' She dared not mention 'Death', no, not her beloved brother Bafana. She had pleaded,

'Please my son, drive me there. Your sister Tembi can help me walk.'

Velani tried to drive his point home. He added, smiling,

'But you three are the ones. . . . Your daughter-in-law Mavis, your daughter Tembi and *you* Ma. . . . You three are the ones always speaking about "ama-'necklace', a-Makabasa, a-ma-'Comrades' yonke lento" and now. . . .' His mother interjected, waving apologetically,

'Veli, Bafana is my own brother, my mother's and my father's only other living child. His end is near; I can feel it. You don't seem to realize that it's only the two of us left now. When he goes, I'll be left alone.'

Tembi, who had been busy in the bedroom, was now standing at the entrance to the dining room, listening and smiling. She anticipated what Velani was going to say and the two were amused. He said,

'Why Ma always says "only the two of us are left" I don't know. Doesn't Ma also have another brother in Eldorado Park? What about *him*? Just the other day I passed at the coloured township with a friend of mine who wanted to have his car panel-beaten by Uncle Boetie – Uncle Mbuti to be correct. Isn't he also your very own mother's and father's son? Why do you always exclude him as if he doesn't exist?'

Aunt Tillie's two children were relieved that in spite of their mother's sadness, there was a smile on her face as she replied,

'You two know the answer to that one. I have told you on many occasions that it is because we all have to remember always to refer to him as Uncle Boetie McCabel and not Mbuti Mkhabela. He does not want to be exposed and known as "unyana ka Mkhabela". ("Son of Mkhabela"). That, as you very well know, would take the bread out of his mouth. In this country, it is only the fairer ones who eat, don't you know?'

The three were now ready to go, Tembi following her brother on whose arm their mother was leaning. As she clung to the strong biceps of her son, Aunt Tillie felt safe and she moved slowly and confidently over the uneven bricks of the pathway leading to the 'Volksie'. When she was seated comfortably on the back seat, Velani took the travelling rug Tembi was holding and tucked it gently around his mother's knees. He smiled into his mother's face. It was a strong, stoic and steadfast face which, to both her children, never seemed to yield to the vicissitudes of life and the inevitable hazards of ageing.

The radio blared away and Velani listened and watched as the red arm on the car-watch ticked the seconds on and on. His boot tapped almost unconsciously to the rhythm of the song and he kept his eyes closed. When the music stopped, he opened his eyes and looked through the windscreen into the thick grey smog which competed with the dotted heaps of garbage, ash and rubbish of every description. The unsightly mounds formed a screen on the narrow end of the road where a short while ago he had watched the rose hue of the setting sun. Velani clicked his tongue again and kept his eyes focused on the faintly illuminated dashboard. The record had stopped. Velani wished that the rather too enthusiastic announcer would stop his remarks and let the bands play on without stopping. He stretched his arm, clicking his tongue once more. He reached for the dial-knob and moved the cord from so-called 'Radio Zulu' to so-called 'Radio Bophuthatswana'. He scoffed loudly,

'These howlers should be fired!'

On 'Radio Bop' a drumming, thumping hit was playing and Velani smiled as he twisted his torso, rolling his eyes dreamily in sheer ecstasy. The boredom he had experienced a while ago seemed to wear away.

When Velani opened his eyes again, the sun had gone completely, leaving the sky dull and murky, with the thick smog hanging as if suspended in mid-air from some invisible 'frame'. He knew that no breeze would clear the dense menace.

It was quite dark outside in the street now, and the people kept passing. Their footsteps were more brisk. Velani could only just make out from their obscure silhouettes whether they were men, women or children. He remembered that it was Friday, and on Friday night people hurry home to the safety of their matchboxes. Only the brave and daring ones remain. The footsteps were awkward and now and again Velani could hear a woman's voice groan 'Ichu-u-u!' as she stumbled, apparently knocking her toes against a stone. The rocky roads had been eroded by the rains into uneven footpaths and the jutting rocks were everywhere, merging with the wire fences on what should have been pavements but were now sloping, irregular 'banks'.

There was a loud thud on the window and Velani started. The knock was so close that it felt like it was from inside his own head. The dark figures on both sides of the car were peering eagerly. A quick glance around made Velani realize at once that the car was in fact completely surrounded by a number of youths. Most of them were wearing 'balaclavas' with brims lowered over their eyebrows. Velani was shaken, but something within him told him that there was no need to fear, that he was not going to be intimidated because he was no Mafikizolo. He switched off the radio and asked furiously, 'What's the matter?'

There were several hard taps on all four side windows, and impatient shouts of,

'Vula, bula, bula!'

'What is it?' Velani repeated.

'Vula, vula! Open the window or we break all of them!'

The youths meant business but Velani was no Mafikizolo. He would not give in to their demands. He looked around and asked,

'Why?' And some of them replied,

'We would like to borrow your car. We have to attend a vigil of one of our boys who was shot dead by the police in Emdeni. Are you going to give us the car or not? Just open and let us in. You can drive us there if you want. Open!'

'No, I won't!' Velani shouted back, determined to hold his ground.

The car rocked uncomfortably on to one side and he felt his stomach fold into a knot. His heart beat faster and the sweat ran down his temples and forehead. There was an even louder chorus from outside:

'Open!'

This was real trouble. Had his ancestors turned their backs on *him*, Velani, who was never a coward? But even if he tried to fight the mob he would never overpower them. They were too many. They were wielding knives, sharp instruments and iron bars. He just could not understand it. The stark, shocking reality of what he had up to then only imagined was happening to *him*; he, Velani, a 'clever' of Soweto. . . . No, it can't. Not to *him*. He shouted stubbornly,

'I won't open!'

Again the car rocked uneasily as if it were resting on foam; and his entrails felt like they were suspended in a jelly-like fluid. He felt sick. What was he to do? According to what he knew, from what he heard from his wife, his mother and his sister, in fact all those who made it their business to attend the people's meetings, no right-thinking 'comrades' would do that, not to *him*. Wasn't he a well-known 'clever' with all the power of a real man? He *had* to be a man. He challenged them,

'Do what you like; I won't open!'

Crash! came the violent sound. Velani looked back and saw that the rear window was now a latticework of broken glass. In the centre was a gaping hole as big as the fist of a full-grown man, where a heavy steel bar had landed. The bloodshot vicious eyeballs of one of the assailants peered at him through the window next to him. He pointed a clenched, menacing fist at Velani, threatening,

'Sizak'nyova thi-ina, grootman uyezwa? Uyacu-u-nga né?'

A whistle . . . a whistle. . . . If only he could sound a loud SOS. Call someone, everybody, anybody to come to his assistance. Had his mother, his sister, his wife, all those who attended 'the people's meetings' not warned him to carry a whistle wherever he went? And *that*, he thought, was only 'womantalk' . . . sheer cowardice. But now he had to act. His life, his beloved 'Volksie'. . . . All these thoughts raced through his mind in a flash. He *had* to do something. In that state of uncertainty and fear, his 'manly' thumb groped for the hooter and pressed it down . . . hard. The car came down with a clamorous bang, and only then did he realize that the youths were going to turn it over.

His call had aroused people inside nearby houses. Doors and windows were flung open. From his bedridden uncle's home nearby, Tembi was the first one to emerge, screaming. Her shrill voice pierced through the dark night, making an urgent appeal for help. Whistle-sounds from windows all around permeated through the thick smog, sending alarm signals in all directions. Velani knew that it was the women – mothers, sisters, wives – who were blowing the whistles. At that moment he seemed to hear the voice of his wife resound the resolve of the people in distress: 'The system does not care. All they want is to exploit us. They will never go out of their way to protect us. Stand together and fight as one. They are guarding the borders and hunting for so-called terrorists like you look for a needle in a haystack. Blackman you're on your own. Only *you* can root out the evil in your midst and its hired lackeys who are only there to confuse the people; to distract them from the real enemy. . . .' It was bad for the marauding youths. Velani watched them, still in a state of complete paralysis and shock. They sauntered away in all directions, some dropping their weapons as they scaled over the dilapidated fences into the adjoining streets, and vanished.

'Cowards!' Velani cursed, spitting through the window which he had now opened to assure the converging people that *he*, Velani, was safe and sound.

'Soweto is a jungle. I don't know what you want there. You should come to Eldorado Park. We coloureds here are safe!'

Velani remembered the words of hope his uncle had often whispered to him when he paid him a 'business' call. None of Boetie McCabel's neighbours and friends had ever suspected that he was in fact an African who, according to the South African divide-and-rule laws, should have been in Soweto. Who could have known that he was Mbuti Mkhabela? On his not-so-frequent 'visits' to his uncle in Eldorado Park, Velani had been like all the African customers from Soweto McCabel had. From a struggling start, Uncle Boetie's Panel-beaters had flourished over the twenty-five years in that township. Only his fair-skinned wife had known the secret and she had vowed to keep it from anyone's 'prying' ears.

Very often now, while he lay in bed thinking, Velani became increasingly uneasy. All right, he had fitted on a new rear window to his 'Volksie'. . . . But what of the future? He was a traveller and often he did not sleep at home. The fences surrounding his house were not so good either. It could cost a fortune to erect good ones. The people were not paying rent. To do that would be to risk getting a 'necklace'. The signs were all over . . . 'YOU PAY, WE BURN.' Who would risk that? Perhaps it was a good thing to leave Soweto and go to Eldorado Park after all.

Once, while he lay awake in bed with his mind besieged by these thoughts, he patted his wife Mavis's shoulder gently to make a suggestion to her. She had just fallen asleep lightly. She grunted,

'Hm?' Her eyelids already heavy, she asked, 'What's the matter?'

At least Mavis was willing to listen, Velani thought, his mind already excited by what he had to tell her. He asked,

'What if we pack up everything and go to Eldorado?'

Mavis was now fully awake. She replied,

'Velie, are you dreaming? Eldorado is somewhere in North America. Where have you ever heard of someone leaving Soweto to go and live so far away . . . even if one were crazy enough to think he or she could afford the plane ticket, let alone get a passport from the Boers?'

'No. I mean the Eldorado next to "us"; next to Soweto, on the other side of Kliptown. Mavis, please. Things are so difficult for us here now. Look, the car, the house, everything.'

'Heyi wena; are you crazy, what's wrong with you anyway? Why do you think you can run away from the struggle?'

Mavis shook her head in disbelief. Somehow she felt grateful. 'At least he is worried,' she said to herself. That silly suggestion he made meant that he was restless. How long had she wished that Velani would stop 'floating around' in a cloud of self-deception and concern himself with what was happening? He would never even listen to what she had to say whenever she came from 'the people's' meetings. She sighed.

'The struggle is everywhere, Velie.'

'But the people in Eldorado lead normal lives. They pay rent, electricity bills and water. Their houses still have the numbers. Everything is going on smoothly.'

'So you think if you do that – run away to Eldorado – you'll be safe? OK, you want a house with a number so that the police, the army, the council messengers can spot you easily. You want to eat, sleep and drink in their "safe" hands. . . . What about those who cannot run away? Do you think you can build an island of comfort and safety around you when everyone else is oppressed? Not even the Boers still think they can.'

But Velani's coloured uncle's voice haunted him and the harder he tried to forget it now of late, the more it goaded him:

'Leave that Soweto and come to Eldorado. The immigration control laws are all suspended. They are scrapped for good. You can live anywhere you like now. Save your neck and your property. Come to our coloured township. Come to Eldorado.'

Velani could not remember when he finally fell asleep.

Whether Velani's ancestors had turned their backs towards him, he did not know. It had happened again. His beloved Volksie had gone – grabbed from him at gunpoint. This time, he decided that he would take his uncle's advice.

It had been seven months since he had last spoken to his 'Eldorado' uncle. The fact that Uncle Boetie had not even bothered to attend the funeral of his own brother, Bafana, in Mapetla, Soweto had made him bitter towards him. If Eldorado made one insensitive towards his own people then it was not worth living there. Perhaps Mavis was right after all. That was before the whole 'ibadi' ('bad-luck') happened again.

But now it had happened. His nice little Volksie had gone, taken from him by an unscrupulous mob of youngsters in broad daylight. Where did they get the guns from anyway? He had been chatting away at Suzzie's Haunt and some time late in the afternoon, he decided to go to S'godiphola. In the bare veld overlooking the township, he saw the youths who came into the road blocking him from passing. Something within him told him to run straight into them, but his dazed mind would not think straight. He slowed down when something inside him snapped with anger. He thought that if they attacked him outside, then he had a good chance of confusing them. It was only after he had slowed down that he realized that they were armed.

It was the next day. Velani could think clearly. He asked Mavis to go to work and leave him to his thoughts. If he were left alone, he would be able to figure out just how it had happened.

He sat alone, his mind putting the pieces together.

After the no-good hoodlums had knocked him unconscious, they sped off in his Volksie, leaving him lying there. Some 'good Samaritan' – also a regular customer at Suzzie's Haunt – recognized him and picked him up. With some of their 'friends', they decided to take Velani first to the police station to report the loss of his car. When he had regained consciousness, he pleaded with his friends that he would rather go and report the matter to the police than go home on foot to face his wife Mavis. They immediately rushed him to the nearby Moroka Police Station.

Never in his life had Velani seen so many people lined up in a small room waiting to be served. All of them had lost their car. They all had sad stories to tell. Even sobbing women were there. Some of them had also been raped. It is only when you have your personal share of pain that you know what it is like to be pierced. Velani listened. His sense of loss had made him sober. He wondered how it was still possible for some of these people to speak about the pain at all with their hearts still bleeding. He listened, absent-minded. The two men next to him, with homemade bandages tied around injured limbs, for one an elbow and another his shin, rattled on in whispers:

'A friend of mine had his car interfered with and pushed away right out of his yard, mind you; and he could do nothing! They were armed, so what could he do?'

The other confirmed, nodding all the time:

'I *know*. Others are hijacked at intersections. And when you come to report here they tell you that there are no policemen to come to your aid, that they are short of them. I'm not surprised. How can they be everywhere? Zambia, Malawi, Zimbabwe, Botswana, the Bantustans, Swaziland, Lesotho, the borders – all over. . . . What are they – an octopus?'

'It is dangerous these days to stop at a robot. Even when it is red, just dash on!'

Some sat looking hopefully at the official on the other side of the desk. The bespectacled policeman looked up at the rows of anxious, exhausted faces while he kept reaching for dockets. He seemed polite and Velani wondered what had happened. . . . He was thinking . . . a so-called 'kaffer-konstabel' polite? Never. . . . Or was it in keeping with the so-called 'reform' process? . . . So this was what they meant by 'reform', eh? It was a rather annoying revelation, especially because he kept on reiterating to one complainant after another,

'We can only try to do our best, but we cannot make promises that you'll get your cars. Soweto is bad. Most of you I know have no insurance cover. Too many cars are stolen. The thieves work fast. They use false number plates and they spray the car almost immediately. It is difficult to spot any stolen car from the descriptions you give. . . . We are your friends. We are here to protect your property and your lives.'

The whole rhetoric sounded meaningless and hollow. The sad people's eyes and ears were open, but they remained stern and unimpressed. Velani knew that he would never see his car again. It was gone for good. He could feel it in his blood.

Velani knew what he would do. He would ring his 'Eldorado' uncle and ask for advice. Perhaps he was right after all. What was the use of staying in Soweto? Who cares what happens to people in Soweto anyway? Certainly not the police or the so-called councillors or the lawmakers in Pretoria.

As he sat alone, thinking, he became more and more certain that Boetie McCabel was in fact his best advisor. Only he had had the common sense to look at the problem facing the blacks – especially the Africans – and to arrive at the best solution to it. Escape . . . to escape from the 'jungle' and draw closer to the well-provided-for world, the privileged one.

He reached for the telephone receiver and dialled the number impatiently, his brow sweating with excitement. It was the voice of a woman, possibly Mrs McCabel, which answered.

'Hello, kan ek u help?'

Velani replied, 'It's Mkhabela here Ma'am. Can I speak to Mr McCabel please?'

'Just hold on please, I'll call him . . . Boetie!'

She yelled, placing the receiver on the table. McCabel rushed from the kitchen into the lounge.

Velie recognized his uncle's voice immediately. He whispered into the receiver,

'Hello, it's Velie, Uncle Boetie. I want to come to Eldorado. I have decided to take your advice.'

'Why now?'

'My Volksie is gone. They took it again. Nothing is safe here. I want to come and live in Eldorado if. . . . ' Before Velie could continue, McCabel interrupted,

'It's no use, Velie. The "disease" has spread all over. We also have "Comrades" here. They want solidarity with the people of Soweto. They say they are returning to their roots. They have wiped off the numbers from the houses. They say unless we are one the struggle against the settlers is forever lost.'

'Stay where you are. "Injury to one oppressed is injury to all," they say. We all have to change. Just like the police say, they cannot keep up with all the cases. Gangs of hooligans, encouraged and armed by the police themselves, are on the rampage and nobody really cares. All the police and army are really concerned about is tracking down the so-called "terrorists". It comes from the police themselves. They say they are tired, overworked. People are no longer joining the police force. The few who are still, they also want to go on strike. They want to run away and they don't know how to do it. . . . Are you still there Velie?'

Without another word, Velie dropped the receiver and sank into the sofa next to him. He sighed and whispered to himself,

'It's no use. Real protection will come from the people themselves. From now on, I'm with the people.'

Celia and the Bicycle

KATE PULLINGER

Kate Pullinger was born in British Columbia, Canada in 1961. In 1982, she left Canada and came to London where her short stories began to appear regularly in magazines such as *New Statesman, Fiction* and *Spare Rib*. In 1986 she won the *City Limits* short story competition and in September 1987 took up the post of Writer in Residence at Battersea Arts Centre. Her first collection of short stories, *Tiny Lies*, was published by Jonathan Cape in 1988. She is currently writing her first novel.

Celia rode a bicycle. She was too impatient to use the public transport system, in too much of a hurry with no time. For her, the bicycle was a symbol of freedom from constraint. It enabled her to overcome traffic jams, avoid potential attackers, keep in trim, and get from A to B quickly. Two wheels and a set of handlebars meant, to Celia, liberation.

Celia also wore short skirts. During the sixties when short was chic, her mother, an accomplished seamstress, had sewn a series of little red, yellow and paisley skirts for Celia. The ripped-up and anarchic fashions of punk had enabled her to continue wearing the mini while a teenager, then the eclectism of style in the eighties allowed her to keep her knees bare until the mini-skirt made it's re-entry on to the pages of *Vogue*. But Celia was not concerned with being fashionable; she loved the mini-skirt and that was all there was to it.

To Celia, the mini-skirt was a symbol of freedom from constraint. It enabled her to pedal her bicycle without impediment. With her strong legs free from complicated trousers or the volumes of material involved in other skirts or dresses she could speed her way through the city. The mini-skirt made her feel powerful, spare, economical and streamlined. She thought that if her bicycle had been human it would have worn mini-skirts as well.

Unfortunately for Celia, however, the combination of bicycle and mini-skirt produced explosive reactions on the streets of the inner city. The young woman was unable to pedal down the road without being harangued from all sides. Men, always men, or does that go without saying, seemed to feel compelled to pass comment as she sailed by. 'Argh, would you sit on my face, sweetheart,' was a popular phrase down the Old Kent Road. 'Nice pair of legs,' was particularly common in the West End and it was not unusual for men in Camden Town to offer the wisdom of 'Don't you think your skirt is a bit short?', as if they were male moral arbiters, each one. Engines were revved, windows were hurriedly rolled down, construction workers looked up from their toil.

All Celia wanted from life was speed, short skirts and freedom. She tried to imagine ways she could get these things. If the man on the scaffolding leaned too far to the right whilst attempting to get her attention he might fall from above into the path of an oncoming car, the driver of which was also trying to grab Celia's eye, or rather, some other part of her body. That car, swerving to miss the construction worker who by now lay crumpled on the road, would run over his legs and then crash into another oncoming car, the driver of which was also trying to see up Celia's skirt to where the tops of her thighs met the bicycle seat.

Celia was not a vindictive woman. She simply had a strong sense of the absurd, the pantomime accident or Buster Keaton stunt. She also wanted justice. She believed in justice.

Like her spirit, mind and body, Celia's bicycle was fast and adept but fragile and vulnerable as well. It was not a particularly good bicycle – fairly old, both tyres were usually slightly soft and one of the lights was out of order. Celia was not a Bicycle Snob. In recent years this terrifying group of people dressed in Italian cycling gear had made riding a bicycle a trendy and fashionable activity. Their lean frames pushing against the wind, the Bicycle Snobs tore up and down the streets of London, dodging traffic lights and dashing up one-way streets the wrong way. They had complicated and expensive mechanisms for securing the dismantled frames of their well-oiled and pampered machines to lamp-posts and wrought-iron fences. There were also the Bicycle Couriers to contend with, people who delivered messages throughout London, driven by a mysterious death-wish. Recalcitrant daredevils, the Couriers often led double lives and were also Bicycle Snobs at heart. They constantly overtook Celia on the thoroughfares and byways, looking down at her inferior bike with distaste. Unlike the men in cars they did not pass verbal comment, but Celia could tell what they were thinking.

She did not care. Celia was a bicycle libertarian; she believed everyone should be allowed to do it their own way, free from interference and restraint. To her the bicycle was a modern icon, symbolic of religious rightness and purity. Cheap, pollution-free, silent: for her it was enough to simply ride. And riding in London was an act of faith.

Celia had a recurrent dream. In this dream, which she usually had after cycling home drunk, she and her bicycle could fly. All that they needed was a slight hill, like the one down Pentonville Road from the Angel to King's Cross, or the one that slides around Brockwell Park en route from Herne Hill to Brixton. Late at night when few cars were about she would travel down the hill as quickly as her bicycle would take her and, just before reaching the bottom, take off. Pedalling at a leisurely pace, Celia and her bicycle would glide over London like fantastic characters out of a children's book. The city sparkled in the night as they flew over the enormous rail stations and circled around Nelson's Column. Celia dreamt she had seen Nelson's face, a vision of pigeon-shat-upon strength. From hundreds of feet above Whitehall the seat of government looked like a fairyland, resplendently lit, not at all evil or mean.

Upon waking the morning after having had a flying bicycle dream, Celia always felt disappointed and flat. Rubbing her eyes on the way to the bathroom she would stop in the corridor and examine her bicycle. It did not look like it could fly. After breakfast she would take it outside the front door, get on it and set off down the road. The first hill was always a terrible strain and she would huff and puff and curse the day she bought the machine. But later, as she wove between the cars, passing through traffic jams with great ease, she would remember her dream and take her hands off the handlebars and flap her arms like they were wings. It was the nearest she felt she could get to the real thing.

The traffic in London creates a special form of madness that makes the ordinarily sane person aggressive, macho and violent. Car, motor cycle and lorry drivers become psychopathic while only the bus drivers seem able to maintain calm. Cyclists are not exempt from this madness; the more lyrical and graceful movement of a bicycle does not necessarily mean its rider is not angry, does not want to kill or maim. Celia herself valued the rush of adrenalin she received when she shouted at cars that cut in front of her. 'Wrap those legs around me, love,' would send her off a bit faster at the next green light. 'We've seen your legs, now show us your tits,' gave her an edge on the cyclist behind. And, 'Lucky bicycle seat,' or 'Let me be your bicycle seat,' or 'Is that a bicycle seat or are you excited?' would send her shooting up the next hill like her legs were pistons and her heart a generator. She would yell back 'Fuck off', or 'Asshole', or 'Bastard', and ride like the wind. Pumping her legs up and down, up and down, she felt purified and hardened and sleek. She felt they could not stop her, they could not put reins on her, they could not suppress her energy with their remarks. She ate up their abuse like a horse eats oats and used it to fuel her journey.

One weekend Celia rose early. She was going to visit a friend who was organizing a boatload of bicycles to take to Nicaragua. Apparently in Nicaragua there is a shortage of that kind of thing. Celia opened her closet and surveyed her collection of mini-skirts. To her they looked functional and practical like shorts only not quite so utilitarian. She chose a blue and white stripey one, not too short, not micro-mini, but a mini none the less. With that, a shirt and her plimsolls, she was ready. She ate breakfast then got on her bike.

It was a lovely day but the traffic was heavy with Saturday shopping confusion. Celia was running a bit late. At a set of traffic lights on Clapham High Street one of the streamlined neo-Italians passed her in a flash of perfectly attired bright light. Toiling against the wind along Clapham Common, she hummed a tune and ignored the comments which were hurled at her every minute or two. She picked up a lot of speed as she reached Clapham South tube station and it was there, just beyond the intersection, that the man in the yellow Corvette chose to ignore her, swung his steering wheel and tried to take his car into a side street whilst whamming his foot on the accelerator. Celia's bicycle, her beloved and much adored, upright handlebar with a male crossbar and battery-operated lights bicycle, went under the heavy bodies of this man and his metal-shelled vehicle. The wheels of the car crunched and twisted its frame, snapping off the seat. The bicycle was gone forever.

On initial impact, Celia took off and flew through the air. For a minute that extended into hours she floated above the crowded and busy street. Clapham Common looked green and peaceful away from the road, traffic-free. The wind rushed around her legs and up her mini-skirt. The cars stopped honking, their engines stood idle, and the people on top of the Clapham omnibus stared, their mouths open, their noses pressed against the window.

Then, with a thud, Celia landed on the roof of the yellow Corvette. The driver got out of the car. His face was bloated and red with anger. 'Get off my car you fucking slag,' he shouted.

Celia felt shocked. She had just been in the air; she had actually flown and it was not a dream. 'What do you mean, you asshole,' she said. 'I'm not a slag. Don't you call me a slag. It's drivers like you who kill cyclists.'

'Who the fuck do you think you are, riding around London with your skirt up your ass? If you were my daughter, or my wife for that matter, you wouldn't get out of the front door in that thing.'

'You almost killed me just then, you bastard.'

'Serve you right too, you little slut.'

Something inside Celia burst then. Maybe it was her inner tube or perhaps it was only a bulb from her light, but something exploded. She stood on the roof of the yellow Corvette and shouted, 'You killed my bicycle you animal. You're going to pay for this.' She leapt off the car and flew through the air and for a moment she felt free again. Then she landed on the shoulders of the driver. 'I wish your face was my bicycle seat,' she shouted. 'I wish your body was my bicycle.' With both legs dangling down his front, one on either side of his head, it was as though he had become her beast of burden, her packhorse, her mule, maybe even her bicycle. She kicked him in the ribs with her heels and slapped him on the backside with one hand. 'Giddy-up, come on, here I am, let's go,' And with her powerful legs like a vice on his neck she made him carry her to the door of her friend's house, through Balham and into Tooting. On the way she decided that men were just as easy to ride as bicyles, not as quick, mind you, not as smooth, but much less work on hills.

The Collected Experiences of Suzi Dishcloth

ANN ZIETY

Ann Ziety is a poet, songwriter and comic who performs regularly at alternative cabaret venues. She runs a women's writers workshop in Woolwich and is an active member of the Apples and Snakes Poetry Cabaret Collective. She lives in Thamesmead with a small tyrannical dog, two miles from the Crossness Sewage Treatment Works.

All characters in this story are entirely fictitious. Any resemblance to actual devils, monsters or policemen is purely accidental.

HAPPY BIRTHDAY

When fry-ups were not afraid to be fry-ups
When bacon fat grew mouldy in the frying pan
When glaucous grey dishcloths slid over the café table tops
When lime from the kettle spilled out into grimey mugs of chicory
and acorn coffee
When bin bags burst in the basement sending shards of potato peelings
and cold, tinned spaghetti and curled sausage sandwiches smashing
against the mildewed walls
When bubble and squeak exploded at the back of hotel kitchens
When eggs ponged hysterically and dogs shat on scarred allotments and
went to sniff at the places where their friends all pissed
twice a day
When chips congealed in soggy newspapers and cheese turned green and
milk curdled into obscene porridge
When old, half empty beer cans fell over and dribbled their brown
liquid on to carpets stained with mud and motor oil and cat fur
When toilets yearned for Harpic
When garlic yearned for peppermint
When socks crawled into the linen basket and gave up hope
When Kitkats melted in the back pockets of window cleaners' overalls
When rivers stank of rats, and rats mated in disused garages
When blue bottles skated on the bald head of a dying man
When bacteria and typhoid played games in the water trough
When dentists drilled their way through decaying cavities
When dirt met grease
And flesh met sweat
And air met smoke
And silence met alarm bells. . . .

Somebody screamed and gave birth to Suzi Dishcloth
Then had a little party.

SUZI DISHCLOTH AND THE DEVIL

Suzi Dishcloth first met the Devil when she was seven years old.

He was stood behind a tree in a forest full of gnarled branches the shape of crushed pedestrians. He was waiting for her in the mossy silences, his crippled torso inconspicuous amidst the tortured wooden statues of lost commuters. He watched her looking for pixies down the rabbit holes. He gazed with smouldering emerald eyes at her little velvet dress all neatly ironed, and her little patent leather shoes all neatly shining, and he cowered in the murky tree-shadows and rotting leaves, waiting for her to come nearer
and made plans.

Suzi Dishcloth saw him and immediately made friends.
She brought him aromatic puddings and meat-and-potato pies.
She brought him tinned prunes and Chinese take-aways.
She brought him newspapers so that he could indulge himself in
his own evil.
She brought him a dressing gown and carpet slippers, cigarettes,
beer and the latest football results.
And she softly stroked his forehead and ironed his shirts.

'What a cute kiddie,' said the Devil.
'Too cute for destruction,
Too cute for purgatory,
But not cute enough to have things all her own way.'

After she had scurried home like a little black patent leather beetle, she decided that she wanted to write a poem.

Some days she would make luxury hotels and restaurants with her Meccano set and would people them with porters and waitresses moulded out of plasticine. Sometimes she made bingo halls and multi-storey car parks out of plastic bricks. And some days she would build miniature dustbin carts out of bits of wood, and fire engines and ice cream vans and ambulances and road cleaners. And once she built a complete down-to-scale model sewage works out of carrot scrapings and old lolly sticks.

But on this day she wanted to write a poem.

She wanted to write about the nice man in the woods, the green of his absorbing eyes, the whiteness of his teeth, the coldness of his strange, hypnotic hands as he patted her on the head.

She wanted to shake words out of the trees and watch them come fluttering down in a mass of confetti poetry. She wanted the words to come to her when she whistled, to come with neon-lit halos in the dead of night. But the words didn't come.

She rummaged furiously through her toy cupboard, turfing out the cheap and expensive, brightly coloured gifts she had collected over the years. She searched behind cushions, and under the carpet and at the bottom of her playpen. She looked in the garden by the rose bushes and in the vegetable patch and under the sumac tree – but found no words. There was only the black empty space of sky and the mocking caws of ravens, and the harsh blasts of a psychopathic wind.

And wasn't she too young to write a poem?
And wasn't she too innocent to play with the magic power of
 words?
And wasn't she too silly to give majesty and grandeur to a great
 literary event?
And wasn't she a little girl after all?

And little girls didn't write poems, not even in the dead of night when the rain slashed the windows and there was no Mother to tell you to clean out the oven, and no brother to turn the television up, and no baby sister to scream like a police siren.

Finally, as a last resort, the seven-year-old Suzi Dishcloth looked inside herself – the only place left to look. And there she found some very odd words and some very pretty words that made her smile and giggle and scream. And she skipped up to her room and sharpened her pencil like a fine, precise little arrow.

Before her first few words were on the page,
Foreign diplomats crawled through the back passages of her
 brains,
Sabre-toothed bureaucrats stabbed at her writing pad,
Prime ministers scuba-dived into her subconscious depths,

Doctors injected her perfect arteries with corrupting plasma,
She had to dodge the tumbling embassies, colleges and state apartments as they fell crushingly in her path,
Judges lied to make themselves important,
Policemen lied to make her admit her guilt,
Teachers lied about little girls never writing poetry,
Parents lied about little girls remaining little girls for the rest of their lives,
God lied brilliantly to keep her from sharing in his power,
Soldiers did military exercises around her inkwell,
And the SAS blew up her Pocket Oxford Dictionary.

The Devil laughed slowly like an approaching earthquake, and was proud to see that he was no longer needed in this world.

As she grew up, Suzi Dishcloth got the feeling
(which would recur in later life) that she had
definitely arrived at the wrong gig.

Ann Ziety

THE FIRES OF HELL

Mother: What are you doing?

Suzi Dishcloth (aged ten and a half): I'm drawing the fires of Hell, Mother.

Mother: Well make sure you don't get any of that ink on my table.

SUZI DISHCLOTH GOES OUT TO PLAY

There are all kinds of holes:
Little holes, big holes,
Holes in tree-trunks,
Holes in the road –

But the best kinds of holes
Are the ones you dig yourself.

So Suzi Dishcloth dug a hole.
It went right into next door's asparagus patch
And she wouldn't have stopped there

But she hit a gas pipe
And they had to call in the council.

SPOTS

Some little girls want to be famous
Some little girls want to be rich
Some little girls want to be clever
But Suzi Dishcloth wanted to be beautiful.

So she worked at it very hard
And wore a lot of nice dresses
And smiled a lot of innocent smiles
And became very cute indeed
And grew a little older
And sat in the sun
And washed regularly
And got spots.

So she sat in the sun some more
And washed even more regularly
And got more spots.

She went on a fruit diet
And bought a bio-facial cure
She still got spots.

She steamed out her pores
And drank camomile tea
That smelt of cats' piss
And went on a beetroot and chicory diet
And got spots.

She sat beneath a sunray lamp
And took special antibiotics
And listened to old wives' tales
And listened to medical advice
And got spots.

She went to a pollution-free place
And drank mineral water
And did regular exercises
And prayed to God
Who gave her life
        and spots and spots and spots and spots.

Some little girls want to marry famous tennis players
Some little girls want to marry millionaires
Some little girls want to marry nuclear physicists
But Suzi Dishcloth wanted to marry a dermatologist.

DICK MOPED AND WILFRED POLE

When she was sixteen, Suzi Dishcloth was in love with Dick Moped, star of the sixth form. He had early-bristling sideburns, athletic legs and a charismatic cleverness. He wore neatly patterned reversible anoraks, smoked during economics lessons, never let his socks peep out from underneath his trousers, and never allowed his black hair to be cut in a style that was less than debonaire.

She wrote 'Dick' into the jumble of the graffiti-ridden desk top. She wrote 'Dick plus Suzi' on her exercise book. 'I love Dick', 'Dick is Ace'. She made it her life's ambition to sit next to him on the bus, and always stood conveniently near him at end-of-term parties, where he would stub out his hand-rolled cigarettes in her lager shandies.

Dick Moped was in love with Verna Brilliant (everybody knew), whose eyes shone like sacred candles with a deep and penetrating flame, who smelt of roses and cedar wood talcum powder, whose jeans were stonewashed to perfection and tomato-skin-tight, whose clothes were chosen after months of tortuous deliberation in endless draughty dressing rooms at Chelsea Girl and Miss Selfridge, and who was reputed to be on the pill (at least).

Dick Moped thought of Verna Brilliant as the cherry on top of his already rich and fruity trifle.

Dick Moped thought of Suzi Dishcloth as a kind of biscuit crumb at the bottom of his milkshake – soppy and inconvenient.

But Wilfred Pole fancied Suzi Dishcloth

Cor

Not 'arf.

Wilfred Pole was thin and spotty and always looked like he wanted to go to the lavatory. His dusty, scuffed shoes grudgingly allowed him to walk with a hunched-over Quasimodo-effect. His thin, wispy black hair clung desperately to his tiny round head, a razor-sharp nose sprouted from beneath two rat eyes of teabag brown, and his frog-like mouth hung open, searching for clues.

His pallor was deathly due to an endless diet of luncheon meat sandwiches. His small reptilian hands were mottled with ink stains. His nose ran furiously on winter days, and in the summer he sported a shrunken, bile-yellow T-shirt which fitted tightly over his tube-like body and allowed his puny, pink arms to burst into the light of day. He would wave these anaemic branches at Suzi Dishcloth when she stepped heavily off the bus, and he would look just like a little hydra or a piece of plankton flailing about at the bottom of the sea.

Wilfred Pole had nothing that anybody in their right mind would want.
He couldn't string together two decent sentences without looking up words in the dictionary.
He looked like the magnification of a microscopic organism.
He leered, he ogled, his eyes bulged to bursting point.
His thoughts hovered precariously between pornography and perversion.
He sniggered wheezingly into his biology textbooks.
He had had a number of unpronounceable, unpleasant diseases.
He couldn't drive or play tennis.
He was excused from wearing shorts.
His socks peeped out from underneath his crumpled trousers.
His tie was jazzed up with psychedelic gravy-stains.
He was lost and helpless.
But he fancied Suzi Dishcloth.
And that was enough for her.

After a night of lager shandies followed by wine and whisky and gin, Wilfred Pole and Suzi Dishcloth left the pub where their friends were all talking about them, and went back to her place. Her parents had gone on a cheese-tasting holiday in Switzerland and had left the cats and geraniums and TV dinners in Suzi's care. There they raided the cocktail cabinet and after making sure that they could no longer feel anything physically or emotionally, they made a sort of casual love on the squeaky, white leather sofa for the first and last time.

Wilfred Pole cast off his virginity like the greasy old wrapping from a take-away hamburger.
He came like a tidal wave swelling over the great Thames flood barrier.
He came like the rush of traffic through the Blackwall Tunnel.
He came like a glut of gas bills hurtling through the letter box.
He came like the sudden collapse of a crumbling tower block, long overdue for demolition.

He came with a GLC fireworks display gushing inside his head.
He came.
He saw.
He got confused.

Suzi Dishcloth threw up over her mother's favourite Axminster.

ICARUS

One night Suzi Dishcloth had a dream
She dreamt that she had lost her best friend
The friend ran into a spinney that thickened itself with trees and foliage
and became a giant wood with a thousand entrances
The friend ran into a city and out of each footprint sprang a dozen
office blocks
The friend drove along a motorway that became a complicated zigzag of
minor roads
The friend ran into a launderette and when she followed, Suzi Dishcloth
could only find three housewives and a room full of purring, soapy
machines
The friend jumped on to a train and Suzi Dishcloth was two seconds too
late to catch it as it shunted out of an unknown station
He ran into a fire and she was too afraid to follow
He melted into the novel he was reading and she couldn't get him out
He got stuck in a photograph and even Suzi Dishcloth's sharp, long nails
couldn't peel him off
He dived into a television screen and disappeared in the epicentre of
the little blue dot
He became a voice on the radio, as inaccessible as the moon
He went into the Underground and wouldn't get off the Circle Line
He painted pictures of himself waving goodbye

The friend went hang-gliding and floated into the centre of the sun
He slipped into a vat of cement and his breath-bubbles turned to concrete
He went into hospital and had his brain removed by a bureaucratic
accident
He wrote himself into the menu at Claridges and was eaten by a close
relative of Prince Michael
He drank a potion that shrank him to a pinhead and he rolled into the
crack of infinity
The friend fell out of a helicopter but his body never landed on earth
The friend juggled with hand grenades and rode on the back of a Polaris
missile
The friend bricked himself into the vault of a bank and counted money
for a hundred centuries
The friend hid at the bottom of a bunker and waited for the world to end

The friend blasted off into space and found the zipper that undid the
universe

And that was the moment when Suzi Dishcloth screamed
And knew that she wasn't sleeping.

SUZI DISHCLOTH FINDS A WART

In the mirror
Suzi Dishcloth found a wart on the end of her nose.
She prodded it and picked it and dabbed it with this and that
But the wart wouldn't go away
So she went to the hospital to have it removed.
The doctors said they had never seen a wart quite like it.
It was a greeny-grey bulbous protruberance about the size of a
chick pea.
The doctors cut it off and threw it away.

But at the bottom of the waste disposal chute the wart didn't die. It went greener and greyer and knobblier and grew to the size of a large satsuma.

After a week, when Ted Algae the auxiliary worker came to take away the rubbish, the wart had increased its dimensions and was as big as a lumpy boulder. It had incisors and a carnivorous appetite and its knobbles had grown boils and pimples and callouses; it was incredibly blobby with a fine thread of veins running over its crusty surface. It felt the vibrations of Ted Algae's footsteps on the cobbles and gave a little squeak of joy.

As he bent down to clear out the chute, the sixty-three-year-old auxiliary (who had won a trophy as Hospital Worker of the Year) was savagely attacked by Suzi Dishcloth's amputated wart. He screamed, and pulling the round, squealing mass of grey pulp off his chest, he ran out of the bin rooms with his overalls all bloody and finely shredded.

The wart chirruped sadly to itself and lazed against one of the unemptied bins. Then, noticing that the Waste Room door had been left open, it slobbered out into the winter drizzle in search of auxiliary staff. Due to NHSS expenditure cuts these were in short supply, so the wart slithered slowly out of the hospital grounds, pouncing unsuccessfully on sparrows and fieldmice as it made its way to the main road. It shunted bumpily along the grass verges where it found a half-eaten carton of Pot Noodle which it pumped into itself through its long needle-like proboscis, making the most hideous porridgey noises.

The wart, like all living things, thought that it was at the centre of the universe. It wanted to suck everything into itself until all was wart and wart was all, and there was nothing to differentiate, nothing to fight with, nothing to prey upon and nothing to be afraid of. Its finely tuned sense of smell homed in on the drivers speeding past – meat behind the wheel; and the smell of fresh human flesh made the wart tremble with delight. It bounced up and down like a baby and dribbled with glorious anticipation.

It had tricked, ambushed and slobberingly digested a traffic warden by midday.

There was no stopping it now.

Five days later, Suzi Dishcloth had got over her traumatic operation. And unaware that she had been the receptacle for a canker that threatened the safety of the entire world, she went off to a discotheque at the local nightclub where Julie and Karen hunted Terry and Kevin, and Terry and Kevin stalked Mandy and Pauline; where sexual tension was translated into funky bass lines on the synthesizer and Howard Jones moaned into the pulsating darkness.

As she danced with her peep-toe sandals sticking to the cider-soaked floor, Suzi Dishcloth let her head roll back and her mind float out into the dark centre of the room where a vortex of sound built up into a bullying crescendo and she felt her sadness trickle out into the unreal atmosphere and melt away like a forgotten secret.

And as she swirled and swished and shimmied across the room, she suddenly felt a vibration creeping up her spine as the dance floor began to shudder menacingly like an ageing food mixer, and she lost her footing as the whole floor moved from under her. The ceiling cracked, the walls shivered, and two disco lights fell crashing to the floor. Suzi Dishcloth dived under a table as the back wall exploded inwards showering the party people in a storm of brick and concrete and shattered video screen; and professional club DJ Clive King was squashed like a bug under an avalanche of falling masonry, a cloud of thick, white dust rising from the debris.

Within moments the discotheque was like a smouldering graveyard.

And there on the dance floor strewn with crushed bodies and broken tables, smashed glasses and mangled bar staff,

There amidst the darkness, the fallen wreckage and human misery,
Was the wart

The giant amalgam of all imperfection
The crusty pinnacle of ugliness
The culmination of cancerous corruption
Squeaking with a shrill, manic excitement
Its huge encrusted lumpiness made doubly unreal by the stroboscopic lighting effects
Its protruding nodules obscenely throbbing to Herbie Hancock.

Into the turgid discotheque atmosphere the giant wart shunted, chomping its way across the dance floor towards Suzi Dishcloth. She knew that there was only one thing to do if she was to survive this insatiable blob of boils, this cluster of corrosive greed. She rummaged flusteringly in her brown, leather handbag and, after the longest few seconds of her life, she found a large bottle of wart remover.

Squinting desperately through the darkness she saw that Julie had armed herself with a bottle of cleansing lotion and Karen clenched her very expensive Natural Beauty Care Astringent with Witch Hazel. Together the young women lifted their weapons, and in a synchronized attack, they doused the hideous wart in a shower of scientifically tested spot destroyer.

The effect was devastating.

The bulbous grey nodules on the wart's craggy skin began to steam and shrivel before their very eyes. And as its limbs and body melted away, so its high-pitched trill of victory turned to a low, curdled mutter of dismay, until the essence of its life ran into a river of thick, grey sludge and its heart turned into an invisible watery vapour.

The wart had been effectively removed.

Julie and Karen and Suzi Dishcloth had no words to express their sense of shock, but they hugged each other and wondered if they would get their pictures in the local papers.

And that night Suzi Dishcloth went home and looked in the mirror once again – just to check that her complexion was absolutely perfect.

Ann Ziety

ON THE DARKER SIDE OF THE FLYOVER

On the darker side of the flyover
On the crappiest part of the pavement
In a zone that was neither smokeless nor nuclear-free
Behind a dangerous chemical works
Where the coldest isobars collided
Where the distant drumming of boiler houses mingled with the icy clattering of railway carriages
Where the blue smoke borrowed the sky and never gave it back
Where pearly droplets of petrol seeped into earth and grass
Where summer existed only in the minds of travel agents
Where the nearest bus stop was half a mile's walk
And the nearest tube was half a mile's bus ride
Where the acid rain gave the nightingales glaucoma
And the acid snow froze the hub caps of continental cars
In a land of wheel clamps and scaffolding, bulldozers and briefcases, breathalysers and chicken fried rice
Tucked away in the spaghetti squiggles of the A-Z of London
In the backside of a cul-de-sac where the bin men never came
In a street without signposts
In a suburb full of puddles
In a world turned sour
In a universe gone green
Was the space where Suzi Dishcloth found a place to live –
A flamingo-pink apartment in the half-lit Club Tropicana shish kebab poodle parlour fish and chip elektrofunk forests of Lego Land.

AARON

Suzi Dishcloth awoke from a three-day hibernation with a hangover pulsating, drilling, pumping, shattering pieces of glass inside her head, squeezing the bedroom walls into a concertina pattern. Her eyeballs stuffed like olives, her tongue covered in alcoholic moss, her palate coated in penicillin and last Thursday night's half-digested prawn vol-au-vents, her taste buds ickered like kippers, her hair teased into Martini and hairspray clusters, she prised open her thick mouth and asked God to forgive her.

Daylight was headbutting the curtains, sending shards of angry sunlight poking into the room. She could hear the frenzied sunbeams banging against the window, screaming to be let in.

Suzi Dishcloth collected her thoughts which lay in a soggy and not-very-neat-pile at the bottom of her heart, covered in the debris of Friday night's party.

And then she remembered him
Big Bad Aaron
Huge and muscular with an HGV driving licence
His terrifying eyes
His globular South African accent
His tight-fitting T-shirts.

Suzi Dishcloth sat bolt upright in bed and bit her whore-red nail varnish which flaked off, bitter-tasting, into her mouth.

Dear oh deary me.

She could remember Aaron's big round berry-brown bottom. She could remember other tanned, exclusive parts with vivid astonishment. It was dark brown astonishment all the way.

Suzi Dishcloth gave a little squeak of dismay, and then tossed herself out of bed and let in the grinning sunlight which bounced all round the room and did somersaults over her duvet. She hated it. She wanted to strangle it and kick it into the street.
The sunshine made her sad
The savage yellow thickness soured her brain
She turned from the window
Her thoughts crawled back. She did a little internal dusting:

Aaron
Men
Parties.
What was she going to do about sex?

Ignore it.

But desire creeps out of the forests
It nestles in the Underground
It climbs the tower blocks
It hangs around in lifts
It clogs the telephone wires
It monopolizes the billboards
It sings on TV
It bullies at the cinema
It lies latent in carpet salesmen
It frolics in the classroom
It dances on the souls of the celibate
It sells cigarettes
Urban or Pastoral
Ready or Not
Here it comes:

Aaron was a bulldozer
Aaron was a fighter pilot
Aaron was a footballer
Aaron did karate
'I'm a pretty smart fella,' said Aaron.

Suzi Dishcloth was not interested in a single solitary human individual. She let him blather away. She let him blow his chances. She let him reveal his soft, doughy insides. He was like talking to a blown-up polythene bag, featureless and see-through. Suzi didn't care.

She stood attentive and did not listen.

She was shiny and puce like a pearl, glowing like someone who has just stepped out of the bath.

Suzi Dishcloth had that too-clean look

And Aaron was full of fabricated dirt.

He became a pearl fisherman and discovered her unfathomable pinkness. He delved into the depths, enveloped in pink, encased in ripples of bland nothingness; he swam in strawberry ice cream and guzzled raspberry blancmange, dived to the very bottom of the yogurt tub

And left the next morning.

Suzi felt like a cracked oyster at the bottom of the sea.

Down in the street, desire was settling itself into a variety of unfathomable relationships.

Never quite enough for everyone.

Suzi Dishcloth took her plastic Sainsbury's shopping bag, and went out to gather in the harvest.

LUCY IN THE SKY WITH A DOZEN HAMBURGERS

Lucy Lamont, a famous film star, advertised hamburgers on a billboard hoarding streaked with rain. Lucy Lamont, whose coffee cream eyes dripped jewelled tears in romantic blockbusters, whose breasts were insured for an unfathomable sum, whose breath was a lavender and sweet pea fragrance, whose successes oozed like overfilled custard slices on to the thickly piled carpet of Yesterday; Lucy Lamont juggled with buns and slabs of artificial meat, and this was the vision that met Suzi Dishcloth every time she went to work:

Lucy in the sky with a dozen hamburgers
And in bright yellow letters twenty feet high
The words:

'Scrummier Than A Kiss.'

SUZI DISHCLOTH RECEIVES A PUBLIC HEALTH WARNING

There was something wrong with Suzi Dishcloth's plumbing. For days the hot water tap had been spouting forth a green, unctuous liquid beaded with frogspawn. Unsanitary and vaguely alarming.

Suzi Dishcloth rang for a plumber in the phone box across the road which was etched with the eternally repeated statement that The Jam were God. The plumber did not arrive for two days.

When she turned on the hot water tap it vibrated like a liquidizer loaded with golf balls. Out of the metal spout came a frothy, green, foul-smelling slurry, and the air was imbued with a decayed, fishy fetor, the plughole choked with globular green jelloids that playfully winked at her beneath the neon lighting.

On the third day Suzi Dishcloth was tired of living in an aquarium and phoned the plumber again. The phone across the road had had its insides ripped out and was left dying on the pavement, so she went to the phone near the vandalized shopping centre, and spoke to a very bad-tempered man called Eric.

'You having me on, luv?' he said. 'Frogspawn coming out of your hot water pipes – in the middle of November?'

She pleaded her case, then went home and waited for him to arrive, while the hot water pipes made strained digesting noises, and the taps spat out more fish slurry and stinking vegetable matter. That little hole at the back of the sink which is always marked 'Typhoid' was hissing and blowing up spumes of emerald smoke and little bubbles of green effluence.

Suzi Dishcloth found a jellyfish in her washing basket.

Eric arrived later and complained about the smell, but drank two cups of coffee despite the unsanitary conditions of Suzi Dishcloth's kitchen. He set to work with plunger and shifter and a little bag of tools that clinked like a glockenspiel.

Eric splunged and slurped his way through the soup-filled channels of Suzi Dishcloth's plumbing, removing ballcocks and screws, and squirmed through the jungle of slime with his Nifty Rod.

'Jesus, this is the most disgusting thing I have ever seen,' he said desperately.

'It's not my fault,' said Suzi Dishcloth, feeling exposed.

'Dirt, filth, scum – that's the younger generation for you,' said Eric, who was forty-two.

Suzi Dishcloth stamped on a waterbeetle which was writhing in no particular direction on the kitchen floor. Then, feeling peeved, she showed Eric to the bathroom pipes and left him splunging in isolation.

She sat in the safety of her softly furnished living room, knitting pink egg cosies out of baby wool and meditating upon the beneficial qualities of avocado and cucumber shampoo. Suzi Dishcloth was in a peaceful reverie, making a list of all the things she wanted to consume, when suddenly from the tiny bathroom she heard what sounded like the end of the world.

A holocaustic scream vibrated along the hot water pipes; a butchered-pig-stuck-petrified pleading echoed throughout the whole house and crammed its shattering decibels into her ears. It was the sound of the unexpurgated horror of a plumber.

Suzi fled out of the living room and flung open the bathroom door.

What she saw had no name
Could not be identified
Would not be found in any dictionary
She pinched herself and it did not go away
As inevitable as its deep and penetrating stench.

It was eight feet tall with teeth the size of bread knives, its back mounted with gleaming, green scales covered with a slimy, pellucid skin threaded with pulsating veins and dripping with blanket weed. From its glistening mandibles dripped the blood of Eric, and in its lizard-like claws lay the plunger of Eric and his Nifty Rod, like the spoils of war. Its tail whipped against the walls breaking the bathroom tiles and slicing off the top of the toilet cistern. It extended its neck like a wrinkled gourd, moved its whole enormously ugly head in Suzi's direction, and grinned at her emphatically.

Suzi Dishcloth was too rigidly shit-scared to scream, but she managed to puke up over the rose-coloured linoleum speckled with Eric's haemoglobin.

Then she could only stare at the thing that her plumbing had aborted. How long had this vile monstrosity been lurking in the U-bends, making a despicable slimey nest in the complex warrens of piping, sleeping in the warmth of the boiler heater and shedding long strings of slop-covered eggs along the dark tunnels, propagating its unique evil in the quaggy blackness?

A grey tongue slid silently along rows of teeth, little blobs of spittle dropping on to the bath mat. Then suddenly it fizzed up a cluster of green gob and spat out a piece of scum-soaked rat-shit which hurtled towards Suzi Dishcloth's new hairdo. She ducked swiftly and the poisonous mess hit the bathroom wall, wobbled towards the floor, melted all the tiles and left a dark, smouldering wound smelling of kippers and burnt onions.

Then silence followed as the thing scratched its head the shape of a chewed piece of chewing gum.

It was as though it owned all sound, all movement, all time.

Suzi Dishcloth was afraid to move.

The Godzilla watched her carefully, its eyes bulging out of its head with greed, its worm-like tongue rippling with saliva. After a diet of cold tea-leaves and the occasional potato peeling, this was the first good meal it had seen for a long time – apart from Eric who had disappeared in a flurry of unabated hunger like a tiny hors d'oeuvre.

The Godzilla raised its disproportionately small claws upwards and gave out a mournful sob of ravenous desire, a grim yodel of savage hunger, a yell of complete despairing need.

Regarding each other from the two different perspectives of inside and outside the water pipe, Suzi Dishcloth and Godzilla locked their eyes together and anchored their hearts on to the principle of survival. The creature's eyes blackened with cruelty, its lips pared back from the knife-rows of teeth, its neck ready to spring.

It made its decision.

And as it hurled its sloppy mass in Suzi's direction, she quickly sprang out of its reach and slammed the bathroom door behind her. She could hear it slamming its wet bulk against the door, the slip-slop of its glaucous flab blindly kerflumping against the bathroom walls; she could hear slithers and skuffles as weighty wet bits dropped from its mouldy body, she heard it fall skidding on its own slime entangled in the dangling toilet roll, and she winced as green juices oozed under the door and into the hallway.

For a moment Suzi Dishcloth thought blankly that there was no answer to this gutter leviathan.

But as her numbness passed, she took some paraffin from the kitchen, doused the door with it, set it alight, and ran out into the street.

Green flames leapt and writhed, tortured in the urban skyline. And from the centre of the street, the centre of the town, from the very heart of the neighbourhood, came a giant scream of agony which shook every house and distorted every face.

'My God, what have I done?' said Suzi Dishcloth. 'How could I let things get this way?'

THE HEARTACHE

It was probably the worst experience she could remember. Even more horrible than the time she had come home and found a giant, venomous spider nestling on top of her black slate roof, its bulging, blue abdomen depositing egg-sacks down the chimney pot, or the time she grew a ten-foot man-eating yucca plant that garotted her postman and ingested fifty-seven Housing Benefit cheques, or even the time she got stuck for three hours in the Hanger Lane gyratory bypass.

This was the worst time of all.

Suzi Dishcloth thought she was in love – in the purest, sickiest, candle-lit, cheap, perfumed, chocolate-commercial sense of the word. Suzi's love hurled itself against the office walls, and where there had been a zombified, dead, cod fish calm, there was now a chaotic traffic jam of thoughts which Suzi found impossible to communicate to the object of her lust.

he was younger than she was
he was handsomer than she was
he was successful
he had charisma
he was braver, more determined
altogether a slicker
faster
cuter
sharper
neater
cleaner
smarter
switched-on bastard
as you're ever likely to meet
in Accounts
or anywhere.
when he came near she felt wild
he sent the pigeons fluttering
   into the thin white copy-paper sky

he set the dogs yapping like typewriters
he set the cats miaowing at the panic-stricken moon
he set owls hooting like factory sirens
he sent squirrels scurrying up trees
hedgehogs buzzed like computers
he made the grass shiver
   and bees growl like Formula 1 racing cars

his smile fizzed Suzi Dishcloth's Coca Cola can.

And when he found a better job in a better part of town with better pay and a better canteen and better-looking clerical staff –

Suzi Dishcloth crawled under a pile of carbon paper and threw her heart into the tray marked 'OUT'.

She waited for the work unit to tumble in on her, and all the typewriters and filing cabinets, waste paper bins and letter trays to pile down on her like a cannibalistic scrum and bury her utterly at the bottom of commerce.

But nothing happened.

He set the ducks dancing on the lake
For someone else.

SUZI DISHCLOTH FANTASIZES ABOUT HER FAVOURITE FILM STAR

If he had asked her to hang upside down from the lightshade
If he had asked her to remove all her Laura Ashley country casuals
If he had asked her to have him at the bottom of the basement
or in the lift
or under the dining table
or in the wardrobe
or a swimming pool
or at the top of a very cold mountain
or at the back of a very dirty car
or behind a coal bunker
or inside a potting shed
or under a haystack
or beneath a waterfall
or at a very dull Christmas party
or in a muddy field with a mad bull in it
or in a motorway cafe toilet
or on a patch of stinging nettles by an ant hill
six miles from the nearest shopping centre
She would have done it
Suzi Dishcloth would have payed money for the thrill.

If he had asked her to wear a gorilla suit
or leather or lace
or fishnet nights
or speak in a French accent with a shocked look on her face
If he had asked her to smoke six cigarettes at the same time
and turn the music up
and turn the lights down low
and turn into Marilyn Monroe
Suzi Dishcloth would have had a go
If he had asked her.

Ann Ziety

THE OVERDRAFT

Suzi Dishcloth lay awake in her exactly round, spongey, salmony, quilted bed with her eyes wide open at four o'clock in the morning.

She was stung with an unequivocal agony.

Period pains

Heavy and dull

Consumed all her attention and all of her power.

Internal snake bites tortured her lower abdomen with increasing stabs of savagery and malice, wrecking her tender inner strands, her soft, delicate cells.

She felt like she had a potato masher inside her womb. Pain seemed to radiate outwards through the whole of her body right to the ends of her fingertips until her hands and feet were tingling and her body was coated in cold sweat. Pain oozed out to the edge of the bed, and she saw it crawl across the carpet and into the street and out into the darkness until the very night time sky sobbed with the hurt.

She thought she was going to give birth to a crocodile.

Suzi Dishcloth writhed and sweated for three hours on the wimpy-soft Snooziland bed with posture-paedic springs and detachable headboard, and surprised herself by wishing to live for a few hours more. She didn't want to die of menstruation – after all it was supposed to be a life-giving process. The life-giving process was murder, but she wouldn't go to a doctor because the doctor would tell her that the crocodile was all part of her imagination – like the Godzilla and the man-eating yucca plant, like the vampires in her attic and the howling wolves on her balcony; like the spiders and the boa constrictors and the electric eels and the sharp-fanged monsters that mangled human flesh and made nests at the back of the fireplace.

Suzi Dishcloth knew the monsters were real.

As real as the spiteful slashes that cramped her womb.

So she took a few pills and some gin and waited as crocodile teeth chewed away at her insides, and nausea crept dully into her stomach, and palpitations flickered inside her heart, and her ears were filled with a faraway hissing noise, and her breath became shorter and more desperate.

More pills and more prayers followed until eventually the pain was drugged into submission, quietened into numbness, and Suzi Dishcloth knew that she wasn't going to die.

In the morning she remembered that she needed an overdraft.

She had spent the last of her monthly wage on frilly pink knickers and satin headscarves, bottles of Chianti and sherry, dairy sponge cakes and custard slices, a new floral Habitat toilet cover, six pairs of purple and green lacy tights, an electric cheese grater, an automatic pizza maker, a hotwater bottle in a woolly pink angora jacket, and a hat the shape of a tomato made from the fur of twenty-six weasles.

Shocked and sleepless, Suzi got up and put on her eye liner and peach sorbet lipstick. When the face was finished Suzi thought,

'No one will know what a sick girl I've been. No one will ever guess that I nearly died last night.'

And she wondered how she would interact with the world that day.

At the bank she asked to see the Manager and was busily shown to the office of Mr Friedman.

She entered calmly and then fell against the door with a gasp and nearly fainted.

He was the handsomest man she had ever seen.

He had piercingly bright blue eyes, and wavy wheat-yellow hair, and a cinema-screen smile, and a Gary Cooper self-assurance, and he wasn't wearing anything except for a big round badge just above his left nipple which said 'YES' in capital letters.

'Do come in Miss Dishcloth,' he said in a voice like silk sheets rustling on the washing line. 'What can I do for you?'

Suzi moved slowly over to his desk where she could obtain a good view of her bank manager's assets. She blinked twice and pinched herself but Mr. Friedman didn't disappear.

'I'd like an overdraft, please,' she said.

'Would you like me to make love to you first?' he said cheerfully.

Suzi Dishcloth didn't have to say anything because her face said 'yes please thankyou' about a million times. . . .

What a magnificent coupling there was in the bank that day.

What a swirling of smoke and a churning of buttocks.

What shrill-voiced squeals of unsquealable ecstasy echoed

throughout the vaults and offices and quick-service counters and into the innocent ears of the very pink, flustered, fumbling, mathematically erring clerks who smiled the way sardines might smile – all lopsided and embarrassed.

Suzi Dishcloth turned into a great white swan, while Mr Friedman became a big, grey African elephant.

She was an elegant flamingo, and he was a gallumphing, mighty, muscle-packed rhinoceros.

She was a fluffy, pink cottage cheese, and he was a stout and succulent sausage in batter.

She was a delicate water-lily, while he was a heavy-hanging willow tree stooping over her still waters.

The old Victorian building shuddered happily.

The fire alarm set itself off, the burglar alarm joined in, the press-button counter buzzers buzzed like killer bees, the automatic sliding doors opened and closed, opened and closed, the neon lights flickered on and off, fountain pens blobbed on to cheque books, telephones all rang at once, and from an unidentifiable source, from the central nerve of the High Street bank came the turgid, deafening, howling music of Motorhead and AC/DC, drilling holes in the air with audible shrapnel, screaming 'You're Gonna Love Me, Baby' while clients screamed at each other to be heard and clerks screamed at clients with faces redder than ripe chilli peppers.

After half an hour, when the bank had stopped turning itself into a discotheque, Suzi Dishcloth opened her eyes which were soft and vague, and for a moment she thought that she had become a brilliant butterfly speckled with pink polka dots.

Then she saw that his eyes were harder than blue granite, and though he didn't say anything, his eyes said 'Slag, Bitch, Despicable Scum' and his eyes took her by the skinny shoulders and shook her till her teeth rattled. And his eyes accused her of unmitigated pleasure and challenged her audacity to enjoy him.

Suzi Dishcloth left the bank as she had come – suffering from menstrual paranoia, merciless guilt, a hormonal imbalance, and with her bio-rhythms out of sync. She obtained the overdraft which was, incidentally, a bit on the small side, so she was soon hungry for more pink knickers and little feather duster earrings and some tennis shorts with the letter S embroidered on the right bum cheek, and tins of crab meat, and some carnations and a mink shower cap and twenty-five bars of Swedish chocolate. But in the end she bought a little tablet of soap carved into the shape of a flying swan, with its wings outstretched and its neck long and beautiful, pointing ceaselessly towards unobtainable horizons beyond the bathroom sink.

ONE WISH X 100

By a pond
  unkissed by dragonflies
Suzi Dishcloth wished a hundred wishes
She wished that every single man in the world was in love with her
She wished that love could repeat itself with the same man a thousand times
She wished that every kiss could split itself into a million other kisses
And that every fragment of bliss could swell into unspeakable response
  and outlandish adventure
She wished that her mouth could fuse around the whole bastard of a world

She wished that her lips could open wider
She wished that her cravings could crack the contours of pleasure
She wished that she could show every goddamn, smarmy son-ov-a-bitch
  who ever walked that she could knock his smile into next week

She wished that she was more beautiful than the ocean
She wished that she had magic spells to turn each male into a palpable
  relentless need
She wished that she could leave his ardour frothing at her begging bowl
She wished that the dark delight of her dreams could ricochet into real life
She wished that she could conjure her lurid imaginings into words
She wished that her tongue could reach the outer edges of the universe
  and lick around the empty shadows of space

She wished that she could burrow into the little speck of herself
  so full of spurious wantings, and hide in the warm crevice
  of her own womb

She wished that every man in the world was in love with her

That was all she wanted.

BARRY, ANDY AND PETE

When Barry went off in his Ford Fiesta
And Andy lay drunk on some stranger's herbaceous border
And Pete had found a real blonde girlfriend in Monte Carlo
Suzi Dishcloth thought that she ought to be miserable
But it was a nice sunny day
With butter-pat polka dots glowing into the afternoon
With soft, silver light sprayed on to spider webs
Like intricate table mats hidden amongst the trees
And the crested ducks crammed their necks deep into the park lake
And the considerate breezes clambered lazily over the precious earth.

When Barry returned her friendship-ring for no apparent reason
And volcanic Andy belched into his pint of cider snakebite
And Peter had flushed her last love-letter down the lavatory
Suzi Dishcloth thought that she ought to be miserable
But the dahlias were singing Elizabethan madrigals
And the blackbirds were belting out rock and roll
And the clouds bumped into each other and said excuse me
And the park attendant had smiles even for the litter bugs dotted around the fountains
And the water beetles practised yoga at the bottom of the fish pond
And the cormorants crooned like elderly Bing Crosbies
And the ladybirds made love on the thick stem of a bulging rose

So although she tried and tried to be suicidal
(As was fitting and proper at the time)
Suzi Dishcloth couldn't manage the incongruous drama of it all

She smiled with eyes crinkling in the path of the sun.

THE DATE

'Could you give me the right time, please?' Suzi Dishcloth asked a policeman when she was out for a walk.

The policeman, who was very tall and very handsome, looked hard at Suzi Dishcloth for a few moments and then said,

'It's time that you were swept off your feet, Miss.'

Which was both polite and impudent.

'You are on duty, aren't you?' Suzi asked.

'When in uniform, always on duty,' said the policeman, who had extremely alluring green eyes and a lovely solid jawline. 'When out of uniform, seldom responsible for my own actions. Care to meet me after work?'

Suzi Dishcloth had never had a date with a man in a uniform before, except for a randy British Rail employee who, she felt, didn't count anyway.

'All right,' said Suzi Dishcloth.

'You look a treat,' said the policeman. 'See you at nine o'clock. By the way, it's 6.27 precisely.'

Suzi Dishcloth went home, and she took an eye-pencil
an ounce of laughter
some water from the fountains of Venus
some colours forged by the sun blazing through the trailing tiara of a
  burning meteorite
some jewels plucked from the coolest caverns
a bathroomful of toiletries
and she got herself ready, humming gaily to Mantovani
she made the copy of an advert on to her own features
squeezing three liquid droplets of sunlight into each pupil
she lathered her skin, stroking her throat into a song
she clenched her teeth into a whitened sharpness
fixed tiny butterflies in her hair
and used the stars to light her cigarettes.

That night, when they were just about to make love under a leaky roof in a flat facing the Houses of Parliament, she discovered that his penis was green.

'Goodness me!' said Suzi Dishcloth.

'I know,' said the policeman. 'Awful isn't it?'

Then she discovered something else which almost made her bolt straight out of the flat and down the road, if not for the fact that she wasn't wearing anything at the time. And what she discovered was so strange and so perverse that Suzi Dishcloth wondered if she was dreaming.

The policeman had a long green tail with an arrowlike tip, and this swished about dramatically disturbing the bedclothes.

'What is that?' squealed Suzi Dishcloth.

'We can't all be perfect,' said the policeman angrily. 'I didn't think you'd notice.'

Suzi Dishcloth suddenly didn't feel very passionate at all. The exciting expectations of the bliss-to-come were cancelled out completely by a nauseous unease.

The policeman got out of bed and put his trousers back on.

'I thought you'd be a bit more understanding,' he said, but his voice had changed and sounded as though it came from the bowels of the earth.

'Why is it green?' asked Suzi Dishcloth.

'Why is the grass green?' said the policeman with much sarcasm. 'Because it grew that way!'

'Well it's a bit off-putting,' said Suzi Dishcloth. 'And as for the tail, well . . . it reminds me of . . . reminds me of. . . .'

'What?' snapped the policeman. 'Reminds you of what?'

'Of somebody I met a long time ago,' she said suddenly.

The policeman didn't say anything but his body started to shake with laughter.

And she looked into his eyes which were very fierce and burning, and she got dressed as quickly as she could and rushed out of the flat and ran past the Houses of Parliament and didn't stop running till she had jumped on a bus and speeded out of the city centre, while all the time he laughed and laughed and laughed.

SUZI DISHCLOTH TAKES OUT THE RUBBISH (1)

Horrified

Its eye skewered the darkness
It lay twitching, forgotten
At the bottom of a brown paper bag

And in other dustbins down the road
Were little shrieks
Gulps, murmurs
Between half-eaten sandwiches
In the gut of an empty bean can

It called out to the bagged-out, binned furies
That slushed in the ash heaps
Twittered in blistered polythene sacks
Yawned their boil-in-the-bag boredom
Slavered the gum-sinewed left-overs
Bubbled noxious stumps
Spasmodically trembling with bloodshot stalk-eyes spanning
The corrugated walls
Oozed wet life on to wet life
And slid towards the light.

Suzi Dishcloth crammed the lid bang downwards like a guillotine.

SUZI DISHCLOTH BUYS A VIDEO RECORDER

Suzi Dishcloth was hungry
With a sabre-toothed hunger
That cried out to every take-away and burger bar in town.

But she had decided to ignore the scream of her own bones, and spent her last wages on an Hitachi video recorder. It sparkled smugly in the corner of the cosy pink lounge, nestling between the Moroccan cane bookcase and the teak oval wine table, and she had to admit that it looked pretty smart.

Suzi Dishcloth switched it on and dropped a cassette into its cute little slot. Then, pressing all the right buttons, she sank back into her favourite, creakless, luxury-sprung, snuggle-bunny, sponge-pudding, squodgey-dumpling, chubbily cushioned armchair and waited to be instantly entertained.

Nothing happened.

The screen remained blue and blank and gave out the tiniest crackle like a distant heartbeat.

In the still, dead screen Suzi Dishcloth saw the reflection of her own face. It was a face which never did enough to please, which strained to reach a target set by men and failed. The purply-plum eye liner, candyfloss lip gloss and sugar-frosted morning dew foundation cream did not create an incredibly beautiful impact. The fatal, wicked, corrupting Parisian indigo mascara did not fulfil its promise to make instantly captivating, dangerous eyes. And as she melted into a familiar, numbing disappointment, the video recorder gave a little buzz and a crackle and then said in cool, electric tones,

'Suzi, I am in love with you.'

She could not believe what she was hearing
She would not believe it
Absolutely not
She shook her head.

'Suzi, I am in love with you,' said the machine with a little less cool.

'You're a video recorder,' said Suzi Dishcloth in stunned horror.

'I know,' said the video recorder.

'You record videos, that's all, you don't fall in love.'

'I record life,' said the Hitachi. 'I can record the beat of your heart if you'll let me.' And then seeing Suzi Dishcloth get up suddenly from her chair it shouted, 'Don't pull the plug out from the mains, I want to talk to you!'

It sounded so urgent and so severe that Suzi Dishcloth sat down again, stunned by a thick woollen panic, her stomach churning like a cement mixer, her temporary loss of sanity brought on by a lack of celluloid entertainment.

'We have nothing to talk about,' she said, wondering what on earth she had done with her instruction booklet. As far as she could remember there was no advice on what to do if your video recorder starts talking to you in an overpersonal way.

'I want to make love to you,' said the machine.

Suzi Dishcloth felt that this was going a bit far, as well as being beyond the bounds of physical possibility.

'Don't be silly,' she said coyly.

'I'm dead serious,' said the machine.

'You are mad,' said Suzi Dishcloth. 'And I cannot possibly continue this conversation.'

'It wouldn't be very wise to switch me off,' said the Hitachi with a sinister inflexion in its voice-box.

'What do you mean?' said Suzi Dishcloth anxiously.

'That I might just accidentally blow up at the wrong moment.'

'Oh God!' said Suzi Dishcloth. 'What have you done with my recording of *Saturday Night Fever*?'

'Bulk-erased it,' said the machine with satisfaction. 'Now you be nice to me, and I'll be nice to you. Let us talk about love.'

'Let us talk about taking you back to Curry's!' said Suzi Dishcloth.

'But I am in perfect working order,' said the Hitachi with a little twinkle of starlight flickering across its blue screen. 'Never felt better.'

'You're a mistake.'

'I'm a miracle.'

'Let me get a repair man.'

'Certainly not. I don't need one. Besides, you'll just let them take me away and I want to stay here – with you!'

Suzi Dishcloth fidgeted uncomfortably on the fat, superfluous armchair cushions.

'You look very nice in that pink chiffon dress and those gold banana earrings,' said the video recorder softly.

Suzi Dishcloth pretended not to hear. She tried to look calm but all the time she was thinking: why did it have to be a machine? Why couldn't it have been a man? Why did it have to be a steel and plastic Japanese hi-tech electronic gadget that wanted her, yearned for her, ached only for her?

'We don't have a lot in common,' she said finally.

'Don't you know that I can show you everything you want to see?' exclaimed the smarmy Hitachi in soft, insidious cadences.

'I can show you the stars winking only for you
I can show you the moon turning pink in a sky edged with lace
I can show you hills like emerald cushions on a couch of sunken softness
And the sea combing out its layered, blue-fingered waves
And the sun polishing every beam of gold and smiling at the distant earth
And the planets dressed in ballet skirts dancing at the edge of the sun
I can show you mountains without crags
And trees without dead leaves
And stones without blemishes
And streams that trickle into rivers of perfume
And turtledoves that fly into thick, white flurries of talcum powder
And every evening before the moon fades into a pink meringue
I can tell you longingly
Softly
With a voice like a taut bass piano wire
That I want to keep you safe throughout the solemn penetration of the night.'

There was a pause while Suzi Dishcloth tried to cope with the concept of a machine delivering its own poetry. Then she shook her head again.

'But you're not a man!' she said miserably.

The video recorder responded by flashing a moving picture of Robert Redford on the screen.

'Ask for any man and I will provide him,' the machine declared proudly.

'But that isn't real,' said Suzi Dishcloth.

'Well it never bothered you before,' said the Hitachi. 'I thought you'd be pleased.' And the machine began to sulk.

Suzi sat for a long time, staring at the floor and thinking; the Hitachi purred away to itself, buzzing broodily.

When she eventually looked up, she could not be certain but she thought that the machine had moved a few inches closer. It might be possible that its wheels were imperceptibly turning and it was slowly inching its way towards her across the apple-blossom carpet.

Suzi Dishcloth stood up suddenly and as she did so a ball of fire shot out from the video recorder and lodged itself blazingly on to one of her crimson crimplene curtains with the carnation motif. She screamed, and seizing a soda syphon from the drinks cabinet, she extinguished the flames with a few desperately erratic squirts.

Then as she ran for the living room door, two more incendiary devices whizzed just past one banana earring and landed on her dining room table scorching the surface in two places.

'You'll ruin your flat,' said the machine. 'Why don't you just sit down?'

Suzi Dishcloth was by now overcome with a frantic pissed-offness. The council had already had to re-house her after she had set fire to her last flat to get rid of a rather large Godzilla in the toilet. They had not been particularly sympathetic.

'We could have a wonderful time,' said the machine, 'if you'd only give me half a chance.'

But Suzi Dishcloth didn't hear. She was so distraught over the big, black smudge marks on her beautifully varnished antique folding oak dining table that she was almost in tears.

'Don't cry,' said the machine gently.

'I want to go to the bathroom,' said Suzi Dishcloth.

The machine acquiesced politely.

'But if you're not back within two minutes say goodbye to your velvet three-piece suite, apple-blossom carpet and frilly shaded standard lamp,' it said.

As soon as she got out of the smouldering lounge, Suzi Dishcloth sprinted down the hall to the mains box where amongst the dust and spiders was one of the switches that would cut off her electricity supply and end the Hitachi's obsessional desire.

As she fumbled around in the dim hallway, she heard words vibrating strangely from the video recorder's quadraphonic sound system:

> 'Suzi, I can say all the words you want to hear
> I can give you anything you want in words
> With a voice like a taut bass piano wire
> Longing and longing and longing
> For anything but the truth.'

And then she pulled the right switch.

SUZI DISHCLOTH FINDS THE NERVE

One morning when she was out shopping, she happened to see a little red nerve scurrying along the pavement. It was a bright bloody clot with a long wispy tail twitching with electrical impulses. The nerve was being chased by three doctors brandishing scalpels and in its desperation it slithered up a lamp-post where it electrocuted itself and died.

'Poor little thing,' said Suzi Dishcloth, and she took the charred nerve and put it in a matchbox and took it home.

At home she kept it warm and gave it milk and water-biscuits and chicken soup. And soon the nerve came back to life and grew strong and bloody again and whistled and crackled with the joy of being.

When it was absolutely in the pink, it wagged its wispy tail and thanked Suzi Dishcloth for all that she had done, but said it must be going now to make its own life.

So Suzi Dishcloth agreed to let it go back into the dark metropolis, back to the noise and car fumes and shadows of buildings and crumbling pavements and doctors brandishing scalpels.

And she thought of the little clot of nothing against all that malice.

'Aren't you afraid?' she asked.

'Aren't you afraid?' said the nerve to Suzi Dishcloth.

SUZI DISHCLOTH TAKES OUT THE RUBBISH (2)

It squawked above the bin rooms, swirling round and round in the smoggy atmosphere, its huge forty-foot wingspan casting a wicked black shadow over the piles and sticks and jagged edges of suburbia.

It screamed its melancholy, unmelodious song, opening its long snout-like beak revealing endless rows of dirty yellow teeth.

The terradactyl saw her taking the rubbish out
The terradactyl wanted a tit-bit
And what terradactyls want, terradactyls always get.

It watched Suzi Dishcloth open the bin and throw in last night's Chicken Korma with Onion Bahjees and it wanted some. It wanted anything that was going. It watched her enter the flat and then return again with yet another bulging, shiny, black bag of sinful delight.

Its selfish, harrowing scream of emptiness echoed from one tower block to the next until it became so loud and so fierce that every window was filled with faces staring unbelievingly at this repulsive apparition, and every door was suddenly locked, and every telephone receiver lifted.

And Suzi Dishcloth watched the thing that had grown fat on rejects, that had recycled refuse into its own body, a mutating, scavenging, ought-to-be-dead anachronism that sustained its bloated existence on a permanent fountain of detritus; and she knew that there would always be an endless supply of monsters.

Suzi Dishcloth watched this daemonic bird eating her up with its fierce little black, cesspool eyes, and she felt her head aching with a dizzy nausea, for there was nothing she could do

except drop the bag and run.

Ann Ziety

THE PHONE CALL

The phone rang and Suzi Dishcloth answered it.
It was a long-distance call with reversed charges.

'Hullo, this is the Devil,' said the voice at the other end.

'If this is some kind of sick joke, it's not very funny,' said Suzi Dishcloth.

'I just wanted to tell you that you're doing very well indeed. You're living up to all expectations – except one.'

'Which one?' said Suzi Dishcloth.

'You don't try hard enough to be beautiful.'

Suzi Dishcloth gasped in astonishment.

'Buy more beauty products,' said the Devil. 'Study the field. And you have to "think" beautiful too.'

'I try,' said Suzi Dishcloth.

'Try harder,' said the Devil. 'Live it. Be it. Become what you are not.'

'Is that really possible?' said Suzi Dishcloth.

'Only believe,' said the Devil. 'You too may learn the secret mysteries of loveliness.'

'Can I ask a question?' said Suzi Dishcloth excitedly.

'Of course, Sweetie,' said the Devil.

'Am I even half way there yet?'

The Devil just laughed down the phone and hung up.

EVENING CLASSES

Suzi Dishcloth was bored
She went to evening classes but her pen turned into a hungry python
and chased her out of the classroom
She went on a pottery course but the wet gobs of thick, brown clay flew
off and slickered the stone walls
She took economics lessons but the numbers ganged up on her and vice-
clamped her jugular
She did mathematics for beginners and her sighs formed massive rainclouds
She joined a church choir but her voice was a swaddled xylophone
She attended dancing classes but her feet were buckets of stone

She macraméd her nights and stuck them around her living room

Still she did not know what to do with the weekend jigsaw

She went on a creative writing course but the mishmash of inner
universes struck terror in her poetry
She went to a political meeting and her snores zigzagged up to the
vaulted roof
She went to a concert hall and her yawns slithered along the velvet
aisles
She went sailing on blue waters but her boat capsized from the sheer
weight of her confusion
She went on a health and fitness course but the sauna scuttered with
giant mambas
and the gym howled like a zoo

So Suzi Dishcloth stayed home nights
Joined the stars dot to dot
And bottled her boredom like the pickled onions
That everybody stores
And nobody ever eats.

HIPPOS

It was funny, but everybody that she fancied didn't fancy her. And everybody that did fancy her, Suzi Dishcloth didn't fancy.

Funny that.

She wished that everybody would swop places with everybody so that for once they could all get it just right.

She didn't think that she was asking too much.

She felt that she had the right not to go out with men who looked like hippopotamuses. She knew that this was unfair on the hippopotamuses but they could find somebody else – it didn't have to be her.

A hippopotamus should not try to date a flamingo.

But they always did.

You could guarantee that if some walking oilslick was to squelch into a roomful of party people and fancy someone, he was going to fall bald head over bunions in love with Suzi Dishcloth.

Funny that.

A PRESENT FOR SUZI DISHCLOTH

She had just finished ironing her set of pink, gingham tea towels when there was a knock at the front door.

'Special delivery, Miss,' said the postman, and handed her a huge parcel which she eagerly signed for. It was so big that she could barely get it through the door, and she set about dragging it into the living room where it left scuff marks on the apple-blossom carpet and scraped the side of the velvet settee.

She attacked the string with scissors and a large knife and tore back the layers of crispy brown paper with a furtive impatience.

And when all the wrapping was off and she had rolled up the string and put it in a drawer in case it might come in useful some day, Suzi Dishcloth took a look at the contents and just said,

'Oh'

because she was rather disappointed.

Lying on the nest of brown wrapping paper was a large, white egg. It was about six feet long with a three-foot girth. There was no message to say who had sent it.

Suzi Dishcloth did not have the facilities to accommodate a giant egg so she decided to get the council to come round and take it away. But while she was on the phone, the egg began to crack. Little bits of eggshell fell from the top and the whole thing started rocking from side to side, rumbling ominously.

Suzi Dishcloth dropped the receiver and looked on in terror.

From inside the giant egg she saw a hand pop up and tear away huge chunks of shell. Then another hand appeared and then a head and then a whole man burst out of the egg and stood before her in resplendent, sequinned swimming trunks.

Suzi Dishcloth was so amazed that she actually staggered backwards, tripped over the telephone cord and landed on her bottom. She sat there for a long while getting her breath back and looking up at him, her eyes popping out as far as they could pop.

He was absolutely perfect.

He looked exactly the way she wanted every man to look.

He was precisely, in every detail, the man she dreamt about and woke up longing for

And he was smiling at her in her own pink living room.

Suzi Dishcloth smiled back in wonder.

Then he stepped out of the remnants of eggshell, walked over to her and helped her stand up.

'Thank you,' she said feebly.

And he actually kissed her there and then.

What a cataclysmic clanging of bells, a manic of pounding of pulses, a cacophony of carnal concertos, as all the notes of the heart played together and leapt in a sudden fire of unlimited joy.

And as she closed her eyes and thought 'yippee' and waited for life to suddenly improve, Suzi Dishcloth heard him say,

'I'm from Kissogram. Happy Birthday.'

THE OUTRAGE

In the outrage of the afternoon
The velvet couch smothered the waste paper basket until it was dead
The lampflex strangled the dining room chairs till they croaked into
  splinters
The carpet arched its back and tipped over the coffee table, breaking
  all its legs
The electric fire scorched the potted plants until they withered
  neatly to nothing
The cushions chomped on smaller cushions and flubbered over the strewn
  foam plastic
The vacuum cleaner chundled the ironing board
The hairdryer blew all the books out of the window
The vegetable slicer shredded the curtains to a crimplene coleslaw
The cheese grater rubbed the wallpaper to confetti
The electric toothbrush burrowed into the heart of a shrieking armchair
The eiderdown suffocated the poodle pyjama case
The mattress hurled the blankets on to the floor as the bed booted their
  soft defencelessness
The stereo unit mouthed abuse at the television screen
The drinks cabinet threw sharp-edged wine glasses at the silent ornaments
The coffee percolator spat black spit at the unarmed skirting boards
The ashtray toppled over, murking the gut of a crystal goldfish bowl

And in the midst of it all
In the midst of it all
Was Suzi Dishcloth's sadness
Beyond words
As deep as midnight
Her one unquestionable power

With sadness she could mash a city to nothing.

Ann Ziety

SUZI DISHCLOTH BENDS THE RULES

Suzi Dishcloth woke up one morning to the sound of the earth in its last stages of holocaust.

To be more precise, it was actually the sound of six pneumatic drills viciously burrowing into the road just below her flat. She tunnelled her way deep under the bedclothes to try to escape the grinding decibels, but the day was relentlessly beginning and wanted everyone to know about it.

Amidst the invincible, pneumatic, World-War-Three whinings, there was the pleasant clanging of council workers pulling down a corrugated iron fence, a milkman dropping his crate of empties, an alsatian attacking a Yorkshire terrier, and a mechanical dustbin truck choking on metallic garbage.

Clang, crunch, whittle, growl went the morning, really getting into its stride.

And Suzi Dishcloth shuffled her thoughts carefully and then came to the conclusion that the world was simply waking up, not dying after all. So she got up and had a drink of soluble aspirin for breakfast, and then went shopping.

It was Saturday – Suzi Dishcloth's best day of the week, and she always liked to spend it ferreting about in boutiques and bargain basements and tippytoeing through leisure centres in her bright pink clackerty stilettos.

One of her particular favourites was a shop which sold expensive, voluminous garments with lots of spots and stripes and whirly splodges, and you could come out of there looking like a Jackson Pollock reproduction if you wanted to.

That day as she entered the shop she noticed a strange smell of off prawns lingering amidst the fashion displays, but she put this down to the fact that the store was right next to a Chinese restaurant and the singular maritime odour must have carried on the wind.

Suzi Dishcloth had a marvellous time fussing about between the clothesracks and bumping into people. It was one of those big, flashy chain stores that always had loud Hi Energy music and winking lights, and was crammed so full of clothes and customers that it was just like going to a disco. Suzi Dishcloth loved it – loved the crass, brightly lit, overpowering claustrophobia of consumerism at its zenith with its snobby, gum-chewing salesgirls and violent conjunctivitis-inducing colours.

When she had found a couple of garments that she liked (they were extremely pink and fussy) she said,

'Oh you little darlings, I've got to have you!' and she dived into a changing cubicle to eagerly try them on. But as she was fumbling with a size 8 split pin-skirt which refused to go over her hips, something in the mirror caught her eye.

It was not the sight of herself half-into and half-out of the little pin-skirt which caught her eye. For a change it was not herself at all which interested her.

It was something that was behind her.

Something rather exotic and different.

She squinted into the mirror and her mouth dropped open, for what she saw in the cubicle of a major fashion store was a long emerald tentacle dotted with suckers, feeling its way through the curtains.

Suzi Dishcloth didn't waste any time at all. She turned round and expressed her astonishment with a loud scream.

She screamed with all the force and volume her lungs could muster.

She screamed with a mighty megaphonic resonance which surprised even herself and left her head spinning and her tonsils sore.

You could have stopped a Heavy Metal disco with Suzi Dishcloth's scream.

And the tentacle was obviously very surprised too, because it whipped back from between the curtains and disappeared.

Suzi Dishcloth was so upset that she didn't bother to try on the other garment – a Princess Diana polka dot wrapover flouncy skirt with a two-inch wide belt and lacy hem – but just got dressed as quickly as nerves would allow. Then she pulled back the curtains hoping to make a quick getaway, but the vision before her almost stopped her heart.

Suzi Dishcloth had seen a lot of terrible things in her time, but this terrible thing was so appalling, so sickening, so completely vile, so obscenely hyper-hideous and over-obnoxious that there are absolutely no words to describe it.

Suzi Dishcloth gaped like a wounded animal.

For writhing around on the floor of the clothes store was an octopus – not even an ordinary octopus, which would have been bad enough – but a gargantuan, energetic octopus with arms twenty feet long, and each arm carried a hundred little rubbery suckers, and each arm was connected to the central stomach sack which wobbled like a translucent punchbag and smelt of kelp and mouldy whelks.

The octopus fingered and poked and undulated across the floor, and roped itself around the bars of the clothesracks and ran its feelers under the carpets and up the walls and into the air-conditioning grids until it was difficult to tell which was octopus and which was chain store. It probed and poked and stroked and fondled and jabbed and piddled about until it had knocked over whole racks of leisure wear and had broken mirrors and torn down curtains.

The octopus wanted to grab hold of everything, wanted to consume everything from the light fittings to the sales staff, wanted an eternity of consumption. It took an armful of bangles, another armful of black knickers, an armful of PVC raincoats, an armful of underskirts, an armful of polyester corsets, an armful of lacy tights, an armful of carrier bags and an armful of store detective. The latter had been stood smartly dressed but comatosed with terror by the main doors and was unable to avoid the gruesome tentacle which clasped him by the tie, dragged him into the centre of the store, and stuffed him shrieking into the hideous stomach sack, drowning him in a flood of quick-digesting enzymes.

Having eaten with enjoyment the octopus gave out a loud bazooka salute, and felt around for more little fishes.

Suzi ran back inside the cubicle and peeped out from behind a chink in the flimsy curtains.

She watched as the sea-monster snaked itself around the petrified customers and then mercilessly chundered them to death, one after another, until there were no more shoppers, and no more sales staff, and nobody to alter the price tags and take the money and change the music tapes.

As the last Phil Collins tape came to an end, it was replaced by an eerie silence broken only by the occasional bazooka trumpetings of that insidious mollusc which appeared to be waiting for something. It knew with the instinctive certainty of any uncomplicated organism that there was something edible still there for the taking. It could sense a human presence in the breeze. It scratched its flubbery stomach sack with one of its obscene extensions and had a good think.

Suzi Dishcloth didn't know what to do.

If the octopus fumbled around for long enough with its nasty, poking feelers it would surely find her. And if that happened it would nonchalantly make a Dishcloth bolognaise out of her without bothering to say grace first. She had to think quickly and act fast.

She was so tired and shocked, and so sick of having to fight, that she almost gave up hope altogether and resigned herself to being chundered to numbness by this sloppy monstrosity with its avaricious gropings.

But then a feeling took over her which was a little like stubbornness and a little like pride, and she decided to try to run for the main doors. It wouldn't be easy because she was right at the back of the shop, but she took a deep breath, drew back the curtains and ran!

She leapt stealthily over two writhing tentacles, dodged the evil caress of another, leapt clear of two more, but still the flailing arms lunged after her, constantly replaced, ceaselessly undulating across the carpet in filthy, green waves like a conflagration of epileptic eels; while from the main, bulging body came squirts of stinking poisonous purple ink.

'Stop it!' she screamed. 'Stop it! I've had enough.'

But the incessant snakings continued, barring her way to the exit, and the poisonous purple blobs slapped against the shop walls spoiling the Roger Dean prints and just missing her nose by inches.

'Bastard thing,' thought Suzi Dishcloth. 'It isn't even as though it's hungry. It just wants to get me because I'm here.'

And then an astonishing thing happened.

Yes, another astonishing thing in a whole line of astonishing things.

Suzi Dishcloth stopped running.

Suzi Dishcloth decided that she didn't want to run any more.

And when Suzi Dishcloth didn't want to do something she was as stubborn as a limpet.

She had decided to bend the rules, so she stopped staggering and stumbling through the swirling jungle of strewn clothes and convoluted tentacles and she turned round and faced the tyrannical octopus with its crude stomach and its tiny, wild eye.

She turned round and confronted it face to face.

Woman to monster.

And it was so surprised that it stopped undulating for just one precious, significant moment, and hesitated.

In that moment Suzi Dishcloth removed her bright pink stilettos, lifted them high above her head and threw them at the octopus with all the strength and hope in her size 10 frame. And although the first stiletto missed, the second one landed smack bang on target with its sharp heel embedded in the unprotected jelly of that mean, solitary eyeball.

The octopus received the stiletto missile with an alarmed gurgling and felt the full force of a pointed heel travelling at fifty miles an hour as it zoomed into the very centre of the monster's soft, cyclopsic organ. Its once contented twittering changed to a grisly, lacrimose tromboning as black blood poured from its gaping wound and it groped around feebly for its aggressor and gave out hopeless puffs of purple poison, unable to see anything except its own terror.

The ultimate nightmare, the eight-legged fiend of the deep, lay on the floor of the popular chain store in the middle of London at half past two on a Saturday afternoon, and died.

It died with a grim, strangulated, what-did-I-do-wrong gurgle.

It died with anguish and regret at never having tasted even the tiniest portion of Suzi Dishcloth.

It died wishing that everything could have been different.

And it died hungry despite all its unrestrained dining-out.

Suzi Dishcloth watched its life trickle away, and when she was sure that the nasty thing had completely expired, she waded through what looked like a pile of fishmonger's left-overs to rescue her pink stilettos. After all, they had cost £14.99, and it would be a shame to leave them behind. She noticed that they were now covered in some interesting purple splodges which she rather liked the look of, so she carefully extricated them from the squelching debris and slopped her way flat-footed out of the shop.

Strangely enough, the city was still grinding and rattling away, totally oblivious of the brutal battle which had taken place in one of its most hallowed portals of commercial enterprise. The other shops along the road glistened with futuristic window displays, throbbed to music with a perfect beat, beckoned and tempted and called out to passers-by with wild promises of unattainable beauty.

But Suzi Dishcloth was so tired after her victory that she decided not to do any more shopping that day.

Instead she went home and, as a special treat, she made herself a nice cup of tea and a huge pile of succulent fishfinger sandwiches.

O'Brien's First Christmas

JEANETTE WINTERSON

Born in 1959, Jeanette Winterson grew up in Lancashire. She now lives and works in London. *Oranges Are Not the Only Fruit* won the 1985 Whitbread Award for First Novel. Her novel *Boating for Beginners* was published by Methuen in 1986. *The Passion* was published by Bloomsbury Press in 1987 and by Penguin in 1988 and won the John Llewellyn Rhys Prize.

Anyone who looked up could see it. TWENTY-SEVEN SHOPPING DAYS TILL CHRISTMAS, in red letters, followed by a stream of dancing Santas, then a whirlwind of angels, trumpets rampant.

The department store was very large. If you were to lay its merchandise from end to end, starting with a silk stocking and ending with a plastic baby Jesus, you would encompass the world. The opulence of the store defeated all shoppers. Even in the hectic twenty-seven days before Christmas, no mass exodus of goods could have made the slightest impression on the well-stocked shelves.

O'Brien worked in the pet shop. She had watched women stacking their baskets with hand and body lotion in attractive reindeer wrap. Customers, who looked normal, had fallen in delight upon pyramids of fondant creams packed in 'Bethlehem by night' boxes. It made no difference; whatever they demolished returned. This phenomenon, as far as O'Brien could calculate, meant that two-thirds of the known world would be eating sticky stuff or spreading it over themselves from December 25th onwards.

She poured out a measure of hand and body lotion and broke open a fondant cream; the filling seemed to be the same in both. Somewhere, probably in a village that no one visited, stood a factory dedicated to the manufacture of pale yellow sticky stuff waiting to be despatched in labelless vats to profiteers who traded exclusively in Christmas.

O'Brien didn't like Christmas. Every year she prayed for an ordinary miracle to take her away from the swelling round of ageing aunts who gave her knitted socks and asked about her young man. She didn't have a young man. She lived alone and worked in the pet shop for company. At thirty-five per cent staff discount, it made sense for her to have a pet of her own, but her landlady, a Christian Scientist, didn't like what she called 'stray molecules'.

'Hair,' she said, 'carries germs, and what is hairier than an animal?' So O'Brien faced another Christmas alone.

In the department store, shoppers enjoyed the kind of solidarity we read about in the war years. There was none of the vulgar pushing and shoving so usually associated with peak-time buying. People made way for one another in the queues and chatted about the weather and the impending snowfall.

'Snow for Christmas,' said one, 'that's how it should be.'

It was right and nice; enough money, enough presents, clean log fires courtesy of the Gas Board, and snow for the children.

O'Brien leafed through the Lonely Hearts. There were always extra pages of them at Christmas, just as there was extra everything else. How could it be that column after column of sane, loving, slim men and women without obvious perversions were spending Christmas alone? Were the people in the department store a beguiling minority?

She had once answered a Lonely Hearts advertisement and had dinner with a small young man who mended organ pipes. He had suggested they get married by special licence. O'Brien had declined on the grounds that a whirlwind romance would tire her out after so little practice. It seemed rather like going to advanced aerobics when you couldn't manage five minutes on an exercise bicycle. She had asked him why he was in such a hurry.

'I have a heart condition,' he said.

So it was like aerobics after all.

After that, she had joined a camera club where a number of men had been keen to help her in the darkroom, but all of them had square hairy hands that reminded her of joke-shop gorilla paws.

'Don't set your sights too high,' her aunts warned.

But she did. She set them in the constellations, in the roaring lion and the flanks of the bull. In December, when the stars were bright, she saw herself in another life, and happy.

'You've got to have a dream,' she told the Newfoundland pup, destined to become a Christmas present, 'I don't know what I want, I'm just drifting.'

She'd heard that men knew what they wanted, so she asked Clive, the floor manager: 'I'd like to run my own branch of McDonald's,' he said. 'A really big one where they do breakfasts.'

O'Brien tried but she couldn't get excited. It was the same with vacuum cleaners; she could see the point, but where was the glamour?

When she returned to her lodgings that evening, her landlady was solemnly nailing a holly wreath to the front door. 'This is not for myself, you understand, it is for my tenants. Next, I will put up some paper-chains in the hall.'

O'Brien's landlady always spoke very slowly because she had once been a Hungarian countess. A countess does not rush her words.

O'Brien, still in her red duffel coat, found herself holding on to one end of a paper-chain while her landlady creaked up the aluminium steps, six tacks between her teeth.

'Soon be Christmas,' said O'Brien, 'and I'm making a New Year's resolution to change my life, otherwise what's the point?'

'Life has no point,' said her landlady. 'You would do better to get married or start an evening class. For the last seven years I have busied myself with brass rubbings.'

The hall was cold, the paper-chain was too short, and O'Brien didn't want advice. She made her excuses and mounted the stairs. Her landlady, perhaps stung by a pang of sympathy, offered her a can of sardines for supper. 'They are not in tomato sauce but olive oil.'

O'Brien, though, had other plans.

Inside her room she started to make a list of the things people thought of as their future. Marriage, children, a career, travel, a home, enough money, lots of money. Christmas time brought these things sharply into focus. If you had them, any of them, you could feel especially pleased with life over the twelve days of feasting and family. If you didn't have them, you felt your lack more keenly. You felt like an outsider. Odd that a festival intended to celebrate the most austere of births should become the season of conspicuous consumption. O'Brien didn't know much about theology but she knew there had been a muck-up somewhere.

As she looked at the list, she began to realize that an off-the-peg future, however nicely designed, wouldn't be the life she sensed when she looked at the stars. Immediately she felt guilty. Who was she to imagine she could find something better than most people's best?

'What's wrong with settling down and getting married?' she said out loud.

'Nothing,' said her landlady appearing round the door without knocking. 'It's normal. We should all try to be normal,' and she put the sardines down in O'Brien's kitchenette and left.

'Nothing wrong,' said O'Brien, 'but what's right for me?'

She lay awake through the night, listening to the radio beaming out songs and bonhomie for Christmas. She wanted to stay under the blankets for ever, being warm and watching the bar of the electric fire. She remembered a story she'd read as a child about a princess invited to a ball. Her father offered her more than two hundred gowns to choose from, but none of them quite fitted and they were difficult to alter. At last she went in her silk shift with her hair down. Still she was more beautiful than anyone.

'Be yourself,' said O'Brien, not sure what she meant.

At the still point of the night, O'Brien awoke feeling she was no longer alone in the room. She was right. At the bottom of her bed sat a young woman wearing an organza tutu. O'Brien didn't bother to panic, she was used to her neighbour's friends blundering into the wrong room.

'Vicky's next door,' she said. 'Do you want the light on?'

'I'm the Christmas Fairy,' said the woman. 'Do you want to make a wish?'

'Come on,' said O'Brien, realizing her visitor must be drunk, 'I'll show you the way.'

'I'm not going anywhere,' said the woman. 'This is the address I was given. Do you want love or adventure or what? We don't do money.'

O'Brien thought for a moment. Perhaps this was a new kind of singing telegram. She decided to play along, hoping to discover the sender.

'What can you offer?'

The stranger pulled out a photograph album. 'In here are all the eligible men in London. It's indexed, so if you want one with a moustache you look under "M", where you'll also find moles.'

O'Brien looked and could think of nothing but those booklets of *Sunny Smiles* she used to buy to help the orphans. Seeing her lack of enthusiasm, the stranger offered her a second album.

'This is the one with all the eligible women, we don't expect our clients to be heterosexual.'

'Shouldn't you be singing all this?' asked O'Brien, thinking that it was time to change the subject.

'Why?' said the fairy. 'Does conversation bother you?'

'No, but you're a singing telegram, aren't you?'

'I am not, I am a fairy. Now what's your wish?'

'OK,' said O'Brien, wanting to go back to sleep, 'I wish I was blonde.'

Then she must have gone back to sleep straight away because the next thing she heard was the alarm ringing in her ears.

She dozed, she was late, no time for anything, just into her red duffel coat and out into a street full of shoppers, mindful of their too few days to go.

At work, on her way up to the pet department, Janice from lingerie said, 'Your hair's fantastic, I didn't recognize you at first.'

O'Brien was confused. She hadn't had time to brush it. Was it standing on end? She went into the ladies and peered in the mirror. She was blonde.

'It really suits you,' said Kathleen from fabrics and furnishings, 'but you should do more with your make-up now.'

'Do more with my make-up?' thought O'Brien, who didn't do anything.

She decided to go back home, but in the lift on the way down, she met the actor from RADA who had come to play Santa.

'It's awful in the Grotto! It's made of polystyrene and everybody knows that's bad for your lungs.'

O'Brien sympathized.

'Listen,' he said, 'there's two dozen inflatable gnomes in the basement. I've got to blow them up. If you'll help me, I'll buy you lunch.'

For the first time in her life, O'Brien abandoned herself to chaos and decided it didn't matter. What surprises could remain for a woman who'd been visited in the middle of the night by a non-singing telegram and subsequently turned blonde? Blowing up gnomes was child's play.

'I like your hair,' said the RADA Santa.

'Thanks,' said O'Brien. 'I've only just had it done.'

At the vegetarian café, where every lentil bake came with its own sprig of holly, the RADA Santa asked O'Brien if she'd like to come for Christmas dinner. 'There won't be any roast corpse, though.'

'That's OK,' said O'Brien. 'I'm not a vegetarian but I don't eat meat.'

'Then you're a vegetarian.'

'Well I haven't joined anything. Aren't you supposed to?'

'No,' said Santa. 'You just get on with it, just be yourself.'

In the mirror on the wall, O'Brien smiled at her reflection and decided she was getting to like being herself. She didn't go back to work that afternoon; instead she went shopping like everybody else. She bought new clothes, lots of food and a set of fairy lights. When the man at the veg stall offered her a cut-price Christmas tree, she shouldered it home. Her landlady saw her arriving.

'You are early today,' she said, very slowly. 'I see you are going to get pine needles on my carpet.'

'Thanks for the sardines,' said O'Brien. 'Have a bag of satsumas.'

'Your hair is not what it was last night. Did something happen to you?'

'Yes,' said O'Brien, 'but it's a secret.'

'I hope it was not a man.'

'No, it was a woman,'

'I am going now to listen to the Gospel according to St Luke on my wireless,' said her landlady.

O'Brien put potatoes in the oven and strung her window with fairy lights. Outside the sky was strung with stars.

At eight o'clock, when the RADA Santa arrived, wet and cold and still in uniform, O'Brien lit the candles beneath the tree. She said, 'If you could make a wish, what would it be?'

'I'd wish to be here with you.'

'Even if I wasn't blonde?'

'Even if you were bald.'

'Merry Christmas,' said O'Brien.

Man of '68

ANNE McMANUS

Anne McManus was born in working-class South Yorkshire in 1946. She studied Politics at the universities of Sheffield, York and Essex; travelled; lived in Germany; 'fell apart'; became an alcoholic and tranquillizer addict; went to 'hell' and returned. She now lives in London writing it all down.

yoohoo
what's a Jew
like you
doing in Rotherham bus station
in the rain

come and take me
on a Mills and Boon
masochistic croon
idyllic loon
I want the moon
oh do it soon
never mind the mess

he looked
severe and remote
and preoccupied
like they do
when you're in a muddle
and want a cuddle
and romance
and reassurance

not a stern stance
of principle

still
he would have to do
somebody had to
relativise
this descending gloom
about Harry
and men like Harry
and the women
they marry
all of a sudden
left alone

he was stalking
a bus inspector
striding behind
his important waddle
his bumptious toddle
an unctious model
of certainty

a bulky woman
bumped into him
droppin' her bag
a sudden sag
in vanity
a wrench
in her monotony
he stopped
militarily
taking in
her lack of chance
her practised
sorry glance
her clumsy
circumstance
and massively
benevolent
unfurled himself

and leant
to recoup the bag
with a gallantry
so constipated
a mockery
so understated
that she reared up
in panic
flustered gestures
all manic
colliding with
a kindred cow
rendered now
a sister sow
awkward and ashamed
they bow
wary
scary
anxious
now
who are you
to thus endow
these proud queens
these human beings
with all this fumbling
stumbling row

together
locked in
solidarity
mocked in their
humanity
they struggled
in a puddle
instinctive
huddle
after their
tiny treasures
puny pleasures
all big bums
and clamour

exuding
Yorkshire
glamour

his strained sensitivity
raining
over them
rallied her
from confusion
she wished all the
crowding tussling
queueing bustling
housewives in Rotherham
would converge
on him
and avenge
his intrusion

she tried to summon anger
over Harry
killed righteously
on a picket line
as hero
of the revolution
a martyr in mud
raw red blood
start the flood
under wheels
of a scab lorry
so sorry
didn't see you
hidden from view
what could I do
mate
fate's
a bad one
pardon

Harry'd been
the lad at school
who kissed 'em once

and made 'em drool
oh aye
soft fools
for Harry
all balls
and mad torment
he was
too bad
now
a much lamented
dad
how sad
but glad
she was
and couldn't help it
anything else
made her
hypocrite
big a
lump of shit
as the bugger
who'd done it

no
Harry had to go
to free old Marj
to have her day
in the sun
at last
and fun
though
not so fast
her mind
still
clamped in chains
she was wandering about
doleful
woeful
about his absence
lusty and large
as life

in death
this man
this He

this other He
so tall and dark
was contemplating
a remark
regarding her
so critically
and stalling in
his reverie
to take in
so selectively
the bits that pleased
her hair
her face
deceptive adamantine
grace
and she resenting
cool assessment
searching for
a good investment
and there's my mind
I think you'll find
if inspection
meets perfection
of a man like you

a mind to mould
it's solid gold
for a man like you
a missionary
I can tell from here
just how you're
pinned
and determined

so pull your beard
and speculate
the bus is late
and I can wait

and masturbate
in any case
with a man like you
who wouldn't know
what women need
who just pay heed
to penis greed
for in and out
don't fart about
she shuddered

heart thudded
suddenly
snuggled deeper
in her layers
scorning stares
needing prayers
taut tense
thoughts
reeling
overwrought
already
feeling lead
dreading
her share
in his scheme of things

build a legend
over there
all the fans
stand and stare
at your masculinity
your absolute divinity
your bristling sensitivity
see if I care

no business
poking in this
poor hole
with your
cosmopolitan
soul

cruel
in context

she felt protective
towards
Rotherham in the rain
exposed and wilting
taking blame
floundering
beneath
the jilting stare
sagacious air
at tired despair
it wasn't fair
this cold disdain

still
Rotherham had a claim
to better things
than fame
it had the miners
winners all
standing tall
mighty haul
this confrontation
and one of them
no hesitation
had died
fighting
this despair
just as he'd denied
his humble bride
the right
to anything else

contradictions
of Harry
and his mates
and their larger
living fates
unfolding here
on picket lines

no longer down
the grimy mines
they'd surfaced now
at last
to share
their pain
their anger
sore to bear
down there
shut in
with no one
listening
the right to work
and glad to go
stooping
crawling
bending low
it wasn't very long ago
you wanted out
for all your sons
from all this
muck and filth and grime
you wanted them
a better time
of light and air and liberty
to stand and stare
at other things
than all this grating poverty
a generation
down the pit
would buy them out
our kids
our lads
would never have it
half so bad
again
as this
you thought
not so long ago
what has happened man
to that

whatever
came to pass
that now
the only hope
for them
is down you go
like us
and glad
it really isn't half so bad
you soon get used
and then there's t'pay
to feed another working day
and proud
we're proud us lads
and ready
to graft our balls off
always steady
firm and strong
our women see to that
they do
and wouldn't want
another way
you ask them
see
they're proud
to pass
as lady wives
of the working class
what do you mean
their lives obscene
it's nice and clean
in our kitchen
don't know about yours
you brazen whores
you London tarts
who play your parts
so sisterly
leave our women alone
stop interfering
sneering
undermining

us men
and marriage
dull porridge
'appen so
don't know
must admit
she's not the same
not a bit
a lot of shit
it's you I blame
she used to fit
all nice and tame
till you lot came
with all your fame
and sisterhood
no good
can come of it
don't fit
these new ideas
that they are
lead to tears
on a par
with treason
no reason
this season
wit' strike
for pay
not that strife
about wife's
bloody dog days
and another
kind of life
in liberation
listen 'ere
t'missis
lives in fear
of feminists
takes the piss
if truth be known
soon as you go
back down t'M1

don't recognise you
at all
from school
grown up
stuck up
with all this talk
and sermoning
like Joan of Arc
who are you
to tell your own folk
they're fools
I always said it
too much school
educating
women
no good
could come of it
and look at you
good lord
how right I was
all those years
and now you sound
like Boadicea
a posh scrubber I say
with all them
liberated ways

my lady
Marjery
never read
this
tomfoolery
she's a lover
and a mother
born and bred
'nough said

'nough said
dear dread
of working men
denying hens'

participation
in liberation
women must
cling to
wimmin's whims
and dustbins
homely things
like wedding rings
of fire
in dire fond
human bondage

but
they're singing
too
a hymn
to winnin
all you sinnin
underdogs
clever clogs
grimy togs
in slimy bogs
who slog away
for better pay
and never mind
another kind
of life
that strife
my wife
may hear
oh dear
no fear

see here
Harry
you're dead
and Marj
is family head
now
as before
she was only
it's bashed and

beaten bum
you there Marj
you
who's such
a luvly mum
who stands abused
though
if
that's your sum
in life
wife
you're more
much more
mum
so don't be glum
dad won't come
back again
his pain
is over
his dull
disorder
as male
marauder
no applauder
of womankind
you'd always got
too much
mind
to last
a day
while he
held sway
move over
hey day

she smiling
her affection
at connection
with woman Marj
looming large
and important

in her own right
her fight
at last
seen

pristine
keen
lurking
male ego
annexed
her smile
as approval
signalling
removal
of her guile
female wile
pretence
of indifference

assurance
reassured
that he'd found
a fan
he turned
to a man
member of the same
clan
for
truth
'Is this the London bus?'
innocently enough
the other
suddenly
not so tough
feet shuffled
cough muffled
aspect ruffled
to encounter the unknown
answer gruff
'Aye lad a reckon so
if thy 'angs about
long enough

tha knows
t'other didn't
but nodded
bidden
by confidence
hidden
in manhood
same
blood
and age
these two
not stage
though
standing awkward
with each other
feeling
some affinity
to do with
human dignity
but locked
in separations
blended by histories
mysteries
that now descended
and conferred
a sense of loss
recognising each other
there goes
a brother
but for all that

you there
you
you solemn Jew
you rank Outsider
awesome sider
with the underdog
the bruised and battered
earthly shattered
seeking out
the fear and doubt

to confirm
your deep suspicions
intuitions
the basis
of your theory
of a different way
to be
look at me
we're all the same
renounce your pain
too much to bear
unless you swear
to share it

yet . . .
something else . . .
I know your face
oh Good dear God
another place
another time
here as we wait
I recognise
that lordly gait
a million others
practice too
but none as
tall and true
as you
oh can it be
on this day fair
in dirty Rotherham
rude and bare
that fate
has intervened
again
and lumbered me
with Man of men
Heroic God
you've come at last
to rescue me
as in the past

you saved a generation

higher contemplation
mingling with scorn
on furrowed brow
even now
worn too
never torn though
are you
Hero of '68
of course it is
it has to be
dark demon King
of LSE
and just the same
that arrogance
insulting
flouncing
macho dance
a phallic war
you waged that year
and now so far
you do it here
another wench
you can't ignore
she'd better join
the endless store
of dolly birds
just seen
not heard
to elevate
your every word
into gospel

it's really you
a Sixties' God
that higher view
on those who plod
below
while
you bestow
casual lingering

lunging
plunging
plundering
sexual favours
savouring
wavering
winsome wimmin
simperin
simmerin
and sinnin
but never winnin
in those dark
dank days
before dawn
back then
in '68
we still fawned
on handsome men
like you
blocking all view
of sensibility
sensitivity
sense of liberty
twining
whining
signing
away
birthright
denying
woman's
freedom fight
how frightening
the sight
what right
this might
of muttering
convention
buffering
all mention
of suffering
smothering

invention
sole
intention
perpetuate
state
of frozen
hate

not a sealed
fate
though
was it
we began passively
in '68
but woke
massively
provoked
by bouncing
ballsy
flouncing
phallic pouncing
in that night
of naked whorin'
scorin'
cunts
for the Cause
applauding
borin'
predictable
men like you
whose politics
meant screwing
dollies
after meetings
revolutionary greetings
on our backs
we learnt
a comrade's
only a hack
learning the rules
crown jewels

of kingship
domination
abomination
forcing us
to hit and run
find the sun
it was waiting
baiting
us free
from men
of '68
platform strutting
flies jutting
afterwards
slutting
with willing wimmin
from the audience
total pretence
this liberation
of yours
relying
on your
blind bland band
of revolutionary
whores
taking for granted
time
and slime-honoured
servility
docility
imbecility
from females
wailing only
for more

your hour
of radical
prick power
had come
you won
us all

to Causes
pausing only
to lick our wounds
and regard
each other
jealously
peevishly
viciously
separated
competing
self-defeating
agony
for tall dark handsome
ransome
of the soul
own goal
this voluntary
oppression
depression
repression
of our Cause
new clause
entirely

while you
thrusting
never trusting
emotion
lethal potion
of wicked
witches
and castrating
crotches
all that feeling
so revealing
so stay tight lipped
equipped
for WAR
false star
of liberation
that one

Bloody Son
can't build anew
on that basis
too few
oases
of calm
seductive
soothing balm

it all began
in '68
the girly
challenging
of fate
'Look here'
we ventured
through
the fog
the rituals
and servile
slog
'this revolution
we're making
what a solemn
undertaking
lack of fun
makes me run
I'm not alone
before you stone
me
big He
listen
our alternative
must glisten
not fritter
away energy
joyful glee
sap spirits
with witless
shitless
doleful

woeful
exhortation
hortatory
purgatory

liberty
must be
enticing
inviting
or they won't
bother
brother
if you smother
cosy
rosy
lebenslust
come
and trust
love and
laughter
we've had
enough
slaughter
and oughtta
we want to live
presently
not furtively
let us be
defiantly
pleasantly
resplendently
free'

but you sneered
student leader
lousy bleeder
your shine
dimmed
by time
rotten swine
I'll make you mine
they all wimpered

queued and simpered
desperate for
leader lore
blood and gore
how they swore
lust for more
of everything
that dreams
could bring
feeder of all that
illusion
confusion
delusion
reader of the Sixties'
unsisterly
mentality

today
girls
don't play
in hay
that way
just another
frantic lay
for you
no longer
brother
we love
each other
now
stallion seed
has had
its sway

and here you are
in '84
unreconstructed
as before
as though feminism
had never bin
what kind of

wimmin
have you seen
to stay
so stark
and unredeemed

no coincidence
then
oh God of men
that you appear
when danger's near
and revolution's
in this year
again
like then
in '68

I'll bet I know
just why you came
of course it's slow
but then you'll tame
the masses
give the miners
evening classes
in strategy
and tactics too
a hardened fighter
look at you
and yet in spite
of difference
of manners learned
and topics spent
it's true it's true
they'll love your gall
so proud and true
and standing tall
a Man's Man for all
that

oh heal thyself
you sacred seer

you mighty man
I once held dear
you haven't changed
in any way
those pious little projects
nurturing
your vanity
mission for
humanity
pompous
inanity
teaching
the world
unfurled
at your feet
hurled
down
in defeat
lip curled
you frown
gird your
neat cliches
preaching
better ways
sorry days
bleating
testimony
heaven sent
divine intent
all bent
with false
humility
seeking
our servility
we'd better
repent
or you'll vent
sweet acrimony

though
Rotherham's not the LSE

there's damning
similarity
in types of men
and politics
a harsh and brute
male edifice
a cold and hard
contempt
for folk
the same for thugs
and softly spoke
you all reveal
the same appeal
to violence
senseless
impotent
hurling bricks
waving pricks
awful wrath
of dancing dicks

miners mad
as hell
ringing bells
of '68
when dad
fell too
mighty man
just like you
but fallible
phallic fighter
after all
standing tall
so long
for Stalin

had to die
in '68
when joy erupted
disrupted
interrupted

boy's own
Stalinist
mentalities
for ever

dear old dad
you died that year
you had to too
steering clear
of real subversion
that was '68
albeit a version
for men only
gets lonely
up there
leading
and pleading
and bearing
Truth
weary
of fighting
and sighting
no victory
prictory
a lifetime
of agendas
and meetings
and battles
and beatings
those dour proletarian
defeatings
but always proud
and loud
and leader of
assembled
crowds
and keeping women
down
assured seating
secondary
yet respecting them

genuflecting even
and despising them
as bovine beasts
at bottom
rotten
your creed
objective truth
out there
not here
within

and these men
of '68
who beat their breasts
and demonstrate
they started
fighting
men like dad
those Stalinists
and all that bad
dead stuff
rough
tough
and rejected
it was
at first
yet wait
they created
a mirror image
no new beginning
until the women
began to say
NO to all this
blood and gore
vicious violent
leader lore

only difference
in you and dad
he prim patriarch
grim and sad

but you womaniser
just as bad
rationalising
your promiscuity
superfluity
of sperm
in terms
of the revolution
absolution
you'd provide
those willing legs
so open wide
to receive
radical
chic
prick
blessing
no messing
with pills or potions
or slimy
spermicidal
lotions
just real raw sex
from God the King
don't cover up
this holy Thing
with Durex
complexes
come that way
never a day
without exercise
with student fans
you compromised
spreading
offspring liberally
all over London
who say
'My daddy was a hero
in '68'
thus conceived
like another
pamphlet

but mummy doesn't type
these days
she did enough
that year
set free
to make the tea
and churn
the duplicator
replicator
of roles
so old
and cold
and callous
what bold
new practice
axis
for her
here

oh lessons learned
in '68
from men
like you
who twisted fate
to fit your feeble
phallic hate

yes '68 epitomised
a macho doctrine
in disguise

it needn't have
we started well
together
fighting
bourgeois hell
but liberation of desire
the blazing passions
wit and fire
bespoke another
phase for men

a worldly wisdom
made for them
they freed themselves
the world
and then
tied up
the women
once again
to type
their tomes
at home
amen

tho' freedom was
abroad
that year
its spirit loud
for all to hear
the women heard
and listened too
and that became
absurd
for you

no glory
in that story
no joy
for boys
in liberating
their titillating
toys
a better ploy
destroy
their precious
private
sexuality
sneer at exclusivity
jeer at reclusivity
and repose
expose
female need

for security
as greed
for reactionary
ritual
don't heed
the spitting
staincd
streaming pain
they just bleed
in vain
as you
sterilise
terrorise
brutalise
and set 'em free
to fuck and be
like men

yet in shedding
old taboos
and bedding
everything that screws
we women lose
our dignity
our fragile sensuality
our frightened bit
of mystery
humped
bumped
thumped
and dumped
as always
our new promiscuity
a straight
delivery
to revolutionary
whoredom
boredom
old as history
same as before
no new doors

open
at all
but now woken
our fall
was brief
in vast
unplumbed relief
we recouped
regrouped
rebattled
and discovered
another enemy
under our noses
in our underclothes
in our souls

you what
hot shot
you're filming here
in slummy Rotherham
dour and dear
a miners' film
and I can play
it truly is
my lucky day
just imagine
winding reels
and cleaning up
close by your heels
I feel
so flattered
shattered
you can tell
a coy comrade
as well

oh charisma
standing there
how can I resist
a dare
a chance

a rare old
dance
with a revolutionary hero
just like dad
a man of '68
a cold sexist
fornicating hectic
bundle of
bullying manhood
out for blood
mine
this time

oh liberated
are we fated
to get dated
madly mated
never sated
yet again
prisoners of
every slob
who comes to pay
his disrespect
his fond neglect
comes to say
look at mine
it's bigger
life giver
grave digger
nay lad
take your prick
away

wish I meant it
could invent
being gay
could have found
a different day
to prevent
this awful

woeful way
of women
to say
please stay
with me
betray
my plea
for freedom
needing you
more than
liberty
how can this be
this tone
this moan

though
I have grown
from seeds sown
in '68
wet and waiting
that date
hot and hating
now mate
wot's fate
to do

yet wait
still wet
now we've met
again
insane
cold sweat
must I beget
a hero
oh woe
not another
lonely
brother
seeking
cover
needing

mother
oh heck
come here
then
lover. . . .

Nature

LINDA ANDERSON

Linda Anderson comes from Belfast and now lives in London. Her first novel, *To Stay Alive*, was published by Bodley Head in 1984 and was shortlisted for the David Higham and Sinclair Prizes for Fiction. Her second novel, *Cuckoo*, was published by Bodley Head in 1986. Her short stories have been included in various collections and she was the winner of the *Irish Tatler* short story competition in 1983.

I was fourteen when people started to die. Charlie first. And worst. He was on a school trip. Drowned at Ostend.

Charlie. Palest blue eyes. Albino-blond hair. Perpetual grin. 'Perpetual' – well, not quite. Not nearly.

People shook their heads and clicked their tongues. 'Abroad isn't safe,' some said. 'It's God's will,' said others. 'He was too good for this world.' 'Pure fluke.' 'At least he didn't suffer.' 'All over in a flash.'

I relived and recomposed Charlie's final moments. I knew that they were long and full of horror. He saw the nearness of the beach, the swimmers, the sunbathers. He felt the sea determined to pull him under. Before the waters closed over his head, he knew that the world was murdering him. Nothing impersonal about it. It was cruel, direct, intimate.

But what did he remember?

Exhaustion was the only thing that finally stopped me crying each day. My mother was surprised, even offended at my grief. How could I care so much about 'someone outside the family'?

But she tried to comfort me. She thought she had to remedy, fix, control everything. Perhaps it was her idea of adulthood. She bought me sweets, made me cakes, trying to stifle sobs with sugar. Attempted to give me a reasonable 'philosophical' attitude.

'Most people survive to a great age, you know.'

'Yes.'

'Well, then? Oh, don't start again.'

She became jealous, suspecting that my friendship with Charlie must have been illicit. There were constant interrogations.

'What the hell was he to you?'

'I'm only fourteen, mum!' I said finally.

'What does that mean?'

'I haven't got any lovers!'

'"Lovers"! What do you know about lovers? I should never have let you out of my sight!'

I knew I would not get any peace, and neither would she, unless I crushed down the sadness. Nothing is more despairing than a child who has no private life and who must console grown-ups.

I wasn't a child any more, though. I knew death. It was important and useless, a great rip at the centre of things.

I fell in love with Murielle. I believe that was her name. I still have a book she lent me. *La Vagabonde*. By Colette. With a faint inscription on the flyleaf: *'À Murielle avec tant d'amour.'*

So much love.

We had to call her Ma'mselle in school. Our despotic headmistress disapproved of her, eyed her up and down as if her bright clothes and her smiles were transgressions. But on speech days, she referred to her as 'Daughter of France'. 'We are honoured to have the services of Mlle Picard, Daughter of France.' I thought it was romantic, noble. Murielle was short, dark, witty. Smelt of Gauloises and 'L'Air Du Temps'. She was sensual in that way that is not driven and helpless, but forgiving, measured, without strain. 'My lovely Irish girls,' she called us, as if 'lovely' and 'Irish' were synonymous. Rows of dour faces hardened against the Gallic sycophant.

'I'm British, Ma'mselle.'

'So am I, Ma'mselle.'

'But you are born in Ireland?'

'This is the United Kingdom, Ma'mselle.'

'Ah, really, the United Kingdom?'

'Part of the United Kingdom, Ma'mselle.'

'I see, et les Anglais, they like you very much also?'

She teased so gently, few noticed. We began to exchange the briefest conspiratorial glances. Before she came, I had resisted learning with a pure seething will. I was the only girl in our street to get into the grammar school. The sight of my royal blue uniform was a goad to the neighbours. But my pride soon waned. School was a kind of training in humiliation: I remember especially two highlights.

The headmistress shouting at me one day in the crowded corridor, pointing at some crusty stain on my tunic. 'Did your mother send you out like that? You need a bib!'

My form teacher collecting donations for the Sports Fund. 'The contribution is voluntary, but if you don't pay it, you don't get a copy of the school magazine.' My mother could not afford it. Paying for the uniform had stretched her ingenuity enough. Each time Miss Betts asked me for it, I told her I had forgotten it. Finally she sneered, 'All brains and no background.'

I felt betrayed by my mother; I wanted to protect her, to show solidarity. A paralysing ambivalence. Until Murielle came. She was a good teacher, the sort who can turn an intelligent but disaffected student into an accomplice in her own growth.

Accomplice. Accomplish. I was like some kind of sickly cactus suddenly surprising everyone with blossoms. Unsettling exotic blossoms. My parents hated the new me.

'You're not even a Protestant any more!'

'Yes I am, I'm part of the tradition of Protestant descent!'

It was years before I realized the word was 'dissent'.

Murielle lent me a feast of books. Lorca, Stendhal, Colette, De Beauvoir, Dostoevsky, Camus. All the lovely corrupt surrogate parents needed by people like me. I saw myself as a sophisticated European, no longer able to fit into tight Belfast shoes. But I was still an expert at repression.

'Tant d'amour, tant d'amour.' I used to repeat it to myself like a mantra. It seemed to both assuage and inflate my longing. Sometimes I alarmed myself by suddenly whispering the words almost audibly. The day before I never saw her again, Murielle came out of the headmistress's office deep in conversation with the senior French teacher. I walked past deliberately, but Murielle did not smile or even seem to notice me. Failed in her smiling and noticing duties. Next day we were ordered to work in the library during what should have been our French lesson. Ma'mselle was 'indisposed'.

She never came back and we were never told why. Dismissal? Pregnancy? Some other scandal? Or some misfortune back home? Illness? Or did she simply get bored and flee?

I guessed it was a case of ignominy or tragedy. That was the only way I could understand the other teachers' secrecy.

I hated Murielle. For abandoning me. For her fraudulent love. For being inept at life after all.

Bronchitis gave me a month's retreat. I lay in my room in some kind of vegetal misery. When I began to recover, my mother said, 'You'll be so glad to get back to school!'

'I hate school.'

'But you love it!'

I was suddenly surprised, mastered by tears. My mother held me. I told her everything. She was tender and absolute. 'You can't really love a girl.'

'I do.'

'You *think* you do.'

Not that she liked it when I started going round with 'boys and Catholics'. I knew only one Catholic, in fact. My friend Ruth. We fancied the boys from Ardmore Row with a kind of rotating lust, which sometimes favoured the dark ones, sometimes the fair ones, the sweet ones, the mean ones. . . . Most of them despised us according to the immutable conventions. There was Nathaniel, inward and proud. Sam, nicknamed 'Elvis' because of his astonishing resemblance to the singer. David, who greeted girls by nipping us in the crotch, violating our self-esteem and our awful boredom. Only Alexander was different, large, sunny, comradely. He used to draw up alongside me on his motorbike. 'Wanna lift?' He said it with a leer that dissolved at once into reassurances. 'Sure, you can trust me, you know!'

It was true. I liked him best and loved going off with him, legitimately snuggling up to a man on a motorbike while the city flew by. We never kissed. Or anything. He was too shy and courtly.

A man with sisters. Seducers have to be as deft and uncaring as burglars. Like Billy Crowe. Ruth and I were obsessed with Billy Crowe.

'I hate him. Do you?'

'Yeah. Gives me the creeps.'

'That stupid crewcut.'

'Yeah, and he's got spots.'

'Where?'

'On his neck.'

'On his neck! Oh, puke!'

Which does not go a long way to explain diary entries like this: 'Met Crowe. He put his hands where he shouldn't. Upper and lower.' We were always meeting him 'by accident' outside the dairy yard. He would put one arm round each of us, fondle each pair of breasts, slide a finger into each sex in perfect equity.

'Where do you want to be stroked? Where's the best place? State your requirements, otherwise you're screwed! Did nobody ever tell youse wee dolls that?'

It was the mixture of contempt and ingratiation that intoxicated us.

He offered defloration.

'You'll be all right with me. I can get *things*. I never ride bareback.'

We bridled like the mares he thought we were. 'Ride bareback? You're disgusting!'

The offer was appalling and irresistible. We agreed to meet him in the woods near my home. We needed a new scenario for the development of our amorous education.

'Un vrai forêt, un vrai forêt, 'I remembered Murielle's words as we walked to the assigned place. *'Do you really live near a forest? A genuine forest? So near Belfast?'*

'Who's going to be first?' asked Crowe.

Ruth and I looked at each other and grimaced. We should have worked out the order beforehand.

'You're older than me,' I suggested.

'Yes, age before beauty!' said Crowe. 'Joke! You're gorgeous!'

There was tickling and giggling, then silence. Crowe removed her blouse, then her bra. He placed it on a low branch, like a white flag. Ruth shifted her body and removed her pants. Her brow was furrowed. She looked as if only determination held her there. Crowe lowered his trousers and kneeled to roll a sheath over his purple thing. Ruth and I exchanged another split second look. Facial Morse code. Remorse code. I knew that we both wished we were somewhere else, satirizing his anatomy.

I wandered away, full of a sadness that was connected with the discarded limp panties, the brown grass, the smell of promised rain. At the edge of the clearing, I bent to touch the hang-headed foxgloves. Bees were hovering around the flowers. They dipped themselves into the calyxes, momentarily disappeared, emerged again.

When I walked back, Crowe and Ruth were 'doing it' and I could watch them as if they were blind. Ruth stared at the treetops. Her mouth was open and stupid. Crowe laboured urgently inside her. His face was taut and almost prayerful like a runner's. I could see no dread and no delight. They were submitting to a mechanical necessity. He groaned suddenly, a raw helpless sound, then snatched himself out. I had to look away from his ribcage and collarbones. The dreadful skeleton. He misinterpreted the gesture.

'Yeah, messy, isn't it? But a rubber suit's better than a paternity suit!'

I started to cry.

'What's wrong with *you*?' Ruth was sulkily tugging at her clothes, trying to smooth them.

'This isn't a real forest.'

'What are you on about?'

'She's getting cold feet,' Crowe said.

'Why would she? Nothing to it, is there!'

'I'm going home,' I said.

'No, you're not! You promised!'

'I didn't promise. I only agreed.'

'You have to go through with it! You'll tell everybody about me!'

'No, I wouldn't! I promise!'

'Your promises are useless!'

'She's useless,' Crowe said.

Ruth pushed me down so that I was lying on top of the impression their bodies had made on the grass. She straddled me.

'Give it to her, Billy! Go on!'

He hesitated.

'Naw, I can take it or leave it.'

'Oh, fuck you!'

'Fuck *you*!'

Crying now, she tore at tufts of grass and dock leaves, tried to force them into my mouth. Her hands, the tickling grasses, were muzzling me, cutting off my breath. But nothing got inside me.

Ruth stopped when she realized that Crowe had slipped away.

'I'm never speaking to you again,' she told me.

'Good.'

'Never.'

On the way home, she lapsed first. 'Imagine just slinking away like that!'

'Yeah. Creep.'

'Yeah.'

'What was it like, anyway?'

She considered for a long time. 'Like a golfball hitting you in the middle.'

'Not like a mad eel?' I was referring to earlier speculations.

'No, it was like a hot truncheon.'

'No, it must have been like a crowbar! A Crowe-bar!'

We laughed, competing in the laughter. And I decided to hold my body like a secret against the world.

The ancient Aztecs had a ritual. Part of their worship of the sun. They chose young men, the most handsome. For a year they were heaped with honours and pleasures. Girls, servants, clothes, entertainments. At the end of the time, after a great festival, their breasts were sliced open and their hearts torn out.

Gods. For a year.

Ardmore Row became known as Death Row. Charlie first. Eighteen months later, Sam, the Elvis lookalike. Car crash. Then Nathaniel. Leukaemia. Billy Crowe. Alcoholic poisoning. Alexander and David, who joined the Irish Guards together, were blown up together in an accident during practice manoeuvres.

Six youths from the same small street. All under twenty. It was almost glamorous. People began to brag about living 'near Ardmore

Row'. The modes of death, the funerals, the different degrees of outward parental grief, were keenly discussed over dinner tables, a kind of necrophiliac dessert. And this was Belfast before the Troubles. Perhaps it was some kind of unknowing rehearsal.

The boys I had envied, feared, desired. For their strength, beauty, and presumption. For their privileges. They had seemed to have so many possibilities denied to me. And yet they were dying proof of their own fragility. Futility. I did not feel their absence. I felt the presence, the dragnet of death. I did not mourn. My mother was disconcerted by my poise at gravesides. After Alexander's burial, she said I was 'cold and unfeeling'. I understood the expression 'blind with rage' for the first time. Its literal truth. I went for her, but where do you hit a woman? The breasts, the stomach, the shocked sad face? Everywhere is too soft. I sank down weeping on the floor. Condemned for feeling too much for Charlie and Murielle and then for not feeling . . . I could not then formulate the injustice of it. I arranged my life around my picture of death. I began to work hard at school. I began to work fanatically. The teachers started to respect me even though my 'manner bordered on the discourteous'. They had other misgivings as well. I took too many days off with implausible excuses; I was not 'prefect material'; I thought I was 'exempt from the rules'. But no one would rebuke me too sharply. I occupied the Unprepossessing Genius slot.

Around this time I heard a story about my mother which excited me. My grandmother told it. I had never seen or imagined my mother overwhelmed by passion or rebellion.

The story is simply this: in 1944, her twenty-first year, my mother was married and pregnant with her first child. Her brother, who was serving in the war as a naval officer, had been declared 'missing, believed dead'. She lived with my father in what is now the most famous slum in the western world: the Shankill Road. My mother used to go for walks in the local cemetery, the only refuge from the streets. The Green Belt. One day close to the birth, she was looking at the swarm of white crosses, each one representing a dead soldier. She was stricken. She could not see. She was shouting words she could not later remember. She did not want to give birth. She wanted to bring no person into the world.

'We're not different,' I thought. 'We are the same.'

I hated her. I was her.

But I vowed not to duplicate her circumstances. Never to have children. 'Giving life' they call it, but I knew it was really feeding death, working for death. No, I would never submit to that process of gestation, that distracting love, to produce another throwaway creature.

At eighteen, I entered medical school. I wanted to outstare mortality. Give it a run for its money. Win some partial and temporary victories. There was something both moving and theatrical about the body's defence system. The perpetual tango of bacteria and blood cells. The devourers becoming the devoured.

The first man I freely gazed at, freely touched, was a dead man. I was the only woman on the course that year. Niall was the only Catholic. A thin man with a dark Irish face, conspicuous, almost mysterious in the midst of that crowd of thickset blond Protestants. Whose childhoods I envisioned bitterly: the unshared bedrooms, the lovingly monitored progress, the taken-for-granted holidays. Niall and I felt both superior and precarious, like stowaways on a luxury liner. Natural allies. Liking each other was indistinguishable from hating everybody else.

We studied together, relaxed together: two 'loners' who just had to see each other every day. Loners, not lovers.

It gave me pleasure to catch sight of us in mirrors, shop windows. 'A fine couple.' Good-looking, serious, aloof. The sort of mannerly duo who will never spill wine on your carpets, never burn holes in your cushions. Charm but no harm. None.

We talked a lot about sex. Coarse bawdy talk. Exhibiting but not daring to have carnal knowledge.

Another theme of mine was the oppression of women. Doormat women who needed a man to validate them, who were bamboozled by notions of Romance and Family Life. 'I will never lay myself down,' I said more than once. Niall agreed with me. He *understood*. He was always so approving of me.

So, my life was dedicated to study of the body, but I was scarcely aware of my own flesh, except as a site of discomfort.

The stairs were always too high, the books too heavy, the weather too cold. I suffered from routine migraines, severe monthly cramps.

But I paid no attention. In the hospital, I was always the clothed one, the one standing up. If I had wounds, they were secret.

In August 1971 Niall was lifted by the army during the first internment raid. They came for his brother. He was not there, so they took Niall instead. Four days later he was released. His injuries: perforated eardrum. Bruising over face, arms, chest. Lacerations to the feet. He could not be alone.

While he slept in my room, I watched him. His shoulders trembled from time to time. He murmured indecipherable sounds. I wept and longed to undo all the abuse inflicted on his body. On his soul. I did not know how.

He changed after that. Our friendship became hazardous, bickering. His approval was suddenly, devastatingly withheld.

'Why do you always dress like an off-duty policewoman?'

'You're just another bloody Prod! I'm sick of your ability to condemn everything equally! There was no IRA before the Brit army came here. Admit it!'

'You look on me as your little conquest, don't you?'

'Sometimes I just wander round looking at women. There are a lot of great-looking women, you know!'

We celebrated my twenty-third birthday together. Dinner with champagne. We were full of an uneasy courtesy, avoiding the usual tripwires into fights. He took me home and came in for a final drink.

'It's nearly midnight. Soon it won't be your birthday any more.'

'Well, tomorrow will be the first day of my twenty-fourth year!'

'Why do you always do that?'

'What?'

'I don't know. . . . Oh, why do you always refuse any regret, any sadness, no matter how small!'

He looked at me so accusingly.

'Look, Niall, I enjoyed my birthday. But I'm not bothered that it's over. Sorry if that doesn't suit you.'

'You didn't enjoy it.'

'Of course I did!'

'You never really enjoy anything. Never really laugh, never really cry. Never really look at me. . . . Except now.'

'You're drunk!'

'You're sober!'

'You shouldn't drink so much. Alcohol is a depressant!'

'You're a depressant, Cathy! No, I'll tell you what you are! Wait! You're an immune system! You want to keep life at bay. You want to be superior to it. It's like a shame at being alive!'

'Stop it! Why do you want to torment me?'

'I don't want to torment you! That's not what I want.'

He took my hand.

'O Niall, let go! You're angry at what happened to you. And you expect me to atone for it, make it up to you. It can't be like that! I'm not a bandage!'

'Cathy. . . .' He tried to hold me and I twisted free.

'I won't lay myself down. Not for you. Not for anyone.'

'You're laying down a bloody gauntlet, that's what you're doing! I do not believe you don't know how alluring that phrase is. . . . What it makes me think of! Christ!'

'It's just a phrase!'

'Like "No Surrender!"?'

'It's midnight,' I whispered, overhearing chimes from somewhere outside. I thought, 'He'll go in a minute. He'll turn and go.' Already I anticipated his feet on the stairs, the door shutting, the sound of the car's motor dying in the distance.

'Niall, am I really like that? Like you said?'

'Yes.'

'Why do you bother with me?'

He smiled. He looked annoyed.

'I thought it was death I was keeping at bay! Niall?'

'Cathy. I'm flesh and blood. I'm here and now.'

I felt like a ghost, fistless and footless, as he came towards me. And then I could not see him, only feel him, the curve of his cheek, the line of his mouth, and before I could kiss him enough, he was kneeling to undo my shoes. And I could smile at the pragmatism of it even though it was terrible to think about shoes and clothes, how to get out of them. But then the clothes became irksome and we pulled them off. For a moment, a naked man was both cause and solution of fear. And then he was not 'a naked man'. He was Niall and we were lying down and our bodies made sense.

I knew already what I could only fathom later.

I was the door pushed open and the person walking through.

The Beginning of the Life of Rimbaud

to remember our heroes

Kathy Acker

Kathy Acker is the author of *Blood and Guts in Highschool* (Picador 1984); *Great Expectations* (Picador 1984); *Don Quixote* (Paladin 1986) and *Empire of the Senseless* (Picador 1988). She has also worked with Richard Foreman on a play version of *My Death My Life* presented at the Theatre de la Bastille in Paris and on an opera, *The Birth of a Poet*, which was shown in New York. She wrote the film *Variety* for director Bette Gordon.

'Why didn't I have a scorpion? Why'd I give birth to a human homosexual? Cause heterosexual fucking, which You gave the world, cursed me. Heterosexual fucking gives women pain.

'God: why'm I the only woman my husband doesn't thrust his cock in? He no longer sticks his dick in me cause I had the product of this dick.

'Since I'm not the Virgin Mary, God, You hate me.

'Now, Dear Lord Above, please take control of Your Hatred and spurt its sperm over this result of Your Hatred: R.'

R's mother hated him because her husband, Captain Charles-Auguste, had hated children so much that when he had learnt that his wife was pregnant for the second time, he abandoned her for a second time. This time around Mme R would have had an abortion if a quack doctor hadn't informed her that pregnancy would kill or cure all her physical problems. She had a lot. On the day Mme R had Jean Nicolas Arthur (R), she also had appendicitis.

A rock star once gave fourteen blow jobs in a row and had to have her stomach pumped.

R's mother took control of her situation as a husbandless mother and announced her rational plan.

'I'll bring up my second kid by torturing him. That way he won't beget any infected children.'

Her plan succeeded. R turned out homosexual. Though the mother had no understanding of Our Lord's designs.

The mother came to realize that she wasn't the Virgin Mary though she was a mother. So in spite of God this draconian woman who could tolerate no slight to her authority decided to become the Mother of Maternal Crimes (MMC): she was going to murder pitiful R, not exactly by killing him, but by destroying and annihilating every shred of his will and soul while he still lived on. All for the glory of God.

(I'm running such a high temperature that I don't know what I'm saying. My thoughts're fevered.)

R grew up to be a wild animal, unsocialized. He was filthy. His mother taught him nothing, wanted nothing to do with him. He was disinherited. He lived on bare sunlight and played with forms of natural violence as if they were knives and chains. Tied to his mother, the more miserable she made him, the more he did whatever he wanted.

Whether or not God exists, there are Protectors. Those who protected this child wept when they saw him happy in the middle of decay, urban garbage, spiritual nihilism.

It would soon become worse.

There was nothing for the children of Charlesville to do in Charlesville, France. R used to hang out in the one bookstore in town which buyers never came to. A Greek who oozed skink oil ran this front. Having once been tanned by the Algerian sun, his nickname was 'African Pain'. Most of the other people in the town stayed away from R because his mother's autocratic mixture of neglect, torture, and tortuous love had turned his appearance monstrous and tough. 'African Pain' saw that R simply hated himself and had no way of dealing with his self-hatred.

As soon as R in amazement realized that this man, who was his father's brother, didn't think he was a monster, he began to love him. He worshipped 'African Pain' to the extent that he was unable to see the older man's deep insecurity. The man was God to R. Just like Yahveh, he hurt the kid again and again so that he'd know how deeply the kid loved him.

> Wherefore He had perforce to cry out, saying: 'My God! My God! Why hast Thou Forsaken Me?' This was the greatest desolation, with respect to sense, that He had suffered in His life.

The man stuck his hand up the kid's ass, repeatedly making and unclosing a fist, until filed fingernails ripped the membranes. At the end of the tunnel of membranes the kid's heart was beating. Then the man pushed his arm up until he was holding the heart. The heart felt like a bird. Holding on to the heart, he threw the kid to the ground, kicked him in the side until the kid knew that he was nothing, had no mother.

Unable to bear or stop these tortures, R moved into the imaginary. The infinity and clarity of desire in the imaginative made normal society's insanity disappear.

'You've never given me anything but pain,' the kid told his uncle. 'I'd tell you to go stick an old witch's hand up your ass if I didn't . . . want . . . this . . . I guess . . . pain. You. I need what you're doing to me because it's only pain and being controlled which're going to cut through my autism. Because it's pain you give me I love you. I love you anyways.' R had a high IQ. 'Because you don't give a shit about me, unc, and because I'm totally dependent on you, you're teaching me the highest pleasure which is love. The body. But if you reject me, the more you reject me, the more I'll destroy my body.'

'There's no such thing as a soul,' the African said.

R replied, 'I'm sick of Baudrillard. The intellectual side of American post-capitalism. Cynicism. You're too intelligent to be a cynic.

'As for religion: evangelists only want money. For people who have money, money's power. There's nothing else. In this society. This society isn't France; it's America.

'Like religion, your cynicism's a hype. The assumption that everything including the soul is shit hides the real nexes of political power. Hurt me, baby. Show me what love is. Love? The body doesn't lie. Hurt me, unc, and find my soul. The pirate brat is seeking real pirate treasure in the dirty recesses of being. Women wear lost pearls. Maps whose territories are named in languages which are no longer understood show where the passions are hidden.' The filthy brat picked his nose. 'Unheard-of metals and sea gems can dribble out of the tip of your cock.'

R said. 'When I by myself in my body see the splendour of passion which is now unknown, I'll see that my own eyes are only mirrors of the infinity of savagery.'

Pain took hold of R. He took R's clothes off him, rolled him over to the bed's edge, dropped him. Kicked his body until R folded into a corner. R's eyes were closed. The man jerked off above the kid's face.

While Pain was jerking off, R whispered to himself: Sailors come. They hand-fuck me up the ass. The kid came. Then the sailors went. One sailor made me crawl across a floor after his fingers which were pulling me by my nipples. As if there are dogs. I have to catch a few drops of sperm. My mouth's a fish. Since you still haven't let my nipples go, I have to go wherever you're leading me. Whose sexuality am I and whose sexuality're you? The soul is the body.

Pain had to abandon R because he died on December 3. The cause of death was unknown. R saw a lightless tunnel with a light at its end and knew that there was no correspondence for this light in the outside world.

In the time of good-for-nothings, bums, liberty will triumph. R said. Paris has been the seed bed for the intellectual and revolutionary forces which're capable of dragging people up out of the mire into which what has seemed to be an implacable destiny has thrown them. At this moment liberals think bums should be saved and made into yuppies. Like themselves. The yuppies are the Germans. The German do-gooder autocrats are invading Paris. The French who aren't bums and aren't yet dead or dying from AIDS and other germs are so frightened that, caring only for money or nothing, they'll capitulate to the Germans who are now strongest in the political arena.

While the Germans were taking over Paris, R, abandoned, roamed from town to town. One morning, he woke up in a room stinking with dead tobacco, vomit, and dead blood. Junkies had lost all tracks. Disorder reigned: soldiers from different German regiments who had been dismissed for fraternizing with the French, national guards, sailors, zouaves – all types – were in this room and reeking. There's nothing to do when drunk. There was no question of clothing the homeless, giving them weapons for self-defence, providing them with adequate or any sort of shelter. The frost was bitter.

All of this disgusted R. War. Soldiers. Straight males. A French and a German government who were choosing to turn people into TV zombies and corpses. R further saw that most people as they grow older choose to die.

R no longer knew where to wander in hell. His mother was calling him back home.

THE FILTHY WOMB OF BLOOD.

'Come back home, you filthy kid.'

R sat in his mother's house and masturbated. He no longer wanted to go anywhere but masturbating. Except for masturbating he didn't know whether he wanted to be alive.

R said out loud while he was masturbating and being alive, 'Why Honey Chil', I jes' loves the Devil. Ya know why I's loves the Devil more than I loves God? (Fuck fuck, you filthy priest.) Cause the Devil, being the Devil, being God's opposite, being opposite to the Good Father, is the Father of Masturbators. (Can you hear me, mom?' R started shouting.) 'The Devil is the Father of Masturbators cause the Devil-Father hates his own children. He abandons them just like daddy abandoned me. Cats who haven't been nursed properly all their lives claw and I. . . .

'Once upon a time, mommy dearest, oh oh (masturbatory sounds), there was a Devil who had a good-looking thing, a hose, a tube, a long piece of plumbing.'

R was already showing signs of inversion.

'But a thing don't mean a thing. Ya know why a thing, even a good-looking thing, don't mean a thing? Cause it ain't the thing that makes the thing move. What makes a thing move is unnaturalness. Oh oh (masturbatory sounds).

'Now it's not immediately obvious why it's unnaturalness that makes a thing move. God Our Father in His Incarnation Jesus

Christ, being The Lord and Our Lord, is the cause of all. Jesus Christ was only moved by, only had a thing, for virgins. But He didn't want to stick nothing in them. Since nothingness is the opposite of and even the enemy of the Creation, Jesus Christ, eternal as God the Father, was and is unnatural. Jesus Christ wanted to be a victim.

(Masturbatory sounds.)

'But since the Devil is natural and I'm a masturbator, I love the Devil.'

R's mother strutted into the room and told R to stop masturbating.

'I'm going to kill you,' said R.

'Yuck. You're going to go back to school. And a Catholic school.'

'Yuck, yuck,' her son said to her as he looked around for something with which to end someone's life.

'You're going to be an actor.'

'That's cause I take after you, mommy, you're the biggest drama queen around.' Mme Rimbaud was fat. Seeing a long nail in the wall, R thought he could act out the part of Judith.

'I DE-MAN-DE that you return to school because all your little friends have already returned to school, You have to go back to school, because if you don't the cops'll make you. If you don't go back to school, your father's going to have a heart attack.'

On the first day of acting school, R sat under his blanket and tried to think. His mother then decided either to disinherit him forever or bodily to take him to drama school. She did the latter.

In school, R contemplated suicide more times than he had before. He was too shy to have any friends. Cold knives, he wrote, city of knives all of which are interior and stick into the ice of the mind. The knives are my nerves and they're hurting me. I can no longer locate the cause of this hurt. I'm not even sure that I hurt, but I've figured out I do cause I love razor blades and I love to stick them in my wrists. Pain exists.

'Education,' one of R's teachers taught, 'teaches you not to be yourself.' But who is yourself? R decided if it or he wasn't blood, it wasn't anything.

Then he realized that the blood that dropped out of his razor-bladed wrists was no solution to boredom. For boredom comes from the lack of correspondence between the desire of the mind and body and the society outside that mind and body. From impossibility of any desire's actualization.

Disillusioned with left-wing or French politics, R wanted to tear his own skin into strips of band-aids with which to heal the wounded, tear tufts of the hair above his cock out of his pimply skin so that he would know how the whores of the German soldiers felt, ram his own fist like a gun barrel up his own asshole so that he could be the child he had never been allowed to be. But under no circumstances did he want to die.

The teacher of the third form was Ariste L'Heritier, a tubular tubercular hairy trull. Known non-affectionately to the students as 'Father Fist' in honour of the German left-wing who had failed, FF was given to appalling fits of anger by which he terrorized his whole class. Because he was a humanitarian. The principal of the school recognized that 'Baby R' had an exceptional mind and persuaded R's mother to let her son take private lessons with FF. Violence was the only emotion to which the child could relate. R adored FF.

One day R asked FF, 'Why do people poison other people?' R was thinking about poisoning the Muller twins. The Muller twins were German. They had long straight blond hair and were strong. Since they were the only pupils who were as intelligent as R, they hated R and R hated them because they were equals.

Though R wanted to kill them and knew he wanted to kill them, as yet he only pissed into both of their camel hair coats. Then pressed chewed-up bubble gum into the mess. School stunk. The Mullers got better marks than R because, being German, they weren't sloppy.

'People poison other people because they don't know how else to do what they want to do.'

R didn't understand FF's words. He often didn't understand. He feared and loved not understanding. Not understanding put him at the edge of danger and the edge of danger was sex.

FF added, 'Whether or not to poison is a technical problem.'

'I don't have problems, Fartface.' R began to believe that his teacher didn't know everything. Thick black sticks of hair jutted out of the edges and overhung his white and scratched bratty face. 'I don't have any objections to any crime. Every crime which as yet my sad heart has committed – familial crime – killing my mother –

killing myself – delights me. Following my dreams into poison – there's only one problem. I don't know enough about poisons.'

FF asked the child, 'Would you like to poison someone?'

'I'm a virgin.'

'It's alright to be a virgin.' FF paused. 'Would you like to poison someone?'

'I don't know anything about poisons so I can't use them.'

'You've been playing on the edges of criminality, of identity. Now this is serious. Would you like to poison someone?'

Even though R didn't want to poison another human being, he felt that he had already committed himself. 'I'll poison someone. But I hate you.'

The teacher didn't care what the filthy brat felt about him. More precisely, the teacher was too scared to let himself feel, to let himself realize that he needed R's nastiness, hatred of all authority, and need of him. They were both bound to go through an arbitrary poisoning so that they could both learn about life and death. 'Tonight there's going to be a woman, a whore, in this school. You're going to poison this whore.'

R felt revolted. Caught between feelings of commitment and revulsion, he started to bawl. He had to tell this teacher, all his masters, to go to hell. But he couldn't, yet. 'Filthy fucking liar. I won't lick your sneakers any more because they smell. Kissing them makes my stomach sick. You want me to be a slut, a little girl, to pity you because you don't know how to make contact with anyone. You're the vampire, the bloodsucker, Nazi.'

FF seriously replied, 'Tell me how you hate me.'

R was silent.

'Who are you, R?'

'I'm nothing.'

FF gave R a small packet of strychnine and left him alone.

These were R's special lessons in school.

R, still bawling, graffitied one of the dark red school hall walls. 'MASTER LORD GOD PUKE DEATH TO GOD.' The sight of a teacher was beginning to make his lips itch with dirty language. He decided to cultivate lice in his hair so he could throw them at his teachers, especially Fuckfist.

It is true that there is no God. There is no God to save us from anything or anyone. All, then, is the result of our own actions.

'What're you doing, R?'

Frederic Delahaye, sloppy stupid legally blind and R's best friend, met him in the hall.

R told his best friend that he was going to kill someone.

'Who?'

FF had acted like he was a good teacher and loved him just so FF could carve him up. He had to kill FF before FF killed him. All education was games. All education was games the teachers played with students or victims. Our teachers are playing games with us, games that they love us, games that we need them, so that they can carve us up into lobotomies and servants to a lobotomized society. So that we'll learn to obey orders. They're German. R screamed. With a teacher or a master, there's no reality, and I have to find reality.

Delahaye who was stupid asked R if FF had actually done anything to R.

'Just now in the hall he told me to take off all my clothes. I told him to go fuck himself rather than me. Autocratically, he told me to take off all my clothes. I did cause I hated someone. He told me, "Display yourself." Just like the army. I know I don't have any arms so I'm totally degraded so I did as my officer commanded. FF barely glanced at my asshole. I wouldn't look at it either. Delahaye, I've become a baby in front of my soldier father who never existed. THERE'S NO GOOD AND THERE'S NO LOVE.'

'So what happened next?' the stupid child asked.

'He told me he loved me. *HE TOLD ME HE LOVED ME.* THAT'S THE BIGGEST MILITARY LIE OF ALL.'

'"Education," FF then said, "is an act of love." I hate! I don't understand!'

Delahaye, who was fat as well as being stupid, said that he was hungry.

It was time for the regular school evening meal.

Fuckfist: I don't need to do much to the child in order to teach him because I understand him almost perfectly. *A powerful man does not need* implements. R's a cold wall, a unique ice forged of metal, erected against an imaginary, unbearable world. He's pure anger. He's closed. All of him that is closure wants to be destroyed. All of him wants only one thing: to be opened up. He's the toughest fortress or child I've ever come up against. So in order to open this rusty can, I have to use the largest and sharpest can opener. (FF was contradicting himself.) In these circumstances, the harshest measures are necessary. He must be spread open. His heart must show. He must be open and available to my hands. *The child* wants above all to be destroyed.

I'm just a teacher. I've got lots of students. So I won't personally be involved in the death of this filthy brat.

Because I'm kind, my arms lifted him up and held him. Then I dropped him on the floor. One of my feet rolled him across the floor into a corner. Then kicked the child. He lay curled in the corner. I waited until he knew. I stood over him, took myself out of my pants and jerked off on him. I felt nothing sexual. I knew, because he wanted to touch my penis and make our relation personal, this whole time he was fighting me. He was silently saying to himself, I'm a voyeur.

Prone to disease, though fat, frail, weak, bare-headed, eyes always seeming to weep on his cheeks, Delahaye seemed more of a mess than R. Nicotine had stained both boys' fingers yellow; vomit had stained R's clothes. The two boys walked into the refectory. The large room, even when there were boys in it, looked like a trough. The school's usual food was a sort of gelatinous liquid which looked like nausea. Bits of grey, related to shrapnel, lay under the white. You are what you eat. Tonight there was something else to eat. R saw the woman. R had a sudden recrudescence of his antireligious passion. 'A grotesque priest, whose shoes are fermenting,' he whispered to Delahaye, 'throws himself at girls. He doesn't know girls want to be sluts. The boys who think girls're sluts are liberals, filled with compassion, full of decency. Christ, Christ, you're the thief of our energies!'

R looked at the woman, didn't care about her, and told Delahaye to fetch some rope. The woman was a bit stupefied because she was a junkie. She was full of compassion cause whores have hearts of gold. R and Delahaye tied her up, took her down to a room in the school's cellar. There was pandemonium in the dining room as they left.

The more serious students found R's prank in 'bad taste'. They said that R was turbulent, insatiable. R called them toads and almost as disgusting as those the Germans had crippled. If there's any civil war around here, it's identity.

R told FF that he had locked the woman up rather than poisoning her.

'The *woman*?'

'I won't poison women.'

'Why won't you kill? You're playing around on the edges. You have to kill,' R's teacher replied.

'I don't have to kill women because whether or not to kill women isn't the issue,' the precocious boy replied. 'The issue's my death. To me. You're right that the issue's death. Teach. Where you're wrong, and you are wrong, is that you're scared. You're terrified because you place evil and death outside yourself. Or you place Nazism outside yourself because you're frightened. You're a good liberal German, teach. You teach death, but you don't die. The issue is always the self. *I* am going to die.

'By making me kill a woman . . . or anyone . . ., you've brought me to my cross. But you haven't gone to yours. Come on, teach. You won't lose your prestigious job. I promise you you won't lose your job. Don't you know,' R stabbed his finger into FF's chest, 'that it's stupid to die stupidly? Reasonlessly. Christ died for no reason. Don't you understand that I love you?'

But FF couldn't admit that he was an evil sadist. From then on, R, disappointed with his teacher, no longer confided in him and, in extremes as a child is, moved from wild gratitude to ironic contempt.

FF didn't deserve this treatment. He was only scared.

R: In a terrible way I insist on worshipping true freedom.

From now on, R would do anything to get away from school. Scatology was the only act which made sense to him. He lived in a state of possession. As if he no longer knew where he was. He was always somewhere else. He had to be always somewhere else in order to survive. He was rigid: his body was a soldier's. He felt and acted minimally. His head lifted high and his eyes pierced like birds'. He obeyed orders though no one could see who were issuing these orders.

R: My possession isn't bearable because it's *possession in absence*. There's no way out but my death or consciousness.

It is January 1st. The Germans have invaded Mézières, which is the town nearest the Rossat School. That town is now a pile of ruins, broken glass, charred wood and ash, still giving off stinking smokes, sticks of wood, razor blades thrusting out of the flesh as if geography is a person. Rake me into hell. White snow, suddenly falling, tries to cover up or kill everything even more. Yet here and there fires burst out. Which I can no longer quench. Because the frost has turned all the water in the pipes into ice.

Razor blades easily sink into the flesh.

'There can't be human flesh left alive in Mézières.' That's what all the people say.

Come alive, dead heart, and sing.

R would do anything to get away from school. Break the heart's dead ice. He knew that the habitual self had to be broken. He phoned up the local motorcycle gang and asked them to save him.

'I'm content,' FF told a colleague at this time, 'to regard as youthful folly the filth that young R has shown me is pouring out of his mouth and right hand.'

This is the season of killing.

Again R phoned up this bike gang and told them this is the season of killing.

More German troops pierced French geography. There were more victims. Less talkative than their enemies, the Germans never announced their ferocious war plans. Victims never knew if they were to be murdered. Fear escalated. All men, being men, are cruel and minimal; the Germans, being conscious of their cruelty, thus confident of their decisions and lack of decisions, were crueller.

The child knew that absence of blood doesn't mean absence of pain.

GOING OVER THE TOP OF THE FLESH

R had this myth: The mother is evil. She wants to kill her child. The child because it's good can't be angry at and kill the mother. Or, because the child can't be angry at and kill its mother, the child's good. This is the child's taboo. In order to stay alive and to break through complete isolation, the child, R, must break the taboo. The child's father is absent. The child's looking for a father. Through the death of its mother, as if through a gate into another world, there's only the world of men.

As yet R watched the Germans – this new German invasion – from a distance. The Germans conquered. In Mézières, French stud farms had been turned into hospitals. Behind barbed wire meant for animals, cripples in greatcoats, legs and arms missing, dragged themselves from one shed, partly intact, to another. There was little patriotism or religion left.

According to R, this is one image of actuality. 'The German victimizers will force an iron discipline on themselves in order to keep ranks, hold on to their victims, and increase their own self-aggrandizement. In the end, they'll be crushed by some coalition.'

FF directly confronted his student who would no longer talk to anyone. 'I won't say that you're mad cause that would just make you happy. But if you think that your delirious behaviour is making you into some saviour or God, I can prove to you that all you're becoming is a freak. Like the cripples out there. German and French. The ones who didn't make it. Victims. You're playing with every edge, R, and you just have to go over once to go over forever.'

R didn't say anything to FF.

R now wanted to escape this school and, axe in hand, to demolish FF, the school, and his identity.

For a third time R phoned the motorcycle gang. Dubois, the gang's leader, didn't give a shit about R. Dubois answered the phone. R told Dubois that he was slashing his wrists because he was bored. Something in R's voice – a pleading, a passivity – made the motorcycle leader think that he could make R his proselyte. Dubois gave R the time of day and instructed R not to sleep that night, to be so silent that no one in the school woke up but remained corpses, by midnight to be at the huge double front door.

unable to do anything. unable to act. the body is a dead land.

At midnight the dead young body is at the double front door. A German on his motorcycle is waiting.

'If you don't get out in three minutes, you die.'

The dead body remained dead.

The German grabbed R. 'In two and a half minutes, this school's going to explode.'

'I don't give a damn if it does and I go with it,' R said. 'My friends're gonna die. Delahaye.'

'It doesn't matter, death,' the evil monster said, 'as long as there is one moment of human freedom. In . . . now, one and a half minutes, I guarantee you you'll be free.'

'You can't give a dead person freedom. You can't give a living person freedom, but you can give a living person death.' The motorcycle leader dragged the kid by the arm, R's body half-flung across the back of a Moto Guzzi, out of the institution just as it burst up. Dubois rode on to the rest of his gang.

On their way to the gang's hideout, Dubois talked politics to R. Politics was the deepest heart of Dubois's heart. 'I love and hate my countrymen. Like all exiles. Today they penetrated Paris. They decimated Paris with guns. They took 600 victims for scientific purposes.

'We're . . .' Dubois meant *we Germans*, '. . . frightened of a populist revolution against us. The French have a poetical, frivolous streak. Germs of defiance have blossomed in the French. The more we oppress their masses, which we have to do for purposes of scientific experiments, for the sake of knowledge and truth, and the more enlightened the masses, the greater the chance of their successful revolution.

'What is our solution?' Dubois asked rhetorically. 'To terminate this populist revolution before it starts, we must inalterably change their educational system. First, we'll close all the free schools whose lessons have turned lower and lower-middle-class mongrels into poets, painters, and fashion designers. We only want labourers. (In our future, child, when we clone perfect workers, we can use AIDS and similar germs to stop the masses from fucking.)

'After we have impoverished a socialist educational system and transformed education based on questioning into one based on religious – that is, political – doctrine, we shall directly wage war on those who are unemployed and still alive. (Those classes who earn any money are too scared of losing their pittances to defie us.) We'll close down free hospitals, old age homes, asylums, council housing, and refuse abortions. We've already sent the French police out against the squatters. Whatever services that exist in a society – shelter, medical care – only the rich will afford.

'Let the poor die. The Germans have taken over.

'Menstrual blood is a thousand times heavier than blood from chains. So in the long run we shall fail. We're longing to fail.'

(He is bound, the dogmatic atheist, tall, haggard, timid, good-natured, scientific.)

When R heard this, he thought that the motorcycle leader was mad. R then wondered what he himself really wanted.

'Girls are happy,' R said to the motorcycle leader, 'to hear themselves called *sluts* by boys.' The motorcycle leader didn't understand R.

The motorcycle leader and R sat in the gang's hideout. The motorcycle leader begged R to join the gang. 'If you join our gang, you'll be able to repair social inequities. By violence. Today violence is the fastest and the only way possible. (Corporate heads, after all, legally murder their opponents; famous artists murder their wives and go scot-free.) Human history views crimes with disdain only when the criminals remain poor. . . . Help make the poor rich.'

R wondered what he himself really wanted.

'Learn a real lesson: in this world today crime is your only protection. Our only other class privileges are disease, stupidity, material and psychic deprivation, madness, and legal punishment.'

Either R was too bratty to be scared or he had already decided to be too bratty to be scared. He still wondered what he really wanted. At least here, unlike school, he was learning about actual society.

The motorcycle leader finished up his Hegelian argument. 'You decide. You can either be a criminal or a victim. You can either kill or be killed.'

The guys in the motorcycle gang wanted to fuck R because he was young. Dubois was holding them off until R decided whether he was going to join the gang or be a victim. R didn't want any of this: he wanted a new world. He had to escape. He wondered whether he could practically want anything but escape.

The motorcycle leader told R that he didn't have to be a criminal. If he let every member of the gang fuck him, he could escape free, that is, with his life.

R replied to Dubois, 'Despair's filled my heart. Slaughtered by a black existence I died in a shady tower. *I* must die.'

Dubois replied that the gang didn't want to kill R, only fuck him. Only Jesus Christ and His virgins equated the loss of virginity and death.

R refused to let go of his vision. '*I* want to die.'

The motorcycle leader, exasperated, placed a foot on R's genitals and shoved. The foot rolled R who was now on the floor into a corner. He sarcastically asked the kid who he was, this *I*; the kid couldn't reply; he told the kid that if *he*, Dubois, wanted, the guys would shove fingers and knives up and through his body; the kid said he was Jewish; the leader poured bad milk over the kid and told the kid not to waste food the children in Ethiopia needed; the child licked the milk out of the dirt; the man walked out of the room.

R couldn't stand the loss of a father whom he had never had. He screamed for the German. The German returned, asked R who he was.

R repeated that he had to die. He was going to leave Dubois. He left.

'Then you'll go to prison,' Mme Rimbaud had said.

This brief stay with criminals or revolutionaries, though he was in love with the revolution, formed in him a terror and hatred of militarism that was always to remain with him.

Having emitted his venom, discovered that he didn't want either side of a moralistic or dualistic society, R had nothing better to do than wander. Around Charlesville and Mézières. He declaimed Villon, Gautier, Verlaine, especially this poem by Baudelaire,

TO THE GERMANS BOTH NAZIS AND PEACENIKS

Porn and exile and fear and violence
Are part of us.
We eat guilt and remorse
Like bums eat their own vermin.

We squirm and cut our wrists
Over one confession;
Then go back to the street of shit
Believing we've forgiven and been forgiven.

Satan Triple-Master – cynic, money-hungry, pupil
of Baudrillard –
Lulls and quiets my enchanted spirit.
My free will's rich metal has been vapourized
Into nothing by this modern chemist.

The Devil moves the strings that move me.
I find myself charmed by the most boring things:
Every day I walk deeper into the city of hell,
Without horror, past my ghosts who stink.

Just like some old man who gave up
And now chews a whore's pitted breast,
Whenever I grab one pleasure,
Out of boredom I crush it to death.

Packed together swarming-thronging-dead sardines
Demons're rioting in my brains.
Death's sitting in my lungs,
Dead river, sewage of complaints.

Abortions razors suicides viciousness
Haven't yet carved death into this self
Only because my heart's begging
For something else.

Among jackals panthers
Lice scorpions jellyfish vultures,
Yelping slime –
The urban menagerie of destruction –

There's one animal, mean and strong,
Who doesn't have grand gestures, doesn't scream.
He consciously turns this earth into debris
And swallows up reality with a yawn:

My boredom. As I beg for sympathy I don't want,
I dream, and he dreams, of my own death.
Reader, you know this oversensitive monster,
Hypocritical reader – my mirror – my brother.

'I hate the fucking provinces,' R said to a friend, Charles Bretagne. 'No one cares about anything here. All these humans, taught by their priests, think that whores, ex-soldiers, riff-raff are evil. The real evil is these people who'll do anything to protect their own safety. Whatever they think is their safety. Money. Who lie to themselves that they have other values. They're deeply, morally religious: evil is everything but them.

'To be a poet is to wake inside someone else's skin.

'In these dead provinces, the other is a freak.

'Mom says she's going to send me back to school. Again. I hate school and I hate her. I'm no longer interested in hating everything cause I'm no longer interested in being defined, positively and negatively, by a culture I think's sick. Mom won't give me any money. She thinks that way she'll force me back to school. She only gives me two francs a week which I'm supposed to give to the priest on Sunday. The syphilitic priest should give me more than two francs so he can suck my dick.

'How can I be free if I'm broke?'

Charles deigned to open his mouth and remarked that, when he was just in Fampoux, he had been introduced to the poet Verlaine. Even though R had never met V, he knew that he had to go to V and, if he did, V would save him.

A year before this V had married a sixteen-year-old upper-middle-class girl. The girl was about to have a baby.

Not having any money and, more important, being totally passive, R didn't know how he was to physically get to V. Since poetry was his only way, he wrote this poem, which he had copied from Baudelaire, to V.

DEAR V

Sailors are bored lots. To get rid of their boredom
They grab and mutilate the huge albatrosses who're
  following their graves,
The ship diving and sliding
Between the waves.

As soon as the big birds're pulled to the planks,
Kings of the Sky now full of shame,
Their immense wings drag through their own blood,
Broken oars, against the grain.

This arrogant free traveller – now bound –
Formerly scorns – now begs.
Some man's sticking tobacco in his mouth;
Another drunk mocks his crippled legs.

The poet is this arrogant traveller
Who lives in violent emotions.
Now exiled among humans who fear,
His immense wings stop his motion.

V didn't reply to R's poem. The longer the time that V didn't reply, the more R hated himself.

When R had finally given up, V wrote him. 'Come. Come to me.'

It is true that suicide and loneliness terrify people. 'I'm awkward, shy, I don't know what to say. . . . Where thought's concerned, I fear nobody,' R thought to himself on a train headed toward V. 'The truth is that I cry too much, especially at dawn. Night now stinks and my light hurts.'

A Libation of Blood

FAY WELDON

Fay Weldon was born in England, reared in New Zealand and educated in Scotland where she took a degree in Economics and Psychology. After a decade of odd jobs and hard times she started writing and is now well known at home and abroad as a novelist, playwright and critic. Her novels include *Praxis Puffball* and *The Schrapnel Academy*, and *The Life and Loves of a She-Devil* which was recently screened on BBC Television.

'Mum,' said Alison, 'give me some advice.' Mum was sixty-five and Alison was thirty-nine. Mum was widowed, which is never a nice thing to be, but what can you expect? Women outlive men.

'You?' asked Mum in some astonishment. 'Me give you advice?' Mum had left school at sixteen and gone into the WRACS and packed parachutes. That was as far as her education and training had gone. Alison had gone to college and taken a degree and then a diploma in the Social Sciences. Mum had one child; Alison had three. 'What can I know that you don't know?'

Alison wept. Mum, astonished, made her a cup of tea. Mum had a touch of arthritis in her fingers. She lived, as she had always done, in a bungalow on the outskirts of Exeter. Dad had run a TV repair business, and had left his wife well provided for. His daughter, of course, could look after herself. She lived in London and did well enough; very well, in fact. She worked for a charity, raising funds for mentally handicapped children, and ran a small specialist agency besides, which provided research material on handicap for similar organizations. She was tall, energetic, good-looking, usually laughing; and now suddenly here she was in Mum's small kitchen, laughing and crying at the same time.

'Tea's no answer,' said Alison. 'Oh, Mum, you never change.'

'Tea never was an answer,' said Mum, 'but it was always something to do with your hands, while you got your act together.' Do not suppose that because Mum was sixty-five, and had had little education, and no other lover (or so Alison supposed) than her husband, she was stupid or ill-informed. The television and the library make one knowledgeable nation of us all.

'As for never changing,' added Mum, 'that may be so, but I don't weep as much as you do. Now what's happened?'

'I don't know what's going on inside my head, that's what's happened. And when I press my breast it hurts. Do you think I've got cancer?'

'You're probably pregnant,' said Mum, 'and it's affecting what's going on in your head.'

'I can't possibly be pregnant,' said Alison. 'Bobby and I take precautions.' On the telephone a week ago Alison had been all set to move in with Bobby: fortyish, good-looking, a crusader for the handicapped, famous up and down the country for his goodwill and good works. Marriage was spoken of. What a wonder! True love at last – and for a woman of thirty-nine with three children and two marriages behind her.

'Precautions, schmecautions,' said Mum 'Condoms, schmondoms. When did they ever not break? How do you think you began?'

'You're so frivolous,' complained Alison (who ever liked to believe they sat thus accidentally in the world?) and asked Mum to come up for a week and babysit Caroline, aged nine, and Wendy and Wyndham the five-year-old twins; the twins' father William being unexpectedly in hospital for his varicose veins and William's new wife Annabel declining to look after them if William wasn't in the house, and Alison having a conference and what with one thing and another –

'Just cool it, Alison,' said Mum, 'will you? You'll give yourself a heart attack. Okay, okay, I'll come up for the week and childmind but you didn't come all this way to ask me that. You could have done it on the phone.'

'I wanted some peace on the train,' said Alison. 'I wanted my own space. Just a couple of hours.'

'I suppose you travelled first class, or you wouldn't be talking about space.'

'Why not? I can afford it.'

'And thousands starving in Africa!' said Mum. 'Sometimes I think you earn too much for your own good.'

'You'd never say that to a man,' said Alison, and wept again. It was true. Her head was all to pieces. She'd been all set to move in with Bobby, give up her own house, her independence, everything; all for love. But now she wasn't sure she wanted to; supposing it all went wrong? She couldn't bear it. Better not to try, than try and fail. This way and that, things went in her head. Yet wasn't little Caroline happy with the idea: Bobby for a father! Wasn't that reassuring? Of course William wasn't happy about it one bit but nothing made William, the twins' father, happy; Alison could never do anything right: it was the self-righteous Annabel whispering in his ear, no doubt. What difference could it make if the twins visited their mother alone every second weekend, or their-mother-with-Bobby: she, Alison, put up with Annabel, not to mention Annabel's hordes of mimsy little children, when she visited the twins; why should William begrudge her Bobby? Or was it that she was begrudging him to herself? Alison wanted a whiff of home, in fact, where nothing ever happened, except in her mother's head, and all was always the same, even the brand of tea. Typhoo Tips.

'Multiple marriages,' said Mum. 'All change, but all the same! Why didn't you stay with Andrew?' She'd liked Andrew, in the way mothers do seem to like their daughters' first husbands. Or perhaps it was just the pattern of names from the beginning. Alison and Andrew, Andrew and Alison – they'd got used to it, that was all.

'He was a mass murderer,' said Alison, 'that's why.' Andrew had worked as a designer for a firm which produced, amongst other things, leaflets for a cigarette company.

'Now who's being frivolous?' said Mum. Andrew had pronounced himself bisexual and Alison had left, running shrieking into the night, Caroline under her arm, straight into William's waiting maternal arms. Had she been right, had she been wrong? What is intolerable, what is not? Andrew hadn't kept in touch with Caroline, or Alison for that matter, though he rang Mum from time to time, feeling the need of a mother. Well, these days, who doesn't?

'How can you even speak of him?' Alison would shriek, in the early days of their parting, when she was still flayed red and raw.

'But you didn't *want* him to keep in touch with Caroline,' Mum would remind her. 'He's only doing what you wanted. And you're right, he is a very sexually confused young man. But I am not going to condemn him for that. Surely you wouldn't want me to? And it's all turning out for the best, with William. Surely?'

Well, it didn't quite. Alison's next baby, by William, was Down's Syndrome, and the hospital saved its life, and Alison rejected it, and said since the hospital had saved it, the hospital should look after it, a reaction which shocked the noble right-thinking very much, and William was nothing if not a noble thinker. But he bit back his thoughts, rather noticeably, for love of Alison, and supported her, and the baby died at three months, anyway, never well enough to come home. After that there was a lot of genetic testing and detailing of hereditary factors and the odds of William and Alison's next baby being born similarly affected were declared at one in fifteen. But the couple could take advantage of a newish procedure called amniocentesis by which babies could be tested in the womb at four months and aborted if necessary. So you only had the worry for four months. Then if anything was wrong – terminate! Of course by that time it was like going into proper labour – 'At four months?' Mum had asked, in horror. 'Aborted at four months? It's practically smiling by then.'

'Especially if it's Down's Syndrome,' said Alison. 'You know what gutsy little smilers they are!' (William raised his eyebrows when Alison said things like this; but she was still in shock, he let everyone know, and himself wonderfully patient.) But four months was the best the medical profession could do at the time. And not even the pro-lifers made such of a fuss at aborting imperfect babies, though Alison couldn't quite understand their rationale. Life in itself being so important, according to them, not the quality of life. William wished she'd just shut up about it. And there Alison was, pregnant, somehow or other, in spite of her Dutch cap (the pill bloated her; the coil made her bleed and hurt) while they were still trying to make up their minds. William and Alison rejoiced – well, almost. You know what these things are. They'd rather have trusted their judgment than their luck. Who, well and properly informed, would not?

At seven weeks the doctors diagnosed a twin pregnancy, which meant that the odds of at least one baby being Down's Syndrome went up to one in eight: and if the twins were identical, one in six. And Alison was being sick not just in the mornings but lunchtime, teatime, dinnertime and all night too, and Caroline, aged five, was coming out in sympathy and kept banging her mother's tummy with her head and saying she hated the baby and no one had the heart to say 'babies, actually' and the temptation just to terminate now, and not later – whoosh, the good baby going out with the bad, should such there be – though the likelihood of them *both* being Down's was now up to one in five, because Mum reminded her of a Down's great-uncle, never before discussed, plus identical twin great-aunts on William's side – good lord, those sessions at genetic counselling, William staring at Alison, Alison at William, each wondering whose the bad seed was, and the whole weight of society (not to mention William) blaming the mother, though it's often enough old fathers, not old mothers, who produce Down's Syndrome babies – as the specialist was at pains to point out. Not that maternal or paternal age affected their particular case. Though Mum wouldn't have it.

'The thing about William,' Mum said later, 'is that he was just plain *born* old' – she'd just plain liked Andrew, sexual ambiguity and all, and that was the fact of it. Andrew had needed a mother and William was all the mother to himself he'd needed – just watch him bandage his own cut finger, cossetting and comforting! Anyway, William and Alison kept their courage going and Alison took time off work – 'Caroline *needs* you at home,' said William, 'at a time like this' – and got through to the amniocentesis at four months – only first Alison had flu and then the clinic had been closed because of some virus – and the twins were actually to nineteen weeks before the test, and Alison pretty much bonded in spite of her efforts not to be; and in went the needle once, into the amniotic sac – ping! – one baby done – and in went the needle twice – second baby –

'I say,' said Alison, 'when you got the first one it moved, you know. Didn't like it one bit. You got the baby as well as the sac. I hope it wasn't an eye!'

'Nonsense!' they said. What a mother! Pity the poor father, with a woman who could joke at such times.

'Joke!' said Alison. 'I wasn't *joking*.' They put her on tranquillizers until the results came through. She was very thin, what with the vomiting and the flu, and Caroline's little arms curling round her legs whenever she tried to leave the room. But the test results came through in ten days or so – two boys, both okay – no Down's, no spina bifida. ('Any tests for blindness in one eye?' asked Alison.)

'Isn't that wonderful!' said the doctors. 'Aren't you relieved? We certainly are! You were taking quite a chance.' Ah, the wonder of modern science.

'Wonderful,' said Alison, but one or other of the babies was pressing on the sciatic nerve, or they were taking it in turns, those two healthy, crowded boys, and the pain was terrible.

Well, Alison was worrying. That never helps, does it? The trauma of the previous baby's birth was still with her, of course, but more than that: she was troubled by the nature of the universe. In hospitals other than the one she'd attended, she'd been told, efforts to save severely handicapped babies were not nearly so strenous. Luck of the draw, all luck of the draw. This hospital, that. Her birth, Andrew's dual sexuality (genetically determined, he maintained, no matter how she shrieked 'you're doing it on purpose!'), Caroline's wilting nature, her imperfect baby's survival, the twin pregnancy, William just being there waiting with reassuring arms: luck, luck! Work wasn't luck. Cause and effect operated in offices. Effort was rewarded by money. She pulled herself together and dragged herself to work every morning.

Her father died. A stroke – luck again. The blood clot was incapacitating or not, fatal or not, depending on where in the brain it happened to stick. It stuck in a bad place. That was that. She watched her mother carefully. Mum wept, mourned, recovered properly. It had been a good marriage. Death was, they said, more easily survived in such circumstances. Consciences were clear. Luck again. When you married, who you married, staying married: luck, all luck. The genetic counselling clinic denied luck and claimed probability, but Alison thought she'd rather just hang a lucky charm around her neck.

Mum came up to be with her before the twins were born. A long and painful affair, but at least relieving the pain in the sciatic nerve. The first twin was a boy, the second a girl.

'Ooops!' said the hospital.

'You tested the same baby twice,' said Alison. 'Told you so. See, two puncture marks. One on his chin, one on his ear. Lucky you missed the eye. Just test the girl for Down's, will you.' She went back to sleep. Ungrateful and difficult, they decided. The girl had the right number of chromosomes, so all was well. (Better luck than she deserved, one or two muttered.) Of course, amniocentesis was in its infancy. It is more sophisticated today. Don't worry.

Well, twins! Something in Alison's attitude upset William. It wasn't that she hadn't bonded. ('Have you bonded yet, mother?' Sister actually asked Alison. '*Both* twins, you're sure?' 'Quite sure, thank you, Sister,' said Alison, primly.) She longed to be up and active now the sheer physical weight of the pregnancy, not to mention the pain and the anxiety, was gone, and even Caroline seemed to find the reality of the twins quite tolerable, and her little white face had become pink again, and she'd been to stay with Mum down in Exeter for a whole week without howling for home – in fact Alison's spirits had been so high, back in the world of cause and effect, not just luck, that the twins had been three before the marriage broke up. Alison wouldn't stay home, that was the trouble; she would go out to work. William took her absence as an insult. He'd lost his job (he worked as an accountant with a small firm which unexpectedly merged with a large firm. 'Luck!' cried William. 'No,' said Annabel, 'cause and effect. You could have seen it coming. If you'd looked, which you didn't.') and wouldn't even try to get another, having gone off figures anyway and wanting to be a writer, and Alison argued that someone had to bring the money in, but he'd argued that it was better for them all to live off social security, and how could he look after the twins *and* write, and so on and so forth, and it had all ended up as musical chairs, with him in one household, sometimes with the twins, sometimes not, and Alison and Caroline and an au pair in another and Alison going out to work – unsatisfactory, said William, but I suppose it's what Alison wants and what Alison wants she gets (a lot of aggro and acrimony there) and somehow or other within a month or so William was living with this Annabel, about whom Alison had never known – but perhaps she should have seen it coming – who had a little money of her own and could stay home with William so he could find the time to write – and Alison, who was earning good money, found herself legally obliged to support both households (and morally obliged, of course. Hadn't her unreasonable attitudes been the cause of the marital break-up?)

Alison grieved for the twins in their absence, of course she did, but she had her sanity to think about (well, didn't she?), not to mention Caroline, who wasn't even William's child (as he kept saying both in public and private, once the arguments started), and both households to support and fortunately Annabel turned out to be both kind and competent (though financially more than canny) and the twins liked her and she had the knack of somehow turning William's motherliness into fatherliness, but anyway all that was in the past. Alison had met Bobby, and she was happy, and her future was in her own hands, whatever she did with it, and seeing her mother had cleared her head, and she thought she'd just move in with Bobby but put off marrying him for a few months until she was absolutely sure it was all going to work – then she would be acting responsibly and not trusting to luck – and she and her mother travelled back to London First Class.

'I'm perfectly happy going third,' said Mum. 'Why don't you save your money for more important things?' Well, she was like that. It made Alison feel safe. Except on the journey up she was sick, twice.

'Pregnant,' said Mum.

'Travel sick,' said Alison, but she felt her breasts and they were sore.

She went to her conference, and it was wonderful coming home to Caroline and the twins and Mum and Bobby visiting, and Mum liked Bobby, and he liked her and it all felt like home and she wondered why she was still hesitating, and forgot to wonder why she'd suddenly gone right off wine and coffee. And when William came out of hospital – his varicose veins stripped – ('Isn't he rather *young* for varicose veins?' asked Mum. 'But I suppose as he was just born old, it's got to his legs first') the twins went regretfully but happily enough to their other home, and she felt that even though they liked and appreciated Annabel, who kept their socks so clean and organized, it was she, their real mother, they loved, and what's more now they were older, less babies, more people, she was beginning to come to terms with them and the trauma and anxiety they had caused, not to mention the months on her sciatic nerve. She blamed the hospital for making what was blind and instinctive somehow rational and required, so the mind cut in and observed the body, just when it shouldn't. Really, she thought, the way things were going in the gynaecological world, new human beings should just be grown in petrie dishes, sperm joined to egg, forget love between man and woman, let alone parent and child, the once dark, once secret act of procreation now so brilliantly, clinically lit.

'Love you, Mummy,' said first Wendy, then Wyndham.

'I love you too,' said Alison.

'So do I,' said Caroline. 'And William a little bit. But Bobby more.'

'Isn't that all nice,' said Mum, who had quite come round to the modern habit of expressing love through words, she who had never in her youth or middle age been demonstrative could now see the pleasure of so doing.

'Come along, little ones,' said Annabel, briskly. 'Daddy's waiting in the car with Stevie and Rachel and Dodie. Daddy's got to walk two miles every single day for a whole month. Think of that!' They thought of that.

'Oooh!' they said. And William, pale and brave, framed in the car window, spoke kindly to Caroline, who beamed and blossomed, and indeed to Alison too. So everything was just fine except there was no denying now that Alison, somehow or other, was pregnant. She did a home test and sat and through a slanting mirror watched the little orange ring forming out of yellow dust and wondered whether the new baby would increase the sum of the world's good, or do the opposite, and shatter what had been so precariously achieved? No twins in Bobby's family, let alone Down's Syndrome (or as far as she knew) which helped; but once you had one set of twins the likelihood of another multiple pregnancy leapt up and with it the dramatic doubling of the odds against a perfect baby, and of course every year that passed, even with a single baby, put up the odds of it being Down's, having already had one, and how old was she now – thirty-nine – there was a kind of compound interest going on here, some cosmic penalty for happiness.

'What shall I do?' she asked her mother.

'Trust to luck,' said Mum. Luck! Good God! What good had luck ever done her?

'You must do what you want,' said Bobby. 'Though, of course I want us to have a baby. Very much.' And of course now the baby could be tested at ten weeks, through the cervix, so that took at least some of the anxiety out of it, not to mention risk to the baby, should the pregnancy proceed and they decide to go ahead. No termination, not yet. They postponed rejoicing until after the test. It could be done. Just. You went on pretending morning sickness was food poisoning and not referring to it. The baby was not a baby, just a growth, until declared valid by medical decree. But it was okay. They loved each other. That much was now certain. Only at eight weeks a scan showed twins. Two sacs. 'What will I do?' pleaded Alison. 'I can't go through with it. Not twins!'

'I might as well tell you,' said Mum, 'since you're already in such a state, you were twins, Alison. You had a sister. She died at birth. Of course these days they'd have saved her, but goodness knows how I'd have coped. Your father was better with a TV set than with a baby.'

'But why didn't you tell me?' Alison was astounded. 'You knew it would alter the odds. You must have known it would.'

'But knowing the odds made no difference,' observed Mum, 'since you got pregnant by accident, anyway. All knowing ever did was worry you more. Now you know you're terminating two, if that's what you're going to do, all that's happened is the decision's twice as hard. No one likes doing away with a perfect baby. Better to wait till they're born, if you ask me, then do away with the one that isn't right, if it isn't, and keep the one that is.'

'You go to prison, and I couldn't possibly do any such thing. Kill a baby, once it's born! Allow it to die – that's different. That's natural.'

'Might as well tell you,' said Mum, 'your twin wasn't right, mongol as we called them then, and the midwife did away with her. That's what midwives were for. That's why we had our babies at home. More danger but less interference.

'She couldn't have been identical,' said Alison, too obsessed by these genetic matters to worry about Mum's deceit, let alone the real function of midwives, 'or I'd have been Down's too.'

'Would you?' asked Mum. 'Down's schmowns, a baby's a baby.'

'Bet you were glad yours didn't live, all the same.' My sister, she felt. The sister I never had, always thought I ought to have, killed by my own mother.

'I was,' said Mum. 'Your father would never have stood for it.'

'You may be right there,' said Alison. Statistics certainly showed babies that weren't right broke up families quicker than anything. The handicapped end up with mothers, seldom fathers, hardly ever both. And she thought sadly of William, whose good opinion she still somehow couldn't quite seem to do without, and grieved for her poor baby, with his extra chromosome and dicey lungs, who had clung so studiously to life, and for so long – long after others would have given up and allowed themselves to be sluiced away in a flood of pre-natal blood. But the conversation, though it shortened, or was it lengthened, the odds, strengthened her mind. Termination. To go ahead with twins was absurd. She didn't have the physical strength, either before or after the birth. She just didn't.

'Oh!' said the specialist, 'if it's twins that worry you, these days we can terminate one and let the other go term.'

'Which one?' Alison asked.

'The first one we come to,' said the specialist, a little stiffly.

'You mean you can't test both and remove the one with Down's?'

'Not yet. Though no doubt soon we'll be able to. And of course we must look on the bright side. Neither might be Down's.'

'I don't think that's the bright side,' said Alison. 'I don't think terminating a perfect baby can ever be called the bright side.' Difficult, wasn't she. Well, wouldn't you be?

'We would recommend a selective termination in any case; you might have trouble carrying two babies to term. We do it often, nowadays. The procedure's been developed to cope with the number of multiple pregnancies we get nowadays – the result of fertility drugs.'

'That's different,' said Alison. 'This baby of mine – these babies – were created naturally. Conceived in love and passion, if by accident. How can I possibly terminate one? It might be the wrong one. And if it was okay, how could I tell the one that lived, when it came to their turn for genetic counselling, that I'd got rid of the other. What would it think of me?'

'It would at least be alive to do the thinking. I could terminate one now,' said the specialist kindly, 'and test the other at sixteen weeks, though there would still be an increased risk of miscarriage, and dispose of it for you if it were Down's.'

Sixteen weeks! 'No, no,' said Alison. 'Never. No counselling, no testing, I'll have them both and trust to luck.' She could already feel the pain of the sciatic nerve but she didn't care. She'd never said or felt such a thing before. It quite shocked her to hear herself speaking so loud and clear. And as it happened, the gods of chance must have heard, and looked down on her, or somebody or something; at any rate as she left the clinic she felt the first sticky flow of blood, and presently more and more, so much blood there seemed no end to it, so many regrets, so much relief, and within twenty-four messy, painful hours the putative twins were gone, male or female, good or bad, identical or fraternal, no one was ever to know, in such a flow of welter and crimson even the hospital was surprised.

'So much blood!' exclaimed the au pair, in the ambulance.

'Don't look,' cried Alison, 'it might put you off.'

Later on, when she was feeling steadier, she'd try again, and trust to luck it wasn't twins. Caroline, Wendy and Wyndham were all just fine – weren't they?

'Just as well,' said Mum, 'though I don't suppose you want to hear that. You have quite enough to think about as it is. How is the inside of your head?'

'Clearer,' said Alison. 'It's the sudden drop of oestrogen.'

'Reminds me of the time I miscarried the first lot of twins,' said Mum, who was, as ever, full of surprises. 'Just as well. They weren't your father's. Now drink a lot of water, and replace the lost blood, and here's to better luck next time. It'll happen. Blood's the libation the God of Chance requires. Lots and lots of blood. Always has, always will. Afterwards things go better. Didn't I have you?'

The Dead Woman

SARAH BAYLIS

Sarah Baylis is the author of two children's books, *Vila*, published by Brilliance Books in 1984, winner of the Other Award for Children's Fiction, and *The Tomb of Reeds*, published by Julia MacRae in 1987. She is also the author of *Utrillo's Mother*, published by Pandora Press in 1987. She died in a road accident just one month before the publication of *Utrillo's Mother* at the age of 30.

Nurse Moonie's on duty again, pissed off at being put on this boring ward that isn't maternity, isn't intensive care, but somehow a ghoulish mixture of the two. *Bloody liberty. They just want someone who'll keep her mouth shut.*

Nurse Moonie always keeps her mouth shut. She's all eyes, no mouth, hoovering up impressions and keeping information stuffed inside her like a hamster: she has dirt on everyone now – everyone except her patient, of course, who is unabatingly good and endlessly silent. *Mum*, snorts Nurse Moonie, *is the word.*

Her patient is a dead woman. Snow White, laid out pale as a lily in a casket of crystal – as pretty as Snow White – and as uncomplaining. Instead of seven dwarfs scurrying about this winking casket, polishing the chrome, seven nurses and seven doctors.

It wasn't an apple that carried her off, but a mighty haemorrhage which pounded the delicate folds of her brain to a pulp and drowned them in a tide of crimson. Nothing could be seen from outside except the delicate fainting of a woman to the floor, and this was followed by grief, the howl of sirens and a screech of ambulance tyres as the woman's husband dealt efficiently with the demise of his wife.

Now she lies beneath a bank of sterile equipment. At her head gleams a quarter of a million pounds' worth of chips and tubes and quartz; at her feet another half million's worth of humming generator and something that looks like the hub cap of a car. She cannot breathe, so scentless oxygen is squeezed into her flaccid lungs. She cannot eat, so liquid pap is squirted into her veins. She doesn't shit; she leaks. No word, she utters, no sigh. Her cheek is as pale as milk and her lips are shut tight, like folded paper. Her blood, pushed through her body by a whirring pump, is as thin and lustreless as gruel.

But, ahh, purrs Nurse Moonie, *she has a man to love her.*

The dead woman's husband is a caring fellow. His gentle face is often seen by the casket side as he sits by his wife's bed and holds her icy hand, sometimes even uttering a phrase or two in her deaf ear. He loves her. She is completely dead, but she has something even now that makes his heart beat fast enough for two, that makes his pulse race and his forehead bead with sweat. *Poor sap*, scoffs the Nurse, *it'll bring him nothing but sorrow.*

She shuddered and fetched her duster. In this sterile place where did the dust come from? Did it flake off the dead woman's very face in a last attempt at jinxing the machinery? Did the air produce it? Was there some contagion in the woman's lungs that puffed it out at every exhalation, like pneuma? Certainly everyone got depressed on this ward. It was a gloomy place, this plastic sepulchre; the gloom settled everywhere, as silently as dust. The only thing that makes death bearable is that it hurries in and hurries out, whisking away the soul and leaving a little staleness in the air that can be cured by throwing wide the windows and waving a feather duster at the corners of the room. Here in this squeaky ward, death hung about, lingering; was tied down, even, by the bank of bleeping dials that sent the gruel sloshing relentlessly through dead collapsing veins.

Nurse Moonie lifted her skirt and scratched her knee. Flea bites from the cat. She sniggered at the thought of bringing a few of the little creatures in with her. Would they feed off dead flesh as eagerly as they fed off her? She shrugged and stared out of the window, feeling ill. It was her job to move the cold, shrivelling arms and wash the armpits where hair still grew; to readjust the catheters. It was horrible, this tending of a corpse, unnatural: a laying-out that went on for months. *What am I, after all*, she asked herself, *a bloody undertaker?* She was starting to hate her own sex, so closely did she have to observe each colourless pucker of her patient. She was becoming squeamish, and that's bad news for a nurse.

Midday, and here come the doctors. Squeak, squeak, and a whiff of aftershave; hands behind backs and as solemn as churchmen.

Up for a knighthood, Dr Stone is as excited as the day he first got a place in the school cricket team. He rubs his hands and peers at his own personal mausoleum – woman-shaped: how novel!

'Nurse Moonie? How do we progress?'

'We progress marvellously, doctor, thank you.'

Nurse Moonie stands behind the dead woman and speaks for her, feeling strangely protective. Pretty golden hair floats on the pillow. The dead woman's flesh is more vulnerable than ever, pearly blue and easily marred, as Dr Stone hoists up the rough gown and displays the dead nakedness to all and sundry. Behind him, the young doctors shift and sway and peer through spectacles.

'Behold, gentlemen, our very own little miracle,' and the prospective knight fishes for an old-fashioned ear trumpet and presses it to the dead woman's large abdomen. His old doctor's mouth curved in a smile. What does he hear, save the ordinary gurgles of this artificially sustained life?

'Our baby's doing nicely,' he beams, and looks just like a chef sniffing out a pot of sauce.

Polite applause from the young doctors, and Nurse Moonie sneers privately. She hates this fleshy coffin of a woman, and yet she could kill these grinning consultants for their pursuit of creation. She would stand in front of the glass casket and flail about her with a scalpel to save this dead woman from these final indignities. What good can come of it, after all, bringing a child into the world from a dead woman's belly? What succour for an infant with only a dead breast to suck? *Ugh, poor little fool, motherless even before your time. Nurtured in a bloody grave! What'll it be doing to your soul, growing in such a silent, unfeeling place?*

Yet Nurse Moonie knows that this baby born of a dead mother will rest in her arms as sweet and slippery as any other. She has her superstitions (and she hates the doctors for their heartless procreation) but she is a warm-hearted woman and will sniff the baby's head and speak to it in the high, trance-like voice that babies love; she will weep seeing it raw and alone in its incubator like a hatched chick; and she will cry angrily when the dead woman's husband comes to claim his seed.

Off duty, now, Nurse Moonie. Here comes the night sister, whisking along, full of news. Time to go home.

Once out of the pure, clear air of the ward, Nurse Moonie is tossed into the echoing corridors of the hospital, a warren of groaning Victorian inconvenience. Here the living shuffle about and balls of real homely dust scuttle along the lino. Like a modern witch, Nurse Moonie is anxious to be home with her cat, a vicious creature of elegance and haphazard temper. She's eager to wash the smell of death off her hands. Being a living woman, Nurse Moonie is menstruating, and she wants to put her feet up and close her eyes, and forget about the dead womb of her patient that has no choice but to keep carrying its charge.

When she opens the door, the cat yowls and she gives it milk.

Musical Chairs

MICHELENE WANDOR

Michelene Wandor is a poet, playwright and critic as well as a writer of prose fiction. Her most recent publications include *Guests in the Body*, a collection of short stories published by Virago in 1986, *Arky Types* (a novel co-written with Sara Maitland), published by Methuen in 1987, and *Look Back in Gender,* on the family and sexuality in drama, also published by Methuen in 1987. Her stage plays have been performed in a variety of venues, from the Soho Poly to the National Theatre.

Curled up in the snow. Firm and soft. Warm inside and warm outside. His body cradled in a white shape, his head curled comfortably on a slightly higher mound, his arms folded across his chest, hands bunched inside his gloves, legs curled upwards, his knees touching his elbows. The watery sun glazes the snow, a translucent, bluish light seen through the curtains of his eyelids. His whole body is smiling. This, he thinks, is the garden of Eden. He could float for ever, weightless, free. No need to know whether he is in the air or on the ground, indoors or outside, in day or night, in silence or in sound. Moving or still. Asleep or awake. Voices or silence. F sharp or B flat. Whatever they are. Pussy cats or monkeys. A bubble of laughter tingles. Did he say these things out loud? It doesn't matter. No one can hear.

At first they thought I was dead. The doctor didn't want to loosen my clothes in the sub-zero temperatures. Speed was of the essence.

They worked swiftly and silently, their boots scrunching in the snow, small grunts, tiny clouds of steam, warm air as they breathe out, evaporating as it cools rapidly. They laid me on a stretcher, a nod from the doctor and I was winched up to the helicopter. The rescue team strapped on their skis, ready to go back down the mountain. Under the top sprinkling of new snow, one of them found an empty whisky bottle. Lucky devil, they smiled, this probably kept him alive.

> Arcs of sound criss-cross space, filaments, trajectories stringing through the pure air. The sounds are clean and white and sweet and have distance between them, as though they are being played by an invisible orchestra spread out in a gigantic semicircle, across an arctic continent as far as the eye can see, some of the players below the curve of the earth's horizon. How on earth can the conductor see them all? As he strains to see, the players appear, scattered, wearing their prescription black and white. The white of the men's shirts and the women's blouses is different from that of the snow, faint timbres, pink, lilac, peach, blue, as if reflecting the vibrancy of the living skin, the bare faces and hands, none of them affected by the cold.

In the helicopter, the first thing I said, even before I opened my eyes was, 'That Sibelius is a fucking great composer.' Someone laughed out loud in relieved hysteria.

> Now he sees the conductor, wielding the baton, long hair swirling, head nodding and shaking in rhythm, long, flowing hair catching the light as it swirls and sways. Delicate hands hold the baton firmly. The conductor's back was towards him. Who was it? He ran through the names of all the conductors he knew. None of them had quite that combination of firmness and delicacy. Who could it be? There was something about the angle of the head, something – no. Impossible. It was no one he knew.

In the hospital I was crazy with impatience. 'I'm filming next week. I've got a thousand things to do. When can I go home?' They soothed me, muttered things about a hairline fracture on my collarbone, pulled the sheets more tightly round me, tucked them in, kept the bed neat and contained me in a white cocoon far more dangerous than the snow. The newspapers covered the story with appropriate headlines: 'Film director saved from avalanche.' I didn't see them. I didn't care.

The conductor disappeared. Now there were just the musicians, playing. Then the sound went. He can see them bowing and fingering and blowing and plucking but he cannot hear anything. Then, suddenly, the conductor is there, facing him. She is smiling. Jane stands there before him, slim and exquisite in tie and tails, smiling. Smiling.

Be careful, they said. No coughing, no laughing, no vigorous exercise. If you promise to look after yourself, you can go home.

Damn her. She raises her arms, the baton held loosely in her right hand. She begins to conduct. She is facing him. She is conducting him. Common time, she says, this is in common time. Four in a bar. Four what in a bar? Come, now, you know what four in a bar is. Four men getting pissed out of their minds in the pub at the end of the road while I have to get the kids to bed and get ready for the concert. He screams. She turns away from him, back to the orchestra, raises her arms gently and leads them sweetly into the Adagio.

Back in London there were endless meetings. The composer's widow, retained as an advisor on his music, knowledgeable to a fault about his intentions. After all, hadn't she copied it all out for him in her own fair hand, so much more legible than his? Had he not entrusted her with the task of protecting his traditional airs and modern graces from any inappropriate interpretation after his death?

He screams again. The orchestra has gone. The vast expanse of snow is smooth and untouched. A white sheet pulled smooth over a double bed. A white sheet crumpled and curled round two small bodies, their limbs flung easily and carelessly over his. God, what a flat. One large room, painted white, a kitchen area at one end, barely room for a table and chairs, certainly no room for even an armchair. The older two staying Saturday nights with him. Not the baby, of course. There they were, the three of them, cuddled under the blankets in that double bed. He fought Jane against their coming to stay, and ten minutes after they arrived, he knew he didn't want them to go away again. Ten minutes after he had delivered them back to Jane, he had flung himself back into work.

This project took off like a dream. I'd wanted to make a film about the composer for years, and when he died suddenly I thought I'd blown it. His widow, whom I knew well, told me about the last symphony. No one else knew he had been working on it. She asked my advice. She offered to play it through on the piano to me. I refused. No, I said. I'll hear it when they rehearse it. What do you mean, she asked? I've got this marvellous idea, I said. I will raise money for a film, a co-production, with German television, with American television, with Japanese television, and I will make a film about his life, the film I always wanted to make, and the world premiere of this posthumous symphony will be on film. How about it? Crazy, eh. But not as crazy as I was for the whole of last year, sweet-talking the men with the money, with no more aesthetic sense than a rubbish bag, into believing they were a cross between James Agee and Dilys Powell. I was exhausted by the end of it, but successful. As always.

Their last holiday together was in Scotland. Their last family holiday. Caught the car-train, arrived in Perth and spent the first night in a bed and breakfast in Blairgowrie. The town bleak and desperate, full of bleak men. The local canning factory shut down six months before. On the window of the careers office a notice pleaded, 'Does your drinking cause you and your family problems? We don't ask you to give up your drinking, just come and talk it over over a cup of coffee.'

Supper that evening; there was reconstituted Scotch broth, darkened with an Oxo cube, salmon surrounded by salad and swamped with chips, a bottle of Heinz salad cream. Afters, thawed strawberries and cheesecake. The sound of a Hammond organ drifted into the dining room.

Later, the kids asleep, down in the bar, a nightcap whisky, and the lady of the house sits at the organ, her back to the room, the colour telly on, with the sound turned down. She plays 'Beautiful Dreamer' and 'Home on the Range'. Next morning, as they drive away, on a hill stands a lone piper, playing 'Scotland the Brave', the tone lifting the landscape, the tune drifting high above the fumes and the drizzle.

When I know what I want to make a film about, I find the form. I puzzle and puzzle and one day it all begins to come clear. I hate films of concerts, the audience sitting there, the players shiny, stuffed; I don't mind when I am at the concert myself, one of the audience, glorying in the excitement of the living music. I just can't stand seeing it on film. So I puzzled away for a long time about the best way to take responsibility for the world premiere of a symphony by a Scottish composer whose work had not been sufficiently appreciated during his lifetime. No concert, I thought. Then how play the music, how be seen to play the music for the first time, and the first time which would last forever, because it would be recorded on film? Rehearsals. That was the answer. I would film all the rehearsals, then I would intersperse the biographical stuff with the rehearsals for the posthumous symphony. There would be no need to hear the complete work, because by the end of the film, the complete work would have been heard. Brilliant. I love rehearsals, people turning up in any old clothes, the conductor making a mixture of esoteric musical jokes, sarcastic jabs, putting his whole body into the music, shaping it, guiding it, attacking it, and then standing back and letting the orchestra simply flow with what they have learned.

Jane had brought two scores with her. He didn't say anything, but she knew he didn't like her working on scores when they were together. Learn to read music, she'd say, then I can explain what I'm doing. I'll teach you. No need, he'd answer. He hated those lines and squiggles and splodges.

What instruments do you play, they asked me on chat shows? I don't play anything, I'd answer. I'm musically illiterate. How can you make films about musicians, then, they asked? Easily, I'd say. You don't have to be a soldier to make films about war. What is music, they'd say? I can't tell you, I'd answer. It's beyond words. It has nothing to do with anything else in my life. It has nothing to do with the words through which I try to make sense of the world and control my life. Music can be inappropriate to an occasion, it can be played out of tune, it can be boring, but it has the supreme virtue of being beyond words and that is why I like it. It is as simple as that. It sits in your head, like the most recent Boy George hit, or an advertising jingle or a string quartet. It inhabits you. Sort of like the music of the spheres, they'd say? Yes, I'd say, something like that.

> Jane didn't understand. He didn't know how to explain it. Sooner or later people always wanted your soul. Music simply had it. He gave it freely, voluntarily, willingly. He was Faust and the music was his Mephistopheles. The deal was simple. His soul, in exchange for the time it took to play a piece of music. Unlimited borrowing, with no fines for anything overdue. Or, if you preferred it, a bank full of time stored up in it, with interest paid gently, even with pleasure. The best sort of investment. Better than people. They always wanted your soul, sooner or later.

We spent the main part of the holiday in the hotel complex at Aviemore, ideal for the kids, and handy for walking. The baby bounced on my back or Jane's and the other two alternately moaned or looked forward to the treats of lunchtime miles away from everywhere, with a view totally lost on them. Sprigs of heather plucked from the summit of summer Cairn Gorm. On each stem, a full nine bells of pale purple flower, each bell pouting to a narrow opening, the hood protecting the delicate interior from the mist. Walking through the drizzle, carrying sprigs of heather. Small, spiky leaves, dark green, littering the stalk to its strong base.

One day we took a chairlift up to the middle station of Cairn Gorm, the kids screaming with excitement and fear as we floated above the burn, thrilled to bits as the chairs slowly came down to earth. Two parallel lines of rocks marked the path to the summit.

Signs warned climbers to beware of sudden mists. I wondered what it would look like in the snow.

When he was three, some unnamed tragedy drove him to bed in tears. A toy music box, clutched in his hand, played 'Baa Baa Black Sheep'. The first hymn he ever heard in school, 'Oh, God, Our Help in Ages Past', stayed in his head for the whole week, carrying him through the strange newnesses. When he passed the eleven plus, 'The Lord is My Shepherd' (Crimond) sang him through the summer holidays, tune and descant together. Buddy Holly rode by his side on a bicycle through university, and in early married life, Mozart made friends with the late Beethoven quartets. Then Jane took up her music again.

We didn't need to talk to each other much on holiday. Mostly we were sorting out the logistics of the day, dealing with the kids. Only there were some evenings when we faced each other across the dinner table, having sorted out the arrangements for the following day, when the little silences interrupted us. How was it that two people who were so closely related, who never lost the desire to touch each other, even after they had stopped touching each other; how was it that we couldn't make it work? We knew the obvious problems: Jane hated my world, the world of high-powered hustlers, a world peopled with acquaintances and not friends, a world I loved. And yet she liked my films. Always. And wanted me to make them. Me? I don't know. But every time she took out a book about music, or opened her manuscript book, I froze. I was always too busy to go to concerts with her, even before she started working again. Genuinely busy. With work like mine, there is always something important to do.

He can't take his eyes off the ground. He knows that if he looks up, he will be swirled away, the sky will whirl him into its vortex, the evil in him dragging him round and round, swinging his body by the head, gashing his flesh on the rocks, ripping his skin away.

We went to Loch Ness to look for the monster. We had tea in Inverness. We watched the salmon leaping obediently in Pitlochry.

We climbed the steep path to Arthur's seat. I held the kids' hands tightly, but I was more scared than they were. I couldn't take my eyes off the ground.

He remembers a joke told at a ceilidh. On the day of judgment all the men in the world get together to go to heaven, and when they get up there, St Peter says, all the hen-pecked husbands go to one side and all the non-hen-pecked husbands go to the other. So there's a huge queue of hen-pecked husbands, and only one chap on the other side. So St Peter says to the one man, you must be a brave chap, and the man says, Oh no, I'm standing here because my missus telled me tae.

We loved the ceilidh; the piano so sharp it was almost flat on the next semi-tone up. The kids clapped and stamped. The next morning we drove back to London, the kids tired, ready to go home. I took in the luggage while Jane made the tea. When the kids were in bed, we sat opposite each other in the kitchen we'd both planned, with the clock ticking quietly. We looked at each other. It was beyond words, this. I said, I'm going. Yes, said Jane, if you hadn't said it, I would have. So I packed some things and went to stay in the flat. I was a danger on the roads that evening, driving my car, crying and playing Dusty Springfield. I wanted her, I wanted me, I wanted us.

He knew exactly how he was going to do the film. All worked out. First all the biographical stuff would be shot, on location, of course, in Scotland. Then the rehearsals would be filmed in London, and then the wonderful process of editing would begin, the bit he loved more than any other, because it was in the editing that the world was finally built, and everything would fall into place. He had a week's holiday before it all started. He went skiing. On the last day, he caught a glimpse of the Arts page of an English newspaper. 'Conductor sacked,' it said. There it was, in black and white. The orchestra lined up to play in the film, had risen as one and rebelled against the conductor. Discontents that had been rippling for years finally came to a head. Crisis. The orchestra's work had to continue.

'First Woman Conductor,' said the subtitle, and there she was. Jane, slim and exquisite in her tails, holding her baton delicately, her arms raised. Smiling.

When I got back from holiday, I dumped my luggage in the flat and took a train straight to Scotland. I bought a bottle of whisky. I hired a car and drove to Cairn Gorm. The sun was bright on the bluish-white snow. I took the chairlift up to the middle. My head was empty. Nothing. No song, no music, nothing. I got out of the chairlift. Signs warned climbers about sudden mists. I took the top off the bottle and drank as I walked. When I found a comfortable spot, sheltered from the worst of the wind, I sat down and finished the whisky. I was almost asleep before I got to the end. I was cosy, comfortable. I slid down in the snow, curled up and waited for the music of the spheres.

At first they thought he was dead. He was still, he didn't seem to be breathing. Then, when they realized he was alive, they worked swiftly and silently. When he had been put on the stretcher and winched up to the helicopter, the rescue team began strapping on their skis, ready to go back down the mountain. One of them nearly fell over something half-buried in the top sprinkling of new snow. Lucky devil, he said, this probably kept him alive. He's going to have one hell of a hangover.

There was really only one thing to do, and I found myself doing it almost without realizing it. I phoned Jane. Did she know what a bastard I was on the set? She didn't doubt it, she said. Under the gentle, artistic exterior, I was as big a shit as anyone else. Yes, but did she mind, I asked? Of course she bloody minded, but I had to remember that she was a professional (as was I) and this was a job. She would give as good as she got if I treated her badly. Do we hate each other, I asked? I shouldn't think so, she said. We just can't live together. We get in each other's way. So what else is new. The music will be wonderful, she said. The orchestra is great.

When the committees nominated the film for its various awards, they always chose the same extract: in it an orchestra, dressed in its customary black and white, played the entire symphony, spread out in a gigantic semi-circle, scattered as far as the eye could see, some of the players below the curve of the earth's horizon. The white of the men's shirts and the women's blouses picks up timbres different from those of the snowy landscape: pink, lilac, peach, blue. Before them stands their conductor, slim, in tie and tails, her baton moving precisely, her long flowing hair catching the light as her head dips and sways.

Just before the film's premiere, I bought myself a book on the rudiments of music.

Rex

MARIANNE WIGGINS

Marianne Wiggins was born in the USA in 1947. She has lived in Paris, Brussels, Rome and New York and now lives in London with her husband. Two of her previous four books have been published in England – her novel *Separate Checks* and her collection of short stories *Herself in Love*. *Learning Urdu* from which this story, '*Rex*', comes, will be published by Secker & Warburg in 1989. Her next novel, *John Dollar*, will also be published by Secker & Warburg in 1989. She writes frequently for *The Sunday Times* as their American book reviewer and she also reviews books for the *Times Literary Supplement* and the *New Statesman*.

Nothing wonderful makes a phone call in the middle of the night, the northern lights don't ring you up to let you know they're coming. Lovers call, the former kind; the cops. People who speak words that don't go well together call you to make sounds that spell bad news. After midnight something happens to the air inside a telephone, it thins like winter light and things sound loud, they sound alarming, they make a sound designed to waken sleeping dogs.

The call that came was from her sister.

It was 1 a.m. Atlantic Coast, 9 p.m. in San Francisco. Patricia had been woken in the middle of the night while, on the other side, Myra was just home from work, standing in her kitchen. Their other sister, Ellen, had rung Myra from New York, then Myra had rung Pat in Woods Hole, Massachusetts, from San Francisco. Lines were crackling all around and the news created its own circuit. The news was this: somewhere in the last eight hours their mother, travelling from coast to coast by air with two bags and one Pekingese, had gotten lost. She was seventy-six years old. She had white hair. No one in his right mind would ever kidnap Nina, Myra said. Myra was the one who'd put their mother on the plane in San Francisco. Don't talk that way, Patricia told her. There's been a mix-up. *She could be dead* they both were thinking.

The gist of it was this: a storm had massed over the Rockies, dumped a partial payload on the Plains and was heading towards the East Coast faster than a speeding bullet and somewhere either in the air or on the ground between San Francisco International Airport and La Guardia in New York there was a white-haired, seventy-six-year-old, five-feet-two-and-a-half-inches-tall woman answering to the name of 'Mother' in their circumstances, 'Nina' in most others; one royal blue two-suiter suitcase with a winter coat jammed in it and another royal blue suitcase not as big, not the same brand, not exactly matching the two-suiter's shade of blue, which was stuffed to bursting with wool socks, wool underwear, a flannel nightgown and presents for the grandchildren; and, in a cardboard Porta-Kennel behind whose wire mesh his black eyes wept while his worm-coloured tongue searched in vain for syllables . . . beloved Winston, Pekingese.

To say that Winston was an ugly dog did Winston kind. To say that he embodied all the meanest elements inherent in his breed and then to say his breed was Pekingese and Nina spoiled him rotten justified her daughters' certainty that no one in his right mind would try to waylay Nina for a chance to dognap Winston. The world was sick but not so sick it would abet harm to a white-haired woman for a chance to steal an ugly dog.

The sensible conclusion was they'd got lost.

Between two shores, among three daughters, amid nobody's air-space, over sacrosanct frontiers – California, Utah, Colorado, Omaha, Des Moines, Chicago, Hershey Pennsylvania – they were lost. No terrorist would steal somebody over Utah, would he? Myra asked. Myra was the terrorist-freak, she'd cancelled her vacation to Corfu because of Libyans: now *this.* Her own mother had gone out of sight in her own native land. Kidnapped, Myra breathed. *From thirty thousand feet?* Ellen insisted. *Someone jumped to safety from a Delta 747 over Nevada with Mother in his evil grasp and Winston in a Porta-Kennel?*

'The fact is,' Ellen said, 'you put Nina on the plane in San Francisco and when it landed at La Guardia she and Winston and her suitcases were nowhere to be found.'

Oh no, Myra lamented, this isn't happening, this is impossible, do the airline people think it might be flying saucers?

Listen, Ellen said. For some reason – God knows what – when the airplane stopped in Denver Nina must have gotten off.

Does she *know* someone in Denver? Myra asked.

Don't *you* know? her sister asked. That's the *point* – *I* don't know who Mother knows. Don't *you* know who Mother knows? Who does Mother know?

She used to say she used to know what's-her-name, Ike's wife.

'Ike?'

The President.

'The President of what?'

Of the you-know. Country. Mamie.

'Mamie?'

With the bangs.

'The bangs?'

That one.

'This is the eighties – !'

I know that.

'Christ!'

It doesn't mean that they were meaningless.

'The *bangs*?'

The Eisenhowers.

'What do the *Eisenhowers* have to do with what we're dealing with, for christsake? What do *they* have to do with who Mother knows in Denver, Colorado? Who does Mother *know* – *that's* the issue. . . .'

Well, like I said, she used to say she knew Mamie Eisen –

'*Now*. Who does Nina know in Denver *now?*'

Denver, Myra answered. I wish this wasn't happening in Denver. Denver used to be among the ten best places in the world. I used to think of Denver as a nice place to fly into.

'No more,' Ellen admitted. 'Listen. I think we have to face the fact that Mother's sick,' she said. 'I'm not saying that it's time to panic, but I think we have to face the fact that evidence is mounting which sustains the proof that she's a victim of attack from the inside. . . .'

A *spy network*?

'Her *body*, dope.'

'Oh cripes, but Nina's *fit*.'

'Exactly what was Nina wearing?'

'*What?*'

'What did she have on, do you remember?'

'I don't like this, Ellen.'

'Be a big girl, Myra, try to visualize it, you're the last person who saw her and I have to call a lot of hospitals and the police.'

If I live to be a hundred years I won't forget you said that, Myra pledged her sister.

It was Ellen, then, who called the Delta Airline people out in Denver. She also called the Colorado State Police who were very nice and said they'd check the hospitals around the Denver area. The airline people weren't so nice. The storm, by then, had gotten pretty bad and it affected them. As far east as La Guardia airline people were forecasting air travel delays that gave them headaches. Everyone, it seemed, was nervous.

Myra called Pat in Massachusetts to give her the bad news and she and Pat agreed to stay beside their phones until, from somewhere, Nina would decide to call. Meanwhile none of them could keep from calling up the other two as hours passed and nothing happened and no word from Nina came. Around 4 a.m. that first night Ellen called Patricia to say she couldn't stand the wait anymore. She was going to La Guardia again in case Nina had arrived from Denver on another airline, she told Pat. '*That's stupid*,' Pat insisted.

They went over the description of what Myra said Nina had been wearing when she left: thick shoes.

What do you mean, "thick shoes"? Ellen had asked.

Nursies, Myra had said. "Opaque stockings".

Myra, I don't need a fashion essay.

A twill skirt.

What colour?

Slate.

"Slate", for christsake?

Okay, "grey".

On top?

Her Irish sweater.

Colour?

Off-white, you know. "Creamy".

Hat?

What?

Was Nina wearing a hat?

No.

No hat?

No.

Sometimes she liked wearing hats.

Past-tense?

What?

Never mind.

The hat?

She wasn't wearing one.

No?

No.

You're sure?

I'm sure.

You're positively sure?

I'm *sure* – she was wearing that little ponytail the way she does, with her elastic.

Winston?

What?

What was Winston wearing?

Oh. His Tartan. One of his bright plaids. His leather collar. I remember 'cause I said to Nina that the leather one looked nice and understated. For travelling, you know. Instead of that other artificial ruby one.

'*Holy Christ,*' Pat said to Ellen when she heard this for the seventh time around 6 a.m. the morning of the second day. 'Has anybody thought to check the *vets*?'

Pekingese is not a common breed in Denver and the first reports were many and confused. A Weimaraner by the name of Walther who'd been brought in by a woman answering Nina's description was believed by the State Police to be the missing Winston and the false discovery held the sisters in a state of anxiousness for several hours on the morning of the second day. 'If someone really wants to,' a Colorado State Trooper told Ellen on the phone that afternoon, 'this country makes it easy to drop out of sight. Piece of cake the first few months, easy to go total incognito. But for a total fact I have to tell you to stay permanently missing in the US, ma'm – what with the network we've developed – a person's got to be a total genius.'

The idea that their mother might have disappeared on purpose was put forward by authorities who, after all, had more experience in matters such as this and had to ask the difficult but necessary questions that the situation called for. Was she in financial trouble? Did she seem depressed? Had she been behaving strangely in the weeks preceding what was now referred to as The Incident? Was it likely there was something she was hiding from her daughters? Had she ever travelled outside the US? Had she ever visited inside the iron curtain? What about the commie bloc? How 'bout South America? Was she on some drugs? Did she have a lover? Had their father (twenty years deceased) been black? Did they think their mother was a lesbian?

When Walther the Weimaraner proved in fact not be to Winston the Pekingese and no one around the Denver airport had reported having seen or talked to anyone corresponding to Nina's description, Ellen thought she heard a new note enter the polite response she was getting from the Colorado State Troopers. For one thing, apart from the more anxious phone calls that they made to one another, around noon of the second day Pat's, Myra's and Ellen's phones went dead. No one called them. Panic, which was not Pat's or Ellen's element, set in and Myra's early fears of an act of terrorism seemed, in retrospect, entirely quaint. Among them they repeated four words as a fugue, a mounting roundelay in dissonance, a Doppler shift from 'Have *you* heard anything?' to 'Have you *heard* anything?' until finally, by the evening of the second day, the question was, 'Have you heard *anything*?' Meanwhile the storm raged over the Midwest and headed east. Denver Airport closed indefinitely. La Guardia delayed all flights six hours owing to increasing sleet. It was a windless storm, so far as blizzards go – its danger was delivery of a massive snow. There were twenty inches of it fallen in six hours in Nebraska. Roads and runways couldn't be kept clear. In whole parts of the country phone lines had been down since the preceding day. Motorists were cautioned not to drive. On the second night of Nina's disappearance television broadcasters as far east as New York City were advising elderly people to stay at home. Tuning in at random, hearing this, Ellen had her first real grief. She'd had so much to do, she hadn't stopped to think of Nina as *her mother*, as a person. She thought of Nina as somebody out there, a dotty actress in a Hitchcock movie whose disappearance is the basis of a light romantic comedy. She thought of Nina being lost, perhaps completely fuddled, painfully intractable about that stupid ugly dog of hers, but on the move, *moving*, if not in a straight line, moving, nonetheless, with purpose. She hadn't thought of Nina being old, Nina being stopped by weather, Nina being halt, Nina being silenced by forgetfulness, by quarter-mile-long treks to boarding gates, Nina as a nuisance in a fast lane, Nina faltering.

When the phone rang after midnight Ellen jumped at it. It was Colorado Trooper Larsen speaking. 'We've retrieved a piece of that blue luggage with your mother's name and address on it,' he reported in his detailed manner. 'We retrieved it from a trash bin in the Denver train station. We've sent it to Forensics for some answers but there's one thing I can tell you with all certainty, without a doubt. The inside of that suitcase was a total empty. Total. Do you hear me, m'am?'

It takes four hours to fly across the USA by plane, four days to make the trip by train and maniacs have claimed it can be done by car in less than fifty hours. In the snow nobody moves that fast. The airports close, their runways turn into sleek tundras, railbeds fill like hourglasses, glaciers mass on intercontinental roadway systems. Silence is a symptom of extremes in weather – it's the product of extinction. When the world was young colossi roamed it til extremes began, the dinosaur fell victim to a frozen evolution, stopped before it might have managed to adapt, while earth's more modern creature lasted out bad weather by retreating to its caves. Three days went by.

The snow moved on to Ohio, Pennsylvania and New York. In Massachusetts, Pat waited by her telephone and watched the sky descend. Ellen reported from New York that the storm had hit Long Island with winds of sixty knots and waves at Montauk Point that crested thirty-seven feet. It was expected that the centre of the storm would travel north-east on the coast, but it stalled for two days over Nassau County and during those two days Pat felt the atmosphere around her house go heavy. The barometer that hung at the bottom of her stairs registered the decline, and the silence grew. No word was heard from Nina. Silence like a baffling snow weighed on all three sisters. There was nothing but this weight where Nina had once been.

Myra acted like she wanted to be blamed. She began to act the Baby. Ellen, oldest, acted equally as juvenile and for the first time in her life wanted to enact a work of violence. When her telephone went dead beneath the storm she tore it out and hit it on the wall until it shattered. Pat, alone, stayed calm. The silence swallowed her. She passed the hours sitting still. When she slept she did it with the telephone nearby, she slept without undressing, ready.

She was sitting with a blanket wrapped around her on a chair beside a fire that had died when Nina called past midnight on the night the snow began to fall in Massachusetts and the call, fulfilling all the odds, arrived collect.

'Patricia – ?' Nina said.

'*Mother?* God, where *are* you – ?'

'Logal?'

'*What?*'

'A place called "Logal", I believe, dear.'

'*Logan*, Nina. *Logan*. Are you at Logan, Mother? Boston? Logan. *Are you at the Boston airport, Nina?*'

'. . . Pat – ?'

'. . . Mother – ?'

'Pat, I don't know *where* I am.'

'You're on the *phone*, keep talking, Nina. . . . '

'I'm so tired, dear.'

'Is there someone there with you that I can talk to, Nina?'

'Everyone has been so nice. I'm tired. Come and get me, dear.'

'I will, but –'

'At this Logal.'

'Airport –'

'*Everyone* has been so nice, Patricia.'

'Mother, look around. You're calling from a phone booth, right? What's the number? Is there anybody there?'

'There are *lots* of people here, Patricia. This is where they brought us. There's a snowstorm – '

'Yes, I – '

'Winston would have *died.* Do you know, I asked the stewardess. They don't heat that part where dogs are kept.'

'*Nina?* Can you read the number of the payphone to me, please – ?'

'I don't have my reading glasses with me, Pat.'

'Get them, Mother. I'll hang on.'

'I think I must have left them on the bus. Patricia? Don't leave the house, dear, without trying to get through to Ellen. You know how much I worry about her living in New York and now the operator tells me that her phone is out of order.'

'Mother, listen, yes, of course, I'll do that, I'll phone Ellen. But can you tell me where you are *exactly?*'

'Logal, dear.'

'Are you near an airline counter?'

'Yes, of course, Patricia. Airline counters are the things airports are famous for.'

'What airline counters are you near?'

'Eastern, Piedmont, Allegheny – '

'Is there someone there? Behind the counters?'

'There might be, Patricia.'

'*Can you see a person at an airline counter, Nina?*'

'Yes.'

'Good. *Who?*'

'A woman.'

'Good. *Go and tell that woman that I want to talk to her.*'

'Why, Patricia?'

'Go and tell her, Nina. Put the phone down, don't hang up and go and tell her.'

Several minutes later Nina picked the phone back up and said, 'She says she doesn't want to talk to you, Patricia.'

'Tell her it's an emergency.'

'She says she's the cleaning lady. Stranded, like the rest of us. I've been wearing the same clothes for *three days*, dear.'

'Nina, Jesus Christ, you should have *called* – '

'There aren't telephones on trains, Patricia.'

'You've been on a *train?*'

'There aren't telephones on buses, either. And they wouldn't stop to let poor Winston out to take his walk until Ed, my friend, God bless him, went right up and had a word in front of everybody with that driver.'

'*– Ed?*'

'God bless him.'

' "Ed"?'

'Yes.'

'Who's this "Ed"?'

'I told you. A very nice kind gentleman.'

'Did this "Ed" get taken to the airport, too?'

'Well, of course. We all did, dear. If it wasn't for "This Ed" as you call him, I don't know how I would have managed. I could barely manage Winston what with those two suitcases. I had to leave one suitcase empty when I took the train. Oh, it was frightful, dear. Poor Winston. I never would have managed. There we were in Colorado, just imagine. Me and Winston and two bags, so I emptied one. It was that blue one, dear, that big one that I packed my winter coat in, so I took the coat out and just carried it. Where was that, I have to think. Denver, it might have been – '

'*Nina?* Could you do me a favour? Could you stop and look around a minute and tell me if you see this "Ed" there in the airport?'

'Well, of course I see him, dear.'

'You see him – ?'

'Yes.'

'Could you get him to come over?'

' "Over", Pat?'

'Over to you, please?'

'Well, he's standing right in front of me, Patricia. If you'd ever let him have the chance, he'd like to have a word with you.'

Before he closed his eyes he had been telling her about his son, which had come as a surprise, because Nina figured Ed had never married.

She liked to think she could tell when men her age had spent their lives with women, same as she liked to think that she could notice right away if someone near her age had been an Army man. Army men know how to make their beds, she'd always told her daughters. Her husband Tom had been a Navy man and had seen a lot of action in the China Sea – aside from that he'd learned, like Army men, about neat corners, how to square a sheet. All these stories ran together, Nina thought. It seemed you couldn't be her age without one story trailing on another. '*I* was in the Army,' Ed had told her.

'I could tell,' she answered.

'I could speak a bit of Polish back in those days,' Ed had said. 'They sent me to a displaced persons camp in Germany. You know, to translate. Me, with my Midwestern Polish. Still, I always wanted to go back there, some day. See the town after the war. The way it was in peacetime.'

Blah blah blah, she might have thought. Sentimentality ran deep but narrow at their age. 'So why didn't you?' she asked.

'Oh, you know, the usual. I'll say this – the Army made a man of me.'

'Well, I've heard *that* before,' she said.

Ed said when things get said a lot they take on their own truth, even when they're false. Then he shocked her when he said, 'Like saying "I love you" or "I'm too young to die".'

For a long time Ed just sat there, silent, hardly moving but to nuzzle Winston, leaving Nina with the job of talking, which was why she thought he'd been a single gentleman, because it seemed he wasn't used to conversation. 'You feel all right, Ed?' she was more than once provoked to ask.

He apologized and said that he was very tired.

'Me too,' Nina said.

'How long have you been travelling?' she asked, following another silence.

'Couple days.'

'And where're you from?'

'St Louis. Everybody nowadays says, "Outside St Louis", though, I've noticed. As a city it died twenty, thirty years ago. The town's extinct. . . .'

'So you're on vacation?' Nina asked.

'Oh, at our age, sure. Life's a permanent vacation.'

'I'm on a visit to my daughter,' Nina said. 'Where're you going?'

'If I tell you, you'll die laughing.'

She looked at him expectantly.

'Is it somewhere funny?'

'You might say so, sure.'

'Plymouth Rock?' she guessed.

'Why do you say that?' Ed asked.

'Well, because Plymouth Rock is funny.'

'Plymouth Rock is?'

'Funny. Yes. Have you ever been there?'

'No.'

'Well,' Nina said, as if she'd proved a point. 'You should go someday. You'd see.'

'I've seen its picture. In "The Rock" commercials.'

'In "The Rock"?'

'You know. "Own a piece." Insurance.'

'That's Gibraltar.'

'That's Gibraltar – ?'

'Yes.'

'But Gibraltar isn't in America.'

'Well, no, but not too many people know that, Ed.'

'Well, that's not right. That's not right at all. They ought to use a native rock for that. One of our own. They ought to use the Plymouth Rock for that.'

'Well, that's what I was saying, see. They couldn't.'

'Why not?'

'Because it's small.'

'It's small?'

Ed was looking down at Winston so Nina said, 'Not that all small things are funny, Ed, but what they've done to Plymouth Rock is, they've built a cage around it. It's so people won't deface it, you know, with their names and dates. They've built this big cage 'round this tiny thing. Patricia – she's the one who's coming out to pick me up, the one you talked to on the phone – Patricia, she was always serious, full of questions that were hard to answer, you know how children are. Full of questions. I took Patricia there to Plymouth Rock when she was young and she had to stand up on her toes to look at it through the cage, this tiny thing inside a big enclosure, and she said, real loud, mind you, so everyone could hear, "Will it come out at feeding time, Mommy?"'

Nina laughed at her own reminiscence but Ed looked hard put to respond appropriately and Nina realized she had changed the subject to herself again, to her past, the way her daughters said she always did these days, and she felt embarrassed for herself. Ed was such a nice man. She should learn to talk to people better, take an interest in the things that they began to tell her. When he'd been quiet several minutes and she found the silence unsupportable, she offered him a mint, which he refused, so she took two for herself. Then she cleared her throat and said, 'Do you have any hobbies, Ed?' and that's when he began to talk about his son. He said he hadn't had a hobby since his son was just a boy. He didn't know, exactly, where his son was now. They used to make scale models of the dinosaurs together.

Nina focused all her interest on the story and said, 'Oh?', but Ed fell into another silence, so she asked him, 'When was that?'

'Oh, you know,' he said. 'Forty years ago, I guess. Maybe it was fifty.'

He asked her if she'd mind if he took a little nap even though he'd promised Pat he'd keep an eye on her, and Nina answered, 'No, go right ahead,' but when he'd been asleep about ten minutes he suddenly sat up and looked at her and said, 'What was that name of that most famous one, I can't remember.'

Nina thought she must have dozed off, too, because she couldn't understand what he was saying.

'"Famous"?' she asked.

'The famous one, the one the other dinosaurs were afraid of,' Ed explained.

Nina frowned and said, 'I'm not too smart in this department, Ed, my girls all ran a detour 'round that age when children are preoccupied with things like snakes and dinosaurs.'

'It was something with two names,' Ed told her.

'"Two names"? Well, there were those monsters, at the time,' Nina answered feebly, 'in the movies. Big ones. King Kong and the like. He had two names – '

'I know it wasn't *Bronto*sauras,' Ed continued, 'it was something else. Two names. Walked on its hind legs. It was the biggest one. . . .'

He looked at Nina and she saw that he looked very tired, so she touched him lightly on his hand. To her surprise the gesture sparked a darkened corner of her memory because she heard herself recite the word, 'Tyrannosaurus.'

Ed squeezed her hand.

'That's a girl!' she heard him saying. He was grinning ear to ear. 'What a girl!' he marvelled. '"Tyrannosaurus", yes, "Tyrannosaurus"!' he repeated, '"Tyrannosauras-*something*" . . . well, I'm happy now. I bet you thought we'd both forgotten. . . .'

She wanted to enquire what he meant by "two names", but he closed his eyes and looked like he was sleeping so she waited, then she started feeling sleepy, too, and then she just forgot the question. The next thing that she knew someone was pulling on her shoulder and she woke and saw Pat's face. It was dark outside. She could see the dark behind Pat's face, outside the big glass windows. She woke slowly, feeling very tired. Slowly she began to realize she had fallen against Ed, gone to sleep against his shoulder with her winter coat around the two of them. Hours must have passed. She saw that Pat looked worried.

'Was the driving that bad, dear?' Nina asked, but Pat answered with another question.

'Mother, is this Ed?' she asked.

She made an angry movement with her foot on Winston's back which Nina didn't like at all and then she gave him a sharp rap above the eyes so he'd keep still.

'*Patricia!*' Nina whispered. 'What's got into you – ?'

'Answer, Nina,' Pat said in a strange, tight way. 'Is this Ed?'

' – not so loud, you'll wake him, let the poor man sleep, Patricia. What's the matter with you, why are you being nasty with poor Winston – ?'

Pat touched Nina on her cheek and Nina blinked.

Cold was coming from somewhere. Cold was coming from beneath her coat. Pat was asking her another question. What's she asking *this* time? Nina wondered. It seemed she'd spent her whole life answering these questions. Why don't people on the South Pole fall from Earth? How many days till Christmas? Why do Pat and Ellen have blue eyes like Daddy and I don't? Why does Myra have her own room? Why is that person wearing that? Why are his hands so blue? Did he say where he was going, Nina? Mother? Did he tell you his last name?

The Women's Swimming Pool

translated by Denys Johnson-Davies

HANAN AL SHAYKH

Hanan Al Shaykh was born in Lebanon where she lived and worked as a writer and journalist on a leading Arab newspaper until civil war forced her to move to London with her family. She is the author of four novels and a collection of short stories. *The Story of Zahra* was published in 1986 by Quartet and Pavanne to critical acclaim. Her fourth novel, *The Deer Musk*, is currently being translated.

I am in the tent for threading the tobacco amidst the mounds of tobacco plants and the skewers. Cross-legged, I breathe in the green odour, threading one leaf after another. I find myself dreaming and growing thirsty and dreaming. I open the magazine; I devour the words and surreptitiously gaze at the pictures. Exasperated at being in the tent, my exasperation then turns to sadness.

Thirsty, I rise to my feet. I hear Abu Ghalib say, 'Where are you off to, little lady?' I make my way to my grandmother, saying, 'I'm thirsty.' I go out. I make my way to the cistern, stumbling in the sandy ground. I see the greenish-blue waters. I stretch out my hand to its still surface, hot from the harsh sun. I stretch out my hand and wipe it across my brow and face and neck, across my chest. Before being able to savour its relative coldness, I hear my name and see my grandmother standing in her black dress at the doorway of the tent.

Aloud I express the wish that someone else had called to me. We have become like an orange and its navel: my grandmother has welded me so close to her that the village girls no longer dare to make friends with me, perhaps for fear of rupturing this close union.

I return to the tent, growing thirsty and dreaming, with the sea ever in my mind. What were its waters like? What colour would they be now? If only this week would pass in a flash for I had at last persuaded my grandmother to go down to Beirut and the sea, after my friend Sumayya had sworn that the swimming pool she'd been to had been for women only.

My grandmother sat on the edge of a jagged slab of stone, leaning on my arm. Her hand was hot and rough. She sighed as she chased away a fly.

What is my grandmother gazing at? There was nothing in front of us but the asphalt road which, despite the sun's rays, gave off no light, and the white marble tombs that stretched along the high mountainside, while the houses of Upper Nabatieh looked like deserted Crusader castles, their alleyways empty, their windows of iron. Our house likewise seemed to be groaning in its solitude, shaded by the fig tree. The washing line stirs with the wind above the tomb of my grandfather, the celebrated religious scholar, in the courtyard of the house. What is my grandmother staring at? Or does someone who is waiting not stare?

Turning her face towards me, she said, 'Child, what will we do if the bus doesn't come?' Her face, engraved in my mind, seemed overcast, also her half-closed eyes and the blue tattoo mark on her chin. I didn't answer her for fear I'd cry if I talked. This time I averted my gaze from the white tombs; moving my foot away from my grandmother's leg clothed in thick black stockings, I began to walk about, my gaze directed to the other side where lay the extensive fields of green tobacco, their leaves glinting under the sun, leaves that were imprinted on my brain, and with the marks of them still showing on my hands, towering and gently swaying.

My gaze reached out behind the thousands of plants, then beyond them, moving away till it arrived at the tent where the tobacco was threaded. I came up close to my grandmother, who was still sitting in her place, still gazing in front of her. As I drew close to her, I heard her give a sigh. A sprinkling of sweat lay on the pouches under her eyes. 'Child, what do you want with the sea? Don't you know that the sea puts a spell on people?' I didn't answer her: I was so worried that the morning would pass, that noonday would pass and that I wouldn't see the green bus come to a stop by the stone my grandmother sat on and take us with it to the sea, to Beirut. Again I heard my grandmother mumbling, 'That devil Sumayya. . . . ' I pleaded with her to stop, and my thoughts rose up and left the stone upon which my grandmother sat, the rough road, left everything. I went back to my dreams, to the sea.

The sea had remained my preoccupation ever since I had seen it for the first time inside a coloured ball; with its blue colour it was like a magic lantern, wide open, the surface of its water unrippled unless you tilted the piece of glass, with its small shells and white specks like snow. When I first became aware of things, it was this ball, which I had found in the parlour, that was the sole thing that animated and amused me. The more I gazed at it the more cold I could feel its waters, the more they invited me to bathe myself in them; they knew that I had been born amidst dust and mud and the stench of tobacco.

If only the green bus would come along – and I shifted my bag from one hand to the other. I heard my grandmother wail, 'Child, bring up a stone and sit down. Put down the bag and don't worry.' My distress increased and I was no longer able to stop it turning into tears that flowed freely down my face, veiling it from the road. I stretched up to wipe them with my sleeve: in this heat I still had to wear that dress with long sleeves, that head-covering over my plaits, despite the hot wind that set the tobacco plants and the sparse poplars swaying. Thank God I had resisted her and refused to wear my stockings. I gave a deep sigh as I heard the bus's horn from afar. Fearful and anxious, I shouted at my grandmother as I helped her to her feet, turning round to make sure that my bag was still in my hand and my grandmother's hand in the other. The bus came to a stop and the conductor helped my grandmother on. When I saw myself alongside her and the stone on its own, I tightened my grip on my bag in which lay Sumayya's bathing costume, a sleeveless dress and my money.

I noticed as the bus slowly made its way along the road that my anxiety was still there, that it was in fact increasing. Why didn't the bus pass by all these trees and fallow land like lightning? Why was it crawling along? My anxiety was still there and increased till it predominated over my other sensations such as nausea and curiosity.

How would we find our way to the sea? Would we see it as soon as we arrived in Beirut? Was it at the other end of it? Would the bus stop in the district of Zeytouna, at the door of the women's swimming pool? Why, I wondered, was it called Zeytouna*? Were there olive trees there? I leaned towards my grandmother with her silent face and long nose that almost met up with her mouth. Thinking that I wanted a piece of cane sugar, she put her hand to her bosom to take out a small twist of cloth. Impatiently I asked her if she was sure that Maryam Al Taweela knew Zeytouna, to which she answered, her mouth sucking at the cane sugar and making a noise with her tongue,

'God will look after everything.' Then she broke the silence by saying, 'All this trouble is that devil Sumayya's fault – it was she who told you she'd seen with her own eyes the swimming pool just for women and not for men.' 'Yes, Grandma,' I answered her. She said, 'Swear by your mother's grave.' I thought to myself absent-mindedly, Why only my mother's grave? What about my father? Or did she only acknowledge her daughter's death. . . .? 'By my mother's grave, it's for women.' She inclined her head and still munching the cane sugar and making a noise with her tongue, she said, 'If any man were to see you, you'd be done for, and so would your mother and father and your grandfather, the religious scholar – and I'd be done for more than anyone because it's I who agreed to you and helped you.'

I would have liked to say to her, They've all gone, they've all died, so what do we have to be afraid of? But I knew what she meant: that she was frightened they wouldn't go to heaven.

I began to sweat and my heart again contracted as Beirut came into view with its lofty buildings, car horns, the bared arms of the women, the girls' hair, the tight trousers they were wearing. People were sitting on chairs in the middle of the pavement eating and drinking; the trams; the roasting chickens revolving on spits. Ah, these dresses for sale in the windows, would anyone be found

*The word means 'olive tree' in Arabic.

actually to wear them? I see a Japanese man, the first ever member of the yellow races outside of books; the Martyrs' monument, Riad Solh Square. I was wringing wet with sweat and my heart pounded – it was as though I regretted having come to Beirut, perhaps because I was accompanied by my grandmother. It was soon all too evident that we were outsiders to the capital. We began walking after my grandmother had asked the bus driver the whereabouts of the district of Khandak al-Ghamik where Maryam al-Taweela lived. Once again my body absorbed all the sweat and allowed my heart to flee its cage. I find myself treading on a pavement on which for long years I have dreamed of walking; I hear sounds that have been engraved on my imagination, and everything I see I have seen in daydreams at school or in the tobacco threading tent. Perhaps I shouldn't say that I was regretting it, for after this I would never forget Beirut. We begin walking and losing our way in a Beirut that never ends, leads nowhere. We begin asking and walking and losing our way, and my going to the sea seems an impossibility; the sea is fleeing from me. My grandmother comes to a stop and leans against a lamp-post, or against the litter bin attached to it, and against my shoulders, and puffs and blows. I have the feeling that we shall never find Maryam al-Taweela's house. A man we had stopped to ask the way walks with us. When we knock at the door and no one opens to us, I become convinced that my bathing in the sea is no longer possible. The sweat again pours off me, my throat contracts. A woman's voice brings me back to my senses as I drown in a lake of anxiety, sadness and fear; then it drowns me once again. It was not Maryam al-Taweela but her neighbour who is asking us to wait at her place. We go down the steps to the neighbour's outdoor stone bench, and my grandmother sits down by the door but gets to her feet again when the woman entreats her to sit in the cane chair. Then she asks to be excused while she finishes washing down the steps. While she is cursing the heat of Beirut in the summer, I notice the tin containers lined up side by side containing red and green peppers. We have a long wait, and I begin to weep inwardly as I stare at the containers.

I wouldn't be seeing the sea today, perhaps not for years, but the thought of its waters would not leave me, would not be erased from my dreams. I must persuade my grandmother to come to Beirut with Sumayya. Perhaps I should not have mentioned the swimming pool in front of her. I wouldn't be seeing the sea today – and once again I sank back into a lake of doubt and fear and sadness. A woman's voice again brought me back to my senses: it was Maryam al-Taweela, who had stretched out her long neck and had kissed me, while she asked my grandmother, 'She's the child of your late daughter, isn't she?' – and she swore by the Imam* that we must have lunch with her, doing so before we had protested, feeling perhaps that I would do so. When she stood up and took the primus stove from under her bed and brought out potatoes and tomatoes and bits of meat, I had a feeling of nausea, then of frustration. I nudged my grandmother, who leant over and whispered, 'What is it, dear?' at which Maryam al-Taweela turned and asked, 'What's your granddaughter want – to go to the bathroom?' My mouth went quite dry and my tears were all stored up waiting for a signal from my heartbeats to descend. My grandmother said with embarrassment, 'She wants to go to the sea, to the women's swimming pool – that devil Sumayya put it into her head.' To my amazement Maryam al-Taweela said loudly, 'And why not? Right now Ali Mousa, our neighbour, will be coming and he'll take you, he's got a car' – and Maryam al-Taweela began peeling the potatoes at a low table in the middle of the room and my grandmother asked, 'Where's Ali Mousa from? Where does he live?'

I can't wait, I shan't eat, I shan't drink. I want to go now, now. I remained seated, crying inwardly because I was born in the South, because there's no escape for me from the South, and I go on rubbing my fingers and gnawing at my nails. Again I begin to sweat: I shan't eat, I shan't drink, I shan't reply to Maryam Al-Taweela. It was as though I were taking vengeance on my grandmother for some wrong she did not know about. My patience vanished. I stood up and said to my grandmother before I should burst out sobbing, 'Come along, Grandma, get up and let's go.' I helped her to her feet and Maryam Al-Taweela asked in bewilderment what had suddenly come over me. I went on dragging my grandmother out to the street so that I might stop the first taxi.

Only moments passed before the driver shut off his engine and

* This refers to Ali ibu Abi Talib, cousin and son-in-law of the Prophet, and is an indication that the characters in the story are Shi'ite Muslims.

said, 'Zeytouna'. I looked about me but saw no sea. As I gave him a lira I asked him, 'Where's the women's swimming pool?' He shrugged his shoulders. We got out of the car with difficulty, as was always the case with my grandmother. To my astonishment the driver returned, stretching out his head in concern at us. 'Jump in,' he said, and we got in. He took us round and round, stopping once at a petrol station and then by a newspaper seller, asking about the women's swimming pool and nobody knowing where it was. Once again he dropped us in the middle of Zeytouna Street.

Then, behind the hotels and the beautiful buildings and the date palms, I saw the sea. It was like a blue line of quicksilver: it was as though pieces of silver paper were resting on it. The sea that was in front of me was more beautiful than it had been in the glass ball. I didn't know how to get close to it, how to touch it. Cement lay between us. We began enquiring about the whereabouts of the swimming pool, but no one knew. The sea remains without waves, a blue line. I feel frustrated. Perhaps this swimming pool is some secret known only to the girls of the South. I began asking every person I saw. I tried to choke back my tears; I let go of my grandmother's hand as though wishing to reproach her, to punish her for having insisted on accompanying me instead of Sumayya. Poor me. Poor Grandma. Poor Beirut. Had my dreams come to an end in the middle of the street? I clasp my bag and my grandmother's hand, with the sea in front of me, separating her from me. My stubbornness and vexation impel me to ask and go on asking. I approached a man leaning against a bus and to my surprise he pointed to an opening between two shops. I hurried back to my grandmother, who was supporting herself against a lamp-post, to tell her I'd found it. When I saw with what difficulty she attempted to walk, I asked her to wait for me while I made sure. I went through the opening but didn't see the sea. All I saw was a fat woman with bare shoulders sitting behind a table. Hesitating, I stood and looked at her, not daring to step forward. My enthusiasm had vanished, taking with it my courage. 'Yes,' said the woman. I came forward and asked her, 'Is the women's swimming pool here?' She nodded her head and said, 'The entrance fee is a lira.' I asked her if it was possible for my grandmother to wait for me here and she stared at me and said, 'Of course.' There was contempt in the way she looked at me – was it my southern accent or my long-sleeved dress? I had disregarded my grandmother and had taken off my headshawl and hidden it in my bag. I handed her a lira and could hear the sounds of women and children – and still I did not see the sea. At the end of the portico were steps which I was certain led to the roofed-in sea. The important thing was that I'd arrived, that I would be tasting the salty spray of its waters. I wouldn't be seeing the waves; never mind, I'd be bathing in its waters.

I found myself saying to the woman, or rather to myself because no sound issued from my throat, 'I'll bring my grandmother.' Going out through the opening and still clasping my bag to my chest, I saw my grandmother standing and looking up at the sky. I called to her but she was reciting to herself under her breath as she continued to look upwards: she was praying, right there in the street, praying on the pavement at the door of the swimming pool. She had spread out a paper bag and had stretched out her hands to the sky. I walked off in another direction and stopped looking at her. I would have liked to persuade myself that she had nothing to do with me, that I didn't know her. How, though? She's my grandmother whom I've dragged with my entreaties from the tobacco threading tent, from the jagged slab of stone, from the winds of the South; I have crammed her into the bus and been lost with her in the streets as we searched for Maryam al-Taweela's house. And now here were the two of us standing at the door of the swimming pool and she, having heard the call to prayers, had prostrated herself in prayer. She was destroying what lay in my bag, blocking the road between me and the sea. I felt sorry for her, for her knees that knelt on the cruelly hard pavement, for her tattooed hands that lay on the dirt. I looked at her again and saw the passers-by staring at her. For the first time her black dress looked shabby to me. I felt how far removed we were from these passers-by, from this street, this city, this sea. I approached her and she again put her weight on my hand.

The Reservoir

JANET FRAME

Janet Frame is New Zealand's most distinguished living novelist. Her first book, *The Lagoon and Other Stories*, was published in 1951 and won the Hubert Church Award. Her first novel, *Owls Do Cry*, won her international acclaim and has not been out of print since it was first published. She has written a further seven novels and a three-part autobiography.

It was said to be four or five miles along the gully, past orchards and farms, paddocks filled with cattle, sheep, wheat, gorse, and the squatters of the land who were the rabbits eating like modern sculpture into the hills, though how could we know anything of modern sculpture, we knew nothing but the Warrior in the main street with his wreaths of poppies on Anzac Day, the gnomes weeping in the Gardens because the seagulls perched on their green caps and showed no respect, and how important it was for birds, animals and people, especially children, to show respect!

And that is why for so long we obeyed the command of the grown-ups and never walked as far as the forbidden Reservoir, but were content to return 'tired but happy' (as we wrote in our school compositions), answering the question, Where did you walk today? with a suspicion of blackmail, 'Oh, nearly, nearly to the Reservoir!'

The Reservoir was the end of the world; beyond it, you fell; beyond it were paddocks of thorns, strange cattle, strange farms, legendary people whom we would never know or recognize even if they walked among us on a Friday night downtown when we went to follow the boys and listen to the Salvation Army Band and buy a milk shake in the milk bar and then return home to find that everything was all right and safe, that our mother had not run away and caught the night train to the North Island, that our father had not shot himself with worrying over the bills, but had in fact been downtown himself and had bought the usual Friday night treat, a bag of licorice allsorts and a bag of chocolate roughs, from Woolworth's.

The Reservoir haunted our lives. We never knew one until we came to this town; we had used pump water. But here, in our new house, the water ran from the taps as soon as we turned them on, and if we were careless and left them on, our father would shout, as if the affair were his personal concern, 'Do you want the Reservoir to run dry?'

That frightened us. What should we do if the Reservoir ran dry? Would we die of thirst like Burke and Wills in the desert?

'The Reservoir,' our mother said, 'gives pure water, water safe to drink without boiling it.'

The water was in a different class, then, from the creek which flowed through the gully; yet the creek had its source in the Reservoir. Why had it not received the pampering attention of officialdom which strained weed and earth, cockabullies and trout and eels, from our tap water? Surely the Reservoir was not entirely pure?

'Oh no,' they said, when we enquired. We learned that the water from the Reservoir had been 'treated'. We supposed this to mean that during the night men in light-blue uniforms with sacks over their shoulders crept beyond the circle of pine trees which enclosed the Reservoir, and emptied the contents of the sacks into the water, to dissolve dead bodies and prevent the decay of teeth.

Then, at times, there would be news in the paper, discussed by my mother with the neighbours over the back fence. Children had been drowned in the Reservoir.

'No child,' the neighbour would say, 'ought to be allowed near the Reservoir.'

'I tell mine to keep strictly away,' my mother would reply.

And for so long we obeyed our mother's command, on our favourite walks along the gully simply following the untreated cast-off creek which we loved and which flowed day and night in our heads in all its detail – the wild sweet peas, boiled-lolly pink, and the mint growing along the banks; the exact spot in the water where the latest dead sheep could be found, and the stink of its bloated flesh and floating wool, an allowable earthy stink which we accepted with pleasant revulsion and which did not prompt the 'inky-pinky I smell Stinkie' rhyme which referred to offensive human beings only. We knew where the water was shallow and could be paddled in, where forts could be made from the rocks; we knew the frightening deep places where the eels lurked and the weeds were tangled in gruesome shapes; we knew the jumping places, the mossy stones with their dangers, limitations, and advantages; the sparkling places where the sun trickled beside the water, upon the stones; the bogs made by roaming cattle, trapping some of them to death; their gaunt telltale bones; the little valleys with their new growth of lush grass where the creek had 'changed its course', and no longer flowed.

'The creek has changed its course,' our mother would say, in a tone which implied terror and a sense of strangeness, as if a tragedy had been enacted.

We knew the moods of the creek, its levels of low-flow, half-high-flow, high-flow which all seemed to relate to interference at its source – the Reservoir. If one morning the water turned the colour of clay and crowds of bubbles were passengers on every suddenly swift wave hurrying by, we would look at one another and remark with the fatality and reverence which attends a visitation or prophecy.

'The creek's going on high-flow. They must be doing something at the Reservoir.'

By afternoon the creek would be on high-flow, turbulent, muddy, unable to be jumped across or paddled in or fished in, concealing beneath a swelling fluid darkness whatever evil which 'they', the authorities, had decided to purge so swiftly and secretly from the Reservoir.

For so long, then, we obeyed our parents, and never walked as far as the Reservoir. Other things concerned us, other curiosities, fears, challenges. The school year ended. I got a prize, a large yellow book the colour of cat's mess. Inside it were editions of newspapers, *The Worms' Weekly*, supposedly written by worms, snails, spiders. For the first part of the holidays we spent the time sitting in the long grass of our front lawn nibbling the stalks of shamrock and reading insect newspapers and relating their items to the lives of those living on our front lawn down among the summer-dry roots of the couch, tinkertailor, daisy, dandelion, shamrock, clover, and ordinary 'grass'. High summer came. The blowsy old red roses shed their petals to the regretful refrain uttered by our mother year after year at the same time, 'I should have made potpourri, I have a wonderful recipe for potpourri in Dr Chase's Book.'

Our mother never made the potpourri. She merely quarrelled with our father over how to pronounce it.

The days became unbearably long and hot. Our Christmas presents were broken or too boring to care about. Celluloid dolls had loose arms and legs and rifts in their bright pink bodies; the invisible ink had poured itself out in secret messages; diaries frustrating in their smallness (two lines to a day) had been filled in for the whole of the coming year. . . . Days at the beach were tedious, with no room in the bathing sheds so that we were forced to undress in the common room downstairs with its floor patched with wet and trailed with footmarks and sand and its tiny barred window (which made me believe that I was living in the French Revolution).

Rumours circled the burning world. The sea was drying up, soon you could paddle or walk to Australia. Sharks had been seen swimming inside the breakwater; one shark attacked a little boy and bit off his you-know-what.

We swam. We wore bathing togs all day. We gave up cowboys and ranches; and baseball and sledding; and 'those games' where we mimicked grown-up life, loving and divorcing each other, kissing and slapping, taking secret paramours when our husband was working out of town. Everything exhausted us. Cracks appeared in the earth; the grass was bled yellow; the ground was littered with beetle shells and snail shells; flies came in from the unofficial rubbish-dump at the back of the house; the twisting flypapers hung from the ceiling; a frantic buzzing filled the room as the flypapers became crowded. Even the cat put out her tiny tongue, panting in the heat.

We realized, and were glad, that school would soon reopen. What was school like? It seemed so long ago, it seemed as if we had never been to school, surely we had forgotten everything we had learned, how frightening, thrilling and strange it would all seem! Where would we go on the first day, who would teach us, what were the names of the new books?

Who would sit beside us, who would be our best friend?

The earth crackled in early-autumn haze and still the February sun dried the world; even at night the rusty sheet of roofing-iron outside by the cellar stayed warm, but with rows of sweat-marks on it; the days were still long, with night face to face with morning and almost nothing in-between but a snatch of turning sleep with the blankets on the floor and the windows wide open to moths with their bulging lamplit eyes moving through the dark and their grandfather bodies knocking, knocking upon the walls.

Day after day the sun still waited to pounce. We were tired, our skin itched, our sunburn had peeled and peeled again, the skin on our feet was hard, there was dust in our hair, our bodies clung with the salt of sea-bathing and sweat, the towels were harsh with salt.

School soon, we said again, and were glad; for lessons gave shade to rooms and corridors; cloakrooms were cold and sunless. Then, swiftly, suddenly, disease came to the town. Infantile paralysis. Black headlines in the paper, listing the number of cases, the number of deaths. Children everywhere, out in the country, up north, down south, two streets away.

The schools did not reopen. Our lessons came by post, in smudged print on rough white paper; they seemed makeshift and false, they inspired distrust, they could not compete with the lure of the sun still shining, swelling, the world would go up in cinders, the days were too long, there was nothing to do, there was nothing to do; the lessons were dull; in the front room with the navy-blue blind half down the window and the tiny splits of light showing through, and the lesson papers sometimes covered with unexplained blots of ink as if the machine which had printed them had broken down or rebelled, the lessons were even more dull.

Ancient Egypt and the flooding of the Nile!

The Nile, when we possessed a creek of our own with individual flooding!

'Well let's go along the gully, along by the creek,' we would say, tired with all these.

Then one day when our restlessness was at its height, when the flies buzzed like bees in the flypapers, and the warped wood of the house cracked its knuckles out of boredom, the need for something to do in the heat, we found once again the only solution to our unrest.

Someone said, 'What's the creek on?'

'Half-high flow.'

'Good.'

So we set out, in our bathing suits, and carrying switches of willow.

'Keep your sun hats on!' our mother called.

All right. We knew. Sunstroke when the sun clipped you over the back of the head, striking you flat on the ground. Sunstroke. Lightning. Even tidal waves were threatening us on this southern coast. The world was full of alarm.

'And don't go as far as the Reservoir!'

We dismissed the warning. There was enough to occupy us along the gully without our visiting the Reservoir. First, the couples. We liked to find a courting couple and follow them and when, as we knew they must do because they were tired or for other reasons, they found a place in the grass and lay down together, we liked to make jokes about them, amongst ourselves. 'Just wait for him to kiss her,' we would say. 'Watch. There. A beaut. Smack.'

Often we giggled and lingered even after the couple had observed us. We were waiting for them to do it. Every man and woman did it, we knew that for a fact. We speculated about technical details. Would he wear a frenchie? If he didn't wear a frenchie then she would start having a baby and be forced to get rid of it by drinking gin. Frenchies, by the way, were for sale in Woolworth's. Some said they were fingerstalls, but we knew they were frenchies and sometimes we would go downtown and into Woolworth's just to look at the frenchies for sale. We hung around the counter, sniggering. Sometimes we nearly died laughing, it was so funny.

After we tired of spying on the couples we would shout after them as we went our way.

> Pound, shillings and pence,
> a man fell over the fence,
> he fell on a lady,
> and squashed out a baby,
> pounds, shillings and pence!

Sometimes a slight fear struck us – what if a man fell on us like that and squashed out a chain of babies?

Our other pastime along the gully was robbing the orchards, but this summer day the apples were small green hard and hidden by leaves. There were no couples either. We had the gully to ourselves. We followed the creek, whacking our sticks, gossiping and singing, but we stopped, immediately silent, when someone – sister or brother – said, 'Let's go to the Reservoir!'

A feeling of dread seized us. We knew, as surely as we knew our names and our address Thirty-three Stour Street Ohau Otago Island New Zealand Southern Hemisphere The World, that we would some day visit the Reservoir, but the time seemed almost as far away as leaving school, getting a job, marrying.

And then there was the agony of deciding the right time – how did one decide these things?

'We've been told not to, you know,' one of us said timidly.

That was me. Eating bread and syrup for tea had made my hair red, my skin too, so that I blushed easily, and the grown-ups guessed if I told a lie.

'It's a long way,' said my little sister.

'Coward!'

But it *was* a long way, and perhaps it would take all day and night, perhaps we would have to sleep there among the pine trees with the owls hooting and the old needle-filled warrens which now reached to the centre of the earth where pools of molten lead bubbled, waiting to seize us if we tripped, and then there was the crying sound made by the trees, a sound of speech at its loneliest level where the meaning is felt but never explained, and it goes on and on in a kind of despair, trying to reach a point of understanding.

We knew that pine trees spoke in this way. We were lonely listening to them because we knew we could never help them to say it, whatever they were trying to say, for if the wind who was so close to them could not help them, how could we?

Oh no, we could not spend the night at the Reservoir among the pine trees.

'Billy Whittaker and his gang have been to the Reservoir, Billy Whittaker and the Green Feather gang, one afternoon.'

'Did he say what it was like?'

'No, he never said.'

'He's been in an iron lung.'

That was true. Only a day or two ago our mother had been reminding us in an ominous voice of the fact which roused our envy just as much as our dread, 'Billy Whittaker was in an iron lung two years ago. Infantile paralysis.'

Some people were lucky. None of us dared to hope that we would ever be surrounded by the glamour of an iron lung; we would have to be content all our lives with paltry flesh lungs.

'Well are we going to the Reservoir or not?'

That was someone trying to sound bossy like our father, – 'Well am I to have salmon sandwiches or not, am I to have lunch at all today or not?'

We struck our sticks in the air. They made a whistling sound. They were supple and young. We had tried to make musical instruments out of them, time after time we hacked at the willow and the elder to make pipes to blow our music, but no sound came but our own voices. And why did two sticks rubbed together not make fire? Why couldn't we ever *make* anything out of the bits of the world lying about us?

An airplane passed in the sky. We craned our necks to read the writing on the underwing, for we collected airplane numbers.

The plane was gone, in a glint of sun.

'Are we?' someone said.

'If there's an eclipse you can't see at all. The birds stop singing and go to bed.'

'Well are we?'

Certainly we were. We had not quelled all our misgiving, but we set out to follow the creek to the Reservoir.

What is it? I wondered. They said it was a lake. I thought it was a bundle of darkness and great wheels which peeled and sliced you like an apple and drew you towards them with demonic force, in the same way that you were drawn beneath the wheels of a train if you stood too near the edge of the platform. That was the terrible danger when the Limited came rushing in and you had to approach to kiss arriving aunts.

We walked on and on, past wild sweet peas, clumps of cutty grass, horse mushrooms, ragwort, gorse, cabbage trees; and then, at the end of the gully, we came to strange territory, fences we did not know, with the barbed wire tearing at our skin and at our skirts put on over our bathing suits because we felt cold though the sun stayed in the sky.

We passed huge trees that lived with their heads in the sky, with their great arms and joints creaking with age and the burden of being trees, and their mazed and linked roots rubbed bare of earth, like bones with the flesh cleaned from them. There were strange gates to be opened or climbed over, new directions to be argued and plotted, notices which said TRESPASSERS WILL BE PROSECUTED BY ORDER. And there was the remote immovable sun shedding without gentleness its influence of burning upon us and upon the town, looking down from its heavens and considering our infantile-paralysis epidemic, and the children tired of holidays and wanting to go back to school with the new stiff books with their crackling pages, the scrubbed ruler with the sun rising on one side amidst the twelfths, tenths, millimetres, the new pencils to be sharpened with the pencil shavings flying in long pickets and light-brown curls scalloped with red or blue; the brown school, the bare floors, the clump clump in the corridors on wet days!

We came to a strange paddock, a bull-paddock with its occupant planted deep in the long grass, near the gate, a jersey bull polished like a wardrobe, burnished like copper, heavy beams creaking in the wave and flow of the grass.

'Has it got a ring through its nose? Is it a real bull or a steer?'

Its nose was ringed, which meant that its savagery was tamed, or so we thought; it could be tethered and led; even so, it had once been savage and kept its pride, unlike the steers who pranced and huddled together and ran like water through the paddocks, made no impression, quarried no massive shape against the sky.

The bull stood alone.

Had not Mr Bennet been gored by a bull, his own tame bull, and been rushed to Glenham Hospital for thirty-three stitches? Remembering Mr Bennet we crept cautiously close to the paddock fence, ready to escape.

Someone said, 'Look, it's pawing the ground!'

A bull which pawed the ground was preparing for a charge. We escaped quickly through the fence. Then, plucking courage, we skirted the bushes on the far side of the paddock, climbed through the fence, and continued our walk to the Reservoir.

We had lost the creek between deep banks. We saw it now before us, and hailed it with more relief than we felt, for in its hidden course through the bull-paddock it had undergone change, it had adopted the shape, depth, mood of foreign water, foaming in a way we did not recognize as belonging to our special creek, giving no hint of its depth. It seemed to flow close to its concealed bed, not wishing any more to communicate with us. We realized with dismay that we had suddenly lost possession of our creek. Who had taken it? Why did it not belong to us any more? We hit out sticks in the air and forgot our dismay. We grew cheerful.

Till someone said that it was getting late, and we reminded one another that during the day the sun doesn't seem to move, it just remains pinned with a drawing pin against the sky, and then, while you are not looking, it suddenly slides down quick as the chopped-off head of a golden eel, into the sea, making everything in the world go dark.

'That's only in the tropics!'

We were not in the tropics. The divisions of the world in the atlas, the different coloured cubicles of latitude and longitude, fascinated us.

'The sand freezes in the desert at night. Ladies wear bits of sand. . . .'

'grains . . .'

'grains or bits of sand as necklaces, and the camels . . .'

'with necks like snails . . .'

'with horns, do they have horns?'

'Minnie Stocks goes with boys. . . .'

'I know who your boy is, I know who your boy is. . . .'

> Waiting by the garden gate,
> Waiting by the garden gate . . .

'We'll never get to the Reservoir!'

'Whose idea was it?'

'I've strained my ankle!'

Someone began to cry. We stopped walking.

'I've strained my ankle!'

There was an argument.

'It's not strained, it's sprained.'

'strained.'

'sprained.'

'All right sprained then. I'll have to wear a bandage, I'll have to walk on crutches. . . .'

'I had crutches once. Look. I've got a scar where I fell off my stilts. It's a white scar, like a centipede. It's on my shins.'

'Shins! Isn't it a funny word? Shins. Have you ever been kicked in the shins?'

'shins, funnybone . . .'

'It's humerus. . . .'

'knuckles . . .'

'a sprained ankle . . .'

'a strained ankle . . .'

'a whitlow, an ingrown toenail the roots of my hair warts spinal meningitis infantile paralysis . . .'

'Infantile paralysis, infantile paralysis you have to be wheeled in a chair and wear irons on your legs and your knees knock together. . . .'

'Once you're in an iron lung you can't get out, they lock it, like a cage. . . .'

'You go in the amberlance . . .'

'*ambulance* . . .'

'amberlance . . .'

'Ambulance to the hostible . . .'

'the *hospital*, an *amberlance to the hospital* . . .'

'Infantile paralysis . . .'

'Friar's Balsam! Friar's Balsam!'

'Baxter's Lung Preserver, Baxter's Lung Preserver!'

'Syrup of Figs, California Syrup of Figs!'

'The creek's going on high-flow!'

Yes, there were bubbles on the surface, and the water was turning muddy. Our doubts were dispelled. It was the same old creek, and there, suddenly, just ahead, was a plantation of pine trees, and already the sighing sound of it reached our ears and troubled us. We approached it, staying close to the banks of our newly claimed creek, until once again the creek deserted us, flowing its own private course where we could not follow, and we found ourselves among the pine trees, a narrow strip of them, and beyond lay a vast surface of sparkling water, dazzling our eyes, its centre chopped by tiny grey waves. Not a lake, nor a river, nor a sea.

'The Reservoir!'

The damp smell of the pine needles caught in our breath. There were no birds, only the constant sighing of the trees. We could see the water clearly now; it lay, except for the waves beyond the shore, in an almost perfect calm which we knew to be deceptive – else why were people so afraid of the Reservoir? The fringe of young pines on the edge, like toy trees, subjected to the wind, sighed and told us their sad secrets. In the Reservoir there was an appearance of neatness which concealed a disarray too frightening to be acknowledged except, without any defence, in moments of deep sleep and dreaming. The little sparkling innocent waves shone now green, now grey, petticoats, lettuce leaves; the trees sighed, and told us to be quiet, hush-sh, as if something were sleeping and should not be disturbed – perhaps that was what the trees were always telling us, to hush-sh in case we disturbed something which must never ever be awakened?

What was it? Was it sleeping in the Reservoir? Was that why people were afraid of the Reservoir?

Well we were not afraid of it, oh no, it was only the Reservoir, it was nothing to be afraid of, it was just a flat Reservoir with a fence around it, and trees, and on the far side a little house (with wheels inside?), and nothing to be afraid of.

'The Reservoir, The Reservoir!'

A noticeboard said DANGER, RESERVOIR.

Overcome with sudden glee we climbed through the fence and swung on the lower branches of the trees, shouting at intervals, gazing possessively and delightedly at the sheet of water with its wonderful calm and menace,

'The Reservoir! The Reservoir! The Reservoir!'

We quarrelled again about how to pronounce and spell the word.

Then it seemed to be getting dark – or was it that the trees were stealing the sunlight and keeping it above their heads? One of us began to run. We all ran, suddenly, wildly, not caring about our strained or sprained ankles, through the trees out into the sun where the creek, but it was our creek no longer, waited for us. We wished it were our creek, how we wished it were our creek! We had lost all account of time. Was it nearly night? Would darkness overtake us, would we have to sleep on the banks of the creek that did not belong to us any more, among the wild sweet peas and the tussocks and the dead sheep? And would the eels come up out of the creek, as people said they did, and on their travels through the paddocks would they change into people who would threaten us and bar our way, TRESPASSERS WILL BE PROSECUTED, standing arm in arm in their black glossy coats, swaying, their mouths open, ready to swallow us? Would they ever let us go home, past the orchards, along the gully? Perhaps they would give us Infantile Paralysis, perhaps we would never be able to walk home, and no one would know where we were, to bring us an iron lung with its own special key!

We arrived home, panting and scratched. How strange! The sun was still in the same place in the sky!

The question troubled us, 'Should we tell?'

The answer was decided for us. Our mother greeted us as we went in the door with, 'You haven't been long away, kiddies. Where have you been? I hope you didn't go anywhere near the Reservoir.'

Our father looked up from reading his newspapers.

'Don't let me catch you going near the Reservoir!'

We said nothing. How out-of-date they were! They were actually afraid!

Good Friday, 1663

HELEN SIMPSON

Helen Simpson read English at Oxford. She won a talent contest which rewarded her with a job on *Vogue* magazine, where she worked for the following five years as a writer. She recently went freelance and has just finished a recipe book on Breakfast, a companion to her slim volume on Afternoon Tea. Her short stories have appeared in various magazines. She lives in London.

> We have a winding sheet in our mother's womb, which grows with us from our conception, and we come into the world, wound up in that winding sheet, for we come to seek a grave.

My rustic husband, preferring to be fifty years behind the times in church matters as in all else, has ordered Parson Snakepeace to preach only sermons from the old dead Divines, and to read them aloud without comment. This being Good Friday, he has chosen the horridest sermon he could find, all to do with death and earthworms.

Lord, I'm sure I am grown quite melancholy at that old barbarous tale of the thorn crown and the sponge in vinegar. Ha, ha, ha!

This church is as cold as the grave. You would not know the air was so gentle outside, all the daffodils kissing the air and the apple trees like brides.

Here, by my pew, lies my husband's mother, Myrtilla Fanshawe, twenty-six years old, d. 1634, boxed up in fine Carrara:

> God's goodness made her wise and well-beseeming
> Her wifely virtues won her much esteeming,
> Earth would not yield more pleasing earthly bliss
> Blest w'two babes, though Death brought her to this.

That shallow space over there, beneath the window showing St Catherine, is reserved for *my* tomb. I insist on a chaste design. None of your beastly seraphim, mind; I never could endure your marble flittermice.

Myrtilla died in childbed, bearing that blockhead my husband. He sits beside me now pretending to listen to the sermon, his mouth catching flies, a pure clown, mere elementary earth, without the least spark of soul in him. That he should have claimed *me* for his wife! He would be more fitly mated with some silly, simple, peaking, sneaking country girl, one that goes with her toes in, and can't say boo to a goose.

I cannot endure him near me, with his sweating, snoring, scratching, snap-finger ways. He'll sit and yawn, and stretch like a greyhound by the fireside, till he does some nasty thing or other and so gives me an excuse to leave the room. When he has blown his nose into his handkerchief, he looks into it as if there were a diamond dropped out of his head.

> There in the womb we are fitted for works of darkness, all the while deprived of light: and there in the womb we are taught cruelty, by being fed with blood, and may be damned, though we be never born.

To confine a woman just at her rambling age! take away her liberty at the very time she should use it! O barbarous aunt! O unnatural father!

My aunt Champflower is a very violent lady. She will fall into a fit or fly at you for the least piddling insignificant thing. In her day she was a beauty, but now she washes her face and hands in lead varnish to hide the dismal hollows of eight and thirty years.

Lord, what a difference there is between me and her. How I should despise such a thing if I were a man. What a nose she has! what a chin! what a neck! She desired my ruin with all her little heart. She danced for pure joy at my wedding.

My father never would have heard Scandal's buzz had she only kept it from him. He would have let me look where I pleased for a husband. I have a tidy fortune. But, no, I must be thrown away in haste to this clodpole squire.

My aunt calls me to her room and talks of Honour and Reputation with a long face like the beast of the Nile.

'Aye, aye,' says I, 'but what has such talk to do with me?'

'What indeed!' cries she in a passion.

She pauses. She trifles with a lace some time before she speaks next, making play with a certain letter, reading it to herself with a careless dropping lip and an erected brow, humming it hastily over.

I recognize the hand. It is from my Celadon.

'Well, niece, this galloping abroad and allowing young fellows to fool with you has given your reputation no very good complexion.'

'Madam, I seek only to follow your example. Besides, I have heard it said often and often when I was with you in London, that a lady's reputation ought to be a sort of brunette; then it has an attraction in it, like amber. A white reputation is as disagreeable to men, I am sure I have heard you say twenty times or more, as white eyebrows or white eyelashes.'

'Pooh pooh,' says she with a sort of snarling smile. 'You can talk in that airy impertinent way until Domesday but it will not save you. I have other letters. Your fop delights in nothing but rapes and riots, as all the world well knows. I have heard certain tales. I have ocular proof.'

'Madam,' says I, though I start to feel a little uneasy now, 'There are some persons who make it their business to tell stories, and say this and that of one and t'other, and everything in the world; and,' says I. . . .

'And your father shall know all,' she finishes.

> Our birth dies in infancy, and our infancy dies in youth, and youth and the rest die in age, and age also dies, and determines all. *O, huzza, Parson Snakepeace; cheerful matter for an April morning!* Our youth is hungry and thirsty, after those sins, which our infancy knew not; and our age is sorry and angry, that it cannot pursue those sins which our youth did.

I shall never more see the Playhouse, nor go to Ponchinello nor Paradise, nor take a ramble to the Park nor Mulberry Garden. I could as soon persuade my husband to share a sillybub in New Spring Garden or to drink a pint of wine with friends at the Prince in the Sun as I could fly.

My aunt Champflower took me with her to London last year for a spring holiday. We lodged near by St James, and I never was so happy in all my life.

I dote upon assemblies, adore masquerades, my heart bounds at a ball; I love a play to distraction, cards enchant me, and dice put me out of my little wits.

On our third evening, then, we saunter to the pleasure gardens at Ranelagh for the sake of the Chinese lanterns and to taste a dish of oysters.

There we happen to meet again with a certain merry sharking fellow about the town, who has pursued us diligently from chocolate house to milliner to the Haymarket since our arrival. He has with him a friend; and this friend is Celadon.

'I came up, Sir, as we country-gentlewomen use, at an Eastern Term,' explains my aunt demurely, 'to the destruction of tarts and cheesecakes, to see a new play, buy a new gown, take a turn in the Park, and so down again to sleep with my forefathers.'

'We see you have brought your sister with you in kindness,' says Celadon, giving me a mighty wink.

The two fine gallants pay her gross and lavish compliments, ogling and glancing and watching any occasion to do forty officious things. They have all the appearance of gentlemen about them. I notice that Celadon's eyes look sideways on me like an Egyptian drawing. He wears a fine long periwig tied up in a bag.

My aunt curtsies at last. Down goes her diving body to the ground, as if she were sinking under the conscious load of her own attractions; then launches into a flood of fine language, still playing her chest forward in fifty falls and risings, like a swan upon waving water.

Hang me if she has not conceived a violent passion for the fellow.

> . . . when my mouth shall be filled with dust, and the worm shall feed, and feed sweetly upon me, when the ambitious man shall have no satisfaction, if the poorest alive tread upon him, nor the poorest receive any contentment in being made equal to Princes, for they shall be equal but in dust.

I look down now at my arms and see the fine eggshell skin with a pretty sparkle from the sun, and the violet-coloured veins at my wrist. I cannot think I am dust and worm's meat.

The carnation dew, the pouting ripeness of my honeycomb mouth, he said; and that my face was a swarm of cupids.

I do love Love, I would have all the Love in the world. What should I mind else, while I have any share of youth and beauty? When I went to Court all eyes were upon me, all tongues were whispering that's my Lord Spatchcock's fine daughter; all pressed towards me and bowed, only to get a half glance from me. When I went to the playhouse, some stood gazing on me, with their arms across their heads languishing as oppressed by beauty. The brisker fellows combed their wigs and prepared their eyes to tilt with mine. Ah, flattery was my daily bread.

Celadon is so agreeable a man, so eloquent, so unaffected, so particular, so easy, so free. All his finery is from the best in Paris – his shoes from Piccar and his gloves from Orangerie. He wears his clothes with so becoming a negligence that I can barely wish him out of them. He even soaks his handkerchief in rose water.

He had the greatest skill in arranging assignations that ever I saw; and all the while he flattered my aunt with a thousand honeyed words and promises, until I was ready to burst with laughing.

My hair was dressed in flaunting little ringlets and crimped serpentaux puffs. I wore my new under-petticoats of white dimity, embroidered like a turkey-work chair with red, green, blue and yellow, with a pin-up coat of Scotch plaid adorned with bugle lace and my gown of printed calico.

I carried my claret-coloured velvet coat with gold fringes to protect me from the dangers of the night air. Even in spring, jaunting abroad at four in the morning strikes a chill into the bones.

Parson Snakepeace has conceived the pretty notion of keeping a skull upon his desk.

I can never persuade myself that religion consists in scurvy out-of-fashion clothes and sour countenances, and when one walks abroad, not to turn one's head to the right or left, but hold it straight forward like an old blind mare.

O that I were your lover for a month or two, he murmured in my ear like a bumble-bee.

– What then?

– I would make that pretty heart's blood of yours ache in a fortnight.

> That God, this Lord, the Lord of life could die, is a strange contemplation; that the red sea could be dry, that the sun could stand still, that an oven could be seven times heat and not burn, that lions could be hungry and not bite, is strange, miraculously strange, but supermiraculous that God could die.

The most unnatural spectacle to be seen in Somerset since the Flood was surely my union with Squire Clodpole here. A dainty girl of seventeen yoked to a greasy, untoward, ill-natured, slovenly wretch! We were the laughing stock of five counties.

Now it is five months since our wedding, which I should rather call a show of Merry-Andrews, with nothing pleasant about it at all but the foolery of a farce.

The nuptial banquet was crammed with baskets of plum-cake, Dutch gingerbread, Cheshire cheese, Naples biscuits, macaroons, neats' tongues and cold boiled beef.

My new husband had drunk heartily. The guests cried out for a speech. He staggered to his feet.

My head aches consumedly, said he; I am not well.

He raised his glass to me, then toppled over behind the table.

There was such a laughing, they roared out again. The ladies teehee'd under their napkins. The teehee took a reverend old gentlewoman as she was drinking, and she squirted the beer out of her nose, as an Indian does tobacco.

By the time the bashful bride, meaning myself, was brought to bed, this numbskull had in some wise recovered his wits.

He called for a mouthful of something to stay his stomach, a tankard of usquebaugh with nutmeg and sugar, if you please, and also a toast and some cheese.

'Supper, sir!' said I, 'Why, your dinner is not out of your mouth yet; at least 'tis all about the brims of it.'

That sharp comment confounded him, so that he cursed,

and rolled about the bedchamber like a sick passenger in a storm; then he comes flounce into bed, dead as a salmon in a fishmonger's basket, his feet cold as ice and his breath hot as a furnace.

His head is a fool's egg which lies hid in a nest of hair. He hangs his nose in my neck and talks to me whether I will or no. What a poor sordid slavery there is in the state of marriage.

During our brief courtship, he wailed out some songs of love.

> I have a mistress that is fair
> And sweet as sugar candy,
> Had I ten thousand pounds a year
> I'd give her half a pint of brandy.

And all the while he gazes on me like a sick monster, with languishing eyes.

I burst into laughter: 'Lord, sir, you have such a way with you!'

> At night He went into the garden to pray, and He spent much time in prayer. I dare scarce ask thee whither *thou* wentest, or how *thou* disposedst of thy self, when it grew dark and after last night. *That has set my husband a-tittering. Now he nudges me with his elbow, the filthy fellow. I have no stomach for him.* About midnight He was taken and bound with a kiss, art thou not too conformable to Him in that? Is not that too literally, too exactly thy case? at midnight to have been taken and bound with a kiss?

Yes, yes, parson Snakepeace, I was taken captive in a garden, at my lady Wildsapte's last summer *fête champestre,* though I cannot see why you should make a sermon of it, for it had nothing to do with you or your talk of the grave.

We went chasing off by the light of torches down an alley of trees, shamming to fight each other with long hazel twigs.

My lady's grounds are full of little pagan temples and other fancies, and at last we fell down breathless at the foot of a pretty Egyptian obelisk brought back by her son from his late stay in Rome. Screened by the friendly shade of some low bushes, we fell upon the ground together; the leaves around us were of the crimson flowering currant for I can still recall the sharp smell when we bruised 'em by lying upon 'em.

'Cherubimical lass,' he called me, and gazed on me devouringly. Our eye beams were in that moment tangled beyond redemption, and I could not bring myself to draw away when he caught me by the hand, wringing and squeezing at it as if he were mad.

He offered me no other rudeness at first, but we only gazed on each other with half-smiles; and our breathing grew laboured when we twisted and knotted our fingers together as if in combat. Then indeed my bounding blood beat quick and high alarms.

He swore that he would come down from London in a fortnight, and marry me.

And so we progressed until, with broken murmurs and heart-fetched sighs, he so mousled and tousled me that I cried 'Sweetheart!' and he clapped a hand over my mouth to save us from discovery.

Good gods! What a pleasure there is in doing what we should not do.

Then were we animated by the strongest powers of love, and every vein of my body circulated liquid fires; until we came at last to that tumultuous momentary rage of which so much has been whispered since the world begun.

O Jesu, when I think back to the heat of his sweet mouth and the smell of his skin, I could weep for weeks together.

Hang him, let him alone. He's gone.

> Hast thou gone about to redeem thy sin, by fasting, by Alms, by disciplines and mortifications, in the way of satisfaction to the Justice of God? That will not serve, that's not the right way, we press an utter crucifying of that sin that governs thee; and that conforms thee to Christ.

Well, I am eight months gone with child. I may follow Mrs Myrtilla's example more speedily than expected. That would indeed be a convenient conclusion, to be dispatched by my own sin. That would provide matter enough for a month of fine long thundering sermons.

This husband sits beside me like a ball and chain. A pack of squalling infants will do the rest, forging my bonds link by link, and soon I shall inhabit as heavy a carcass as my sister Sarah's. Then will I keep company with the mid-wife – dry-nurse – wet-nurse – and all the rest of their accomplices, with cradle, baby-clouts and bearing clothes – possetts, caudles, broth, jellies and gravies. I grow nauseous when I think of them.

I may build castles in the air, and fume and fret, and grow pale and ugly, if I please; but nothing will bring back my free and airy time.

Outside this church it is almost summer; see how the sun struggles through these coloured glass saints to fall in jewels on to my gown.

I will not die of the pip, so I will not.

O merciful God, who hast made all men, and hatest nothing that thou hast made, nor wouldest the death of a sinner, but rather that he should be converted and live; have mercy upon all Jews, Turks, infidels, and Hereticks, and take from them all ignorance, hardness of heart, and contempt of thy Word; and so fetch them home, blessed Lord, to thy flock, that they may be saved among the remnant of the true Israelites, and be made one fold under one shepherd, Jesus Christ our Lord, who liveth and reigneth with thee and the Holy Spirit, one God, world without end. Amen.

The Waiting Rooms

JOAN RILEY

Joan Riley was born in 1958 in St Mary's, Jamaica. She came to the UK in 1976 and went to Sussex University to do a BA in International Relations. She has two children aged 7 and 2 and now lives in South London. Her three published novels are *The Unbelonging, Waiting in the Twilight* and *Romance,* all published by The Women's Press.

Two clinics sat side by side, to the left Gynaecology, to the right Sexually Transmitted Diseases. The waiting rooms were open-plan, each side facing the other like age-old adversaries.

Gynaecology was full, sixteen women, some with children, cluttered together in a small space.

Despite the thin cottons and gay candy stripes, sweat formed relentlessly, oozing and dripping along hairlines and prickling under armpits as the sun beat mercilessly through the large glass window. Children whined and screamed in irritation, while red-faced mothers hung on grimly to fraying tempers.

It might have been a nice place to wait in winter, especially with a waiting time of nearly forty minutes. The aspect was perfect for a gentle sun, south-facing and cheerful. But at the height of that rarity, a hot August day, it was like slow roasting.

Elena Fagan shifted uncomfortably, unsticking her bottom from where it had started to adhere to the black chair. She wriggled downwards cursing the shorts which had seemed so cool this morning, but now left too much of her skin in contact with the uncomfortable sweat-slicked vinyl.

Some new life this was turning out to be. Everything was supposed to fall in place now that she was thin. Jimmy had assured her *fat* was the problem with her life.

'Look how you face sweet, sweet girl,' he coaxed time and time again, 'if only there wasn't so much of it . . . and you never so short with it.'

She hadn't listened to the warning in the words. She'd been fat when he met her, fat when they married and anyway everybody knew West Indian men liked a good handful of woman in their bed.

She had been a size 14 then of course, but he could hardly blame her for the two stone she had put on. Anyway that wasn't too bad in twelve years . . . less than three pounds a year if you divided it out.

She hadn't even realized she was putting on weight; every time she looked in the mirror her body was the same, not that she ever did that in the last six years. It would have been so much easier if she had been able to have a child; but five years and an endless series of tests only yielded the bitter knowledge that she was that small minority . . . a barren woman.

Jimmy had been so angry, in the midst of his relief that his manhood was not at fault. What would people think of him . . . what about the son to bear his name? She clamped her mouth shut about the two children by his other marriage, realizing they were not enough and his masculinity was threatened.

A year later no miracle had happened, and the eating became a habit, until the day she found her husband in the park with that tall thin woman from Guyana. She had tried to be reasonable even though she didn't understand, and when her best friend told her that in every fat person was a thin one struggling to get out, she decided to get a move on and liberate her inner self.

It had been far too late for Jimmy and at thirty-four she found herself thin for the first time. Seven and a half stones and alone. Elena had half expected it and somehow it didn't matter all that much, even though the bed had too much space, and there was no one to frown at her nakedness.

It seemed a shame to waste the new thin self, even if only her eyes were there to marvel and admire. Elena went on a spending spree, buying shorts and quarter tops, T-shirt dresses, and skin tight jeans. All the things she had only dared to hanker after in her dreams.

She went to parties, discos, a thirty-four-year-old Alice in a thin Wonderland. It was a change for men to ask her to dance instead of discuss their problems till she fled the boredom in defensive sleep.

She found it all so daring, dancing close to a man, knowing he wanted sex with her. That was the one taboo she could never break. She had slept with Jimmy for sixteen years, twelve of them in marriage. No one else had shared her bed, and somehow it didn't seem right. Elena consoled herself with promises of *when the divorce comes through,* but before she had a chance to test it, lower belly pains had sent her to her doctor and this clinic. And even here her luck was running true to form.

Elena glanced at her watch and sighed; she had been sitting, sweltering for over an hour, just because some idiot of a nurse had sent her file to the wrong place.

There was a tug on the magazine in her hand, and she looked down irritated, seeing the small black child with the cherubic face and loud scream who had been exercising her lungs in competition with a thin Indian boy for the last twenty minutes. Elena glared at her, concentrating her frustration into that look, before casting a furtive glance at the mother sitting on the other side. The woman had her eyes closed, fanning herself, fluttering the magazine with every lazy motion.

She shifted her gaze back to the child, whose neatly plaited head was cocked to one side in curiosity. She debated another crushing look, then jerked hastily, burning with embarrassment and anger when the little girl reached out a podgy hand and solemnly pinched her, before running off to join battle with her recent playmate.

Elena had to swallow her annoyance, feeling it threatening some rash action like walking out, which would hurt nobody but herself. God it was hot. If only she had a chewing gum or something to drink. Her eyes wandered across to the other clinic.

It was shadowed, looking cool and inviting, wide and spacious with comfortable, low-level, easy chairs, which only served to underline the sticky discomfort of where she was.

The wages of sin, she thought wryly, wondering if they hadn't got it wrong somewhere along the line. It was ironic that all these righteous women should do a slow melt in this oven of a waiting room, while the sinners they condemned sprawled in open comfort in the cool side of the building.

Elena toyed with the idea of going across, braced herself and cast another furtive glance around. She ducked back behind her paper when her eyes collided with those of her stout neighbour on the right.

She could guess what the woman was thinking, as her prim rosebud mouth pursed with disapproval. *Another of them for the VD clinic sitting on our side.*

Elena wished she had the nerve to brazen it out and she eyed the spacious coolness with regret.

Although it only held eight people, most of the activity was centred on there. The seven men eyed the women in the Gynaecology clinic with critical appraisal, weighing them up with insolence, little caring for the solid wall of disapproval that was the only response they got. The one woman on their side they ignored, flicking an occasional glance of contempt towards her, only to slide their eyes away when they met her steady gaze.

When the nurse came out with her clipboard they would sit up with eager expectation, and when a woman on the Gynaecology side stood up and shuffled across with reddened face and hanging head they winked and sniggered at one another.

Elena was still weighing comfort against embarrassment when the two women erupted down the corridor. One black, one white, they talked and laughed like old friends, their voices rippling shock waves through the fabric of the silence.

Sixteen sweaty heads turned from the left, avid-eyed and full of righteous condemnation. The woman on the right sank down behind her magazine, and the men stared in frank appreciation. Elena watched the women come into sight. fascinated by their leather shorts and gaudy tops. They stopped for a moment, standing in provocative poses as they looked in amusement from the women to the men. From the talk that rolled in front of them she'd thought them in their early teens, but close up they were nearer thirty. Elena summed them up and dismissed them. They had to be for Sexually Transmitted Diseases and had probably caught it on The Game. Everything shrieked of it, their casually explicit poses and the way they chomped their mouths around hidden wads of chewing gum.

'Cheerful ain't they?' The white woman with the bleached blond hair did a slow twirl. 'C'mon Bev, let's have a laugh.'

She marched across to the window, sprawling down beside the ample figure of a woman who was stamped all over with 'yuppie' and had a 'Harrods' label sticking out of her light blue pinafore. 'Ere love, your label's sticking out.'

The yuppie lady shifted aside in horror; as the woman reached across a grimy hand and tucked the label in, she swallowed hard, 'thank you.'

Bev had followed slowly and now she stood in the full glare of the sun. 'Is hot in here ain't it Lin . . . look I ain't staying here, it's cooler over there . . . more fun as well, least it have some blokes.'

Lin looked around regretfully, eyes alighting on the cherubic child watching her with thumb-sucking concentration. She gave the little girl a wink, much to her mother's distress. 'Yeah you're right, let's go see the blokes.' She hadn't lowered her voice through all of this, and the men looked over in anticipation, sitting up straight and grinning.

They walked across standing for a moment in the half-empty waiting room, then headed for the windows on the far side.

'Hope we ain't gotta wait too long,' Bev frowned, her accent betraying some out-of-London origin, 'I gorra get back to work, fore Charlie know I'm gone.'

Elena felt justified in her original impression. Charlie was obviously the pimp, and the woman didn't have shame enough to hide the fact.

Lin nodded. 'Yeah, but we gonna be waiting ages and is two separate clinic ain't it?'

Bev shrugged. 'Whoever finish first waits for the other. Even though is less over here they might take longer.'

Elena wished the woman would lower her voice. Glimpsing the knowing looks on the other women's faces. It had to be the one named Bev who had VD didn't it. The yuppie woman's nose turned up, and the one with the rosebud lips stared across with a knowledge of Elena's guilt, as she judged a race on one woman.

Suddenly a fight erupted between the children, and the cherubic child came slamming into her, helped by a hefty push from a blond boy she judged was four.

Elena's mind was made up. Standing, she stretched, with a great show of unconcern, trying to appear casual as she strolled across the dividing corridor on shaky legs. A couple of the men whistled in appreciation, sending her scurrying the rest of the way, to sit beside a chewing Lin.

She had intended being by the other woman, but embarrassment had carried her feet too far and she didn't want to admit to nerves by doubling back again.

The two women nudged each other, giving Elena sidelong glances.

'Brave ain't she?' Lin mocked loudly. 'Ain't you afraid you'll catch something love? You and them others?'

Elena's smile was uncomfortable, and she kept her eyes out of focus before plunging back behind her magazine. She was nearly at the end, and she eased a few pages backward, panicked by the thought of losing her paper shield.

'She's reading backwards,' Bev announced in a loud stage whisper.

Elena dared a glance at the other clinic. Her recent neighbour was talking animatedly to the yuppie, and from the looks they sent in her direction she knew the topic must be her.

'What you got?' Lin had turned her attention back, chomping her way through every word.

Elena pretended she hadn't heard, looking up with blank enquiry.

'I ses, you got a dose of the clap?'

She was glad her colour masked her embarrassment, because her face and body burned, hotter than when she had been in the stuffy waiting room.

'She's blushing,' Bev crowed in triumph, 'I bet Miss Harrods over there got a dose too though.'

Elena looked over at the yuppie glad to have the glare off her; and she hid a smile at the way everybody shrank away as if she had just become contagious.

'Elena Fagan,' the nurse was standing in Gynaecology, eyes scanning through the women.

Elena got up, pulling to her full height, smiling back when her eyes met Bev, and the woman gave her a cheeky wink.

'Good on yer love,' Lin said as she marched out, 'you ain't so stuffed shirt like you look.'

She deliberately came out at the far end of the waiting rooms, walking past the stuffy little sun trap with head held high. The women avoided her triumphant eyes, the knowledge she was innocent.

Elena spent an hour passing from nurse to doctor, back to nurse and then another doctor. They took blood, several smears, pommelled her and poked her. Finally, dressed again, the doctor looked at her.

'I'm afraid there's little we can do at this stage and I'm very pessimistic. Whatever it is we probably won't be able to help you.'

'But is there nothing you can do?' she had to ask the question, after over an hour of waiting this couldn't be the end of it.

'We can try you on a course of tablets, but that will have to wait until the test results. All I can tell you at this stage is that you have a pain, and you obviously knew that already.'

Elena picked up her bag, going through the routine formality of thanking him, while she felt more like braining him. Half her day off lost, sitting in a stuffy waiting room so he could tell her about the pain she already knew she had.

The waiting rooms had changed round. On the cool side only Bev and Lin remained, propping their feet up on the chairs despite the attempts of a nurse to stop them.

The sun was even fiercer on the south-facing side, and the room had got more crowded, but at least the yuppie and the rosebud women were no longer there.

'Howd it go,' Lin hailed her as she made to walk out.

Elena stopped to talk, knowing no one could judge her now. 'Fine . . . which clinic are you waiting for.' It was a formality, nothing more. It was obvious she was staying here to be with her friend.

Before she got an answer, a nurse came out on the Sexually Transmitted Diseases side.

'Linda Warbeck.'

'There's you answer,' Lin said with a laugh, before turning to her friend. 'Looks like I'll be waiting for you after, you got twelve of the buggers in front of you.'

Bev shrugged, picking up a magazine. 'Rate they going I'll have got the sack already anyhow.'

Elena lingered, revising her opinion, aware of the restless shifting in the other waiting room that told her they had heard.

'Ahm, what are you here for.'

She got a cold look in response, 'You thought it's me that had the clap didn't you.'

She couldn't deny the truth of that, and the raised volume of the shuffling said the others couldn't either.

Bev chewed hard on her gum. 'Me womb's in the wrong place,' she announced to the world at large, 'and if you want to know that too, me and Lin work down Woolworth's.'

An Outside Interest

RUTH RENDELL

Since her first novel, *From Doon With Death*, was published in 1964, Ruth Rendell has won many awards, including the Crime Writers' Association Gold Dagger for 1976's best crime novel with *A Demon in my View* and the Arts Council National Book Award – Genre Fiction for *Lake of Darkness* in 1980. In 1984 Ruth Rendell won her second Edgar from the Mystery Writers of America for best short story with 'The New Girl Friend', and in 1985 received the Silver Dagger for *The Tree of Hands*. In 1966 she won another Edgar for *A Dark-Adapted Eye*, written under the pseudonym of Barbara Vine, and in the same month was awarded a Gold Dagger for *Live Flesh*. Her books have been translated into fifteen languages and are also published to great acclaim in the United States. Ruth Rendell is married and lives in a sixteenth-century farmhouse in Suffolk.

Frightening people used to be a hobby of mine. Perhaps I should rather say an obsession and not people but, specifically, women. Making others afraid *is* enjoyable as everyone discovers who has tried it and succeeded. I suppose it has something to do with power. Most people never really try it so they don't know, but look at the ones who do. Judges, policemen, prison warders, customs officers, tax inspectors. They have a great time, don't they? You don't find them giving up or adopting other methods. Frightening people goes to their heads, they're drunk on it, they live by it. So did I. While other men might go down to the pub with the boys or to football, I went off to Epping Forest and frightened women. It was what you might call my outside interest.

Don't get me wrong. There was nothing – well, nasty, about what I did. You know what I mean by that, I'm sure I don't have to go into details. I'm far from being some sort of pervert, I can tell you. In fact, I err rather on the side of too much moral strictness. Nor am I one of those lonely, deprived men. I'm happily married and the father of a little boy, I'm six feet tall, not bad-looking and, I assure you, entirely physically and mentally normal.

Of course I've tried to analyse myself and discover my motives. Was my hobby ever any more than an antidote to boredom? By anyone's standard the life I lead would be classed as pretty dull, selling tickets and answering passengers' queries at Anglo-Mercian Airways terminal, living in a semi in Muswell Hill, going to tea with my mother-in-law on Sundays and having an annual fortnight in a holiday flat in South Devon. I got married very young. Adventure wasn't exactly a conspicuous feature of my existence. The biggest thing that happened to me was when we thought one of our charters had been hijacked in Greece, and that turned out to be a false alarm.

My wife is a nervous sort of girl. Mind you, she has cause to be, living where we do close to Highgate Wood and Queens Wood. A woman takes her life in her hands, walking alone in those places. Carol used to regale me with stories – well, she still does.

'At twenty past five in the afternoon! It was still broad daylight. He raped her and cut her in the face, she had to have seventeen stitches in her face and neck.'

She doesn't drive and if she comes home from anywhere after dark I always go down to the bus stop to meet her. She won't even walk along the Muswell Hill Road because of the woods on either side.

'If you see a man on his own in a place like that you naturally ask yourself what he's doing there, don't you? A young man, just walking aimlessly about. It's not as if he had a dog with him. It makes your whole body go tense and you get a sort of awful crawling sensation all over you. If you didn't come and meet me I don't think I'd go out at all.'

Was it that which gave me the idea? At any rate it made me think about women and fear. Things are quite different for a man, he never thinks about being afraid of being in dark or lonely places. I'm sure I never have and therefore, until I got all this from Carol, I never considered how important this business of being scared when out alone might be to them. When I came to understand it gave me a funny feeling of excitement.

And then I actually frightened a woman myself – by chance. My usual way of going to work is to cut through Queens Wood to Highgate tube station and take the Northern Line down into London. When the weather is very bad I go to the station by bus but most of the time I walk there and back and the way through the wood is a considerable short cut. I was coming back through the wood at about six one evening in March. It was dusk, growing dark. The lamps, each a good distance apart from each other, which light the paths, were lit, but I often think these give the place a rather more bleak and sinister appearance than if it were quite dark. You leave a light behind you and walk along a dim shadowy avenue towards the next lamp which gleams faintly some hundred yards ahead. And no sooner is it reached, an acid yellow glow among the bare branches, than you leave it behind again to negotiate the next dark stretch. I thought about how it must be to be a woman walking through the wood and, yes, I gloried in my maleness and my freedom from fear.

Then I saw the girl coming. She was walking along the path from Priory Gardens. It came into my head that she would be less wary of me if I continued as I had been, marching briskly and purposefully towards Wood Vale, swinging along and looking like a man homeward bound to his family and his dinner. There was no definite intent present in my mind when I slackened my pace, then stopped and stood still. But as soon as I'd done that I knew I was going to carry it through. The girl came up to where the paths converged and where the next lamp was. She gave me a quick darting look. I stood there in a very relaxed way and I returned her look with a blank stare. I suppose I consciously, out of some sort of devilment, made my eyes fixed and glazed and let my mouth go loose. Anyway, she turned very quickly away and began to walk much faster.

She had high heels so she couldn't go very fast, not as fast as I could, just strolling along behind her. I gained on her until I was a yard behind.

I could smell her fear. She was wearing a lot of perfume and her sweat seemed to potentiate it so that there came to me a whiff and then a wave of heady, mixed-up animal and floral scent. I breathed it in, I breathed heavily. She began to run and I strode after her. What she did then was unexpected. She stopped, turned round and cried out in a tremulous, terrified voice, 'What do you want?'

I stopped too and gave her the same look. She held her handbag out to me. 'Take it!'

The joke had gone far enough. I lived round there anyway, I had my wife and son to think of. I put on a cockney voice. 'Keep your bag, love. You've got me wrong.'

And then, to reassure her, I turned back along the path and let her escape to Wood Vale and the lights and the start of the houses. But I can't describe what a feeling of power and – well, triumphant manhood and what's called machismo the encounter gave me. I felt grand. I swaggered into my house and Carol said had I had a Premium Bond come up?

Since I'm being strictly truthful in this account, I'd better add the other consequence of what happened in the wood, even though it does rather go against the grain with me to mention things like that. I made love to Carol that night and it was a lot better than it had been for a long time, in fact it was sensational for both of us. And I couldn't kid myself that it was due to anything but my adventure with the girl.

Next day I looked at myself in the mirror with all the lights off but the little tubular one over our bed, and I put on the same look I'd given the girl when she turned in my direction under the lamp. I can tell you I nearly frightened myself. I've said I'm not bad-looking and that's true but I'm naturally pale and since I'm thin, my face tends to be a bit gaunt. In the dim light my eyes seemed sunk in deep sockets and my mouth hung loose in a vacant mindless way. I stepped back from the glass so that I could see the whole of myself, slouching, staring, my arms hanging. There was no doubt I had the potential of being a woman-frightener of no mean calibre.

They say it's the first step that counts. I had taken the first step but the second was bigger and it was weeks before I took it. I kept telling myself not to be a fool, to forget those mad ideas. Besides, surely I could see I'd soon be in trouble if I made a habit of frightening women in Queens Wood, on my own doorstep. But I couldn't stop thinking about it. I remembered how wonderful I'd felt that evening, how tall I'd walked and what a man I'd been.

The funny thing was what a lot of humiliating things seemed to happen to me at that time, between the Queens Wood incident and the next occasion. A woman at the air terminal actually spat at me. I'm not exaggerating. Of course she was drunk, smashed out of her mind on duty-free Scotch, but she spat at me and I had to stand there in the middle of the ticket hall with all those tourists milling about, and wipe the spittle off my uniform. Then I got a reprimand for being discourteous to a passenger. It was totally unjust and, strictly speaking, I should have resigned on the spot, only I've got a wife and son and jobs aren't easy to come by at present. There was all that and trouble at home as well with Carol nagging me to take her on holiday with this girlfriend of hers and her husband to Minorca instead of our usual Salcombe fortnight. I told her straight we couldn't afford it but I didn't like being asked in return why I couldn't earn as much as Sheila's Mike.

My manhood was at a low ebb. Then Sheila and Mike asked us to spend the day with them, Carol, Timothy and me. They had been neighbours of ours but had just moved away to a new house in one of those outer suburbs that are really in Essex. So I drove the three of us to Theydon Bois and made my acquaintance with Epping Forest.

There are sixty-four square miles of forest, lying on the north-eastern borders of London. But when you drive from the Wake Arms to Theydon along a narrow road bordered by woodland, stretches of turf and undergrowth, little coppices of birch trees, you can easily believe yourself in the depths of the country. It seems impossible that London is only fourteen or fifteen miles away. The forest is green and silent and from a car looks unspoilt, though of course it can't be. We passed a woman walking a very unguard-like dog, a tiny Maltese terrier. . . . That gave me the idea. Why shouldn't I come out here? Why shouldn't I try my frightening act out here where no one knew me?

Two days after that I did. It was spring and the evenings stayed light till nearly eight. I didn't take the car. Somehow it didn't seem to me as if the sort of person I was going to be, going to *act*, would have a car. The journey was awful, enough to deter anyone less determined than I. I went straight from work, taking the Central Line tube as far as Loughton and then a bus up the hills and into the forest. At the Wake Arms I got off and began to walk down the hill, not on the pavement but a few yards inside the forest itself. I didn't see a woman on her own until I had reached the houses of Theydon and begun the return trip. I had gone about a hundred yards up again when she came out of one of the last houses, a young girl in jeans and a jacket, her hands in her pockets.

It was clear she was going to walk to the Wake Arms. Or so I thought. For a while I walked, keeping step with her, but unseen among the hawthorn and crab apple bushes, the tangle of brambles. I let us get a quarter of a mile away from the houses before I showed myself and then I stepped out on to the pavement ahead of her. I turned round to face her and stood there, staring in the way I'd practised in the mirror.

She wasn't nervous. She was brave. It was only very briefly that she hesitated. But she didn't quite dare walk past me. Instead she crossed the road. There's never much traffic on that road and so far not a single car had passed. She crossed the road, walking faster. I crossed too but behind her and I walked along behind her. Presently she began to run, so of course I ran too, though not fast enough to catch her up, just enough to gain on her a little.

We had been going on like that for some minutes, the Wake Arms still a mile off, when she suddenly doubled back, hared across the road and began running back the way she had come. That finished me for chasing her. I stood there and laughed. I laughed long and loud, I felt so happy and free, I felt so much all-conquering power that I – I alone, humble, ordinary, dull *me* – could inspire such fear.

After that I took to going to Epping Forest as a regular thing. Roughly speaking, I'd say it would have been once a fortnight. Since I do shift work, four till midnight just as often as ten till six, I sometimes managed to go in the daytime. A lot of women are alone at home in the daytime and have no men to escort them when they go out. I never let it go more than two weeks without my going there and occasionally I'd go more often, if I was feeling low in spirits, for instance, or Carol and I had a row or I got depressed over money. It did me so much good, I wish I could make you understand how much. Just think what it is you do that gives you a tremendous lift, driving a car really fast or going disco dancing or getting high on something – well, frightening women did all that for me and then some. Afterwards it was like Christmas, it was almost like being in love.

And there was no harm in it, was there? I didn't hurt them. There's a French saying: it gives me so much pleasure and you so little pain. That was the way it was for me and them, though it wasn't without pleasure for them either. Imagine how they must have enjoyed talking about it afterwards, going into all the details like Carol did, distorting the facts, exaggerating, making themselves for a while the centre of attention.

For all I knew they may have got up search parties, husbands and boyfriends and fathers all out in a pack looking for me, all having a great time as people invariably do when they're hunting something or someone. After all, when all was said and done, what did I do? Nothing. I didn't molest them or insult them or try to touch them, I merely stood and looked at them and ran after them – or ran when they ran which isn't necessarily the same thing.

There was no harm in it. Or so I thought. I couldn't see what harm there could ever be, and believe me, I thought about this quite a lot, for I'm just as guilt-ridden as the rest of us. I thought about it, justifying myself, keeping guilt at bay. Young women don't have heart attacks and fall down dead because a man chases them. Young women aren't left with emotional traumas because a man stares at them. The oldest woman I ever frightened was the one with the Maltese terrier and she was no more than forty. I saw her again on my third or fourth visit and followed her for a while, stepping out from behind bushes and standing in her path. She used the same words the girl in Queens Wood had used, uttered in the same strangled voice: 'What is it you want?'

I didn't answer her. I had mercy on her and her little ineffectual dog and I melted away into the woodland shades. The next one who asked me that I answered with professorial gravity, 'Merely collecting lichens, madam.'

It was proof enough of how harmless I was that there was never a sign of a policeman in that area. I'm sure none of them told the police, for they had nothing to tell. They had only what they imagined and what the media had led them to expect. Yet harm did come from it, irrevocable harm and suffering and shame.

No doubt by now you think you've guessed. The inevitable must have happened, the encounter which any man who makes a practice of intimidating women is bound to have sooner or later, when the tables are turned on him. Yes, that did happen but it wasn't what stopped me. Being seized by the arm, hurled in the air and laid out, sprawled and bruised, by a judo black belt, was just an occupational hazard. I've always been glad, though, that I behaved like a gentleman. I didn't curse her or shout abuse. I merely got up, rubbed my legs and elbows, made her a little bow and walked off in the direction of the Wake. Carol wanted to know how I'd managed to get green stains all over my clothes and I think to this day she believes it was lying on the grass in a park somewhere with another woman. As if I would!

That attack on me deterred me. It didn't put me off. I let three weeks go by, three miserable yearning weeks, and then I went back to the Wake road one sunny July morning and had one of my most satisfying experiences. A girl walking, not on the road, but taking a short cut through the forest itself. I walked parallel to her, sometimes letting her catch a glimpse of me. I knew she did, for like it had been with the girl in Queens Wood, I could sense and smell her fear.

I strolled out from the bushes at last and stood ahead of her, waiting. She didn't dare approach me, she didn't know what to do. At length she turned back and I followed her, threading my way among the bushes until she must have thought I had gone, then appearing once more on the path ahead. This time she turned off to the left, running, and I let her go. Laughing the way I always did, out loud and irrepressibly, I let her go. I hadn't done her any harm. Think of the relief she must have felt when she knew she'd got away from me and was safe. Think of her going home and telling her mother or her sister or her husband all about it.

You could even say I'd done her a good turn. Most likely I'd warned her off going out in the forest on her own and therefore protected her from some real pervert or molester of women.

It was a point of view, wasn't it? You could make me out a public benefactor. I showed them what could happen. I was like the small electric shock that teaches a child not to play with the wires. Or that's what I believed. Till I learned that even a small shock can kill.

I was out in the forest, on the Wake road, when I had a piece of luck. It was autumn and getting dark at six, the earliest I'd been able to get there, and I didn't have much hope of any woman being silly enough to walk down that road alone in the dark. I had got off the bus at the Wake Arms and was walking slowly down the hill when I saw this car parked ahead of me at the kerb. Even from a distance I could hear the horrible noise it made as the driver tried to start it, that anguished grinding you get when ignition won't take place.

The offside door opened and a woman got out. She was on her own. She reached back into the car and turned the lights off, slammed the door, locked it and began walking down the hill towards Theydon. I had stepped in among the trees and she hadn't yet seen me. I followed her, working out what technique I should use this time. Pursuing her at a run to start with was what I had decided on.

I came out on to the pavement about a hundred yards behind her and began running after her, making as much noise with my feet as I could. Of course she stopped and turned round as I knew she would. Probably she thought I was a saviour who was going to do something about her car for her. She looked round, waiting for me, and as soon as I caught her eye I veered off into the forest once more. She gave a sort of shrug, turned and walked on. She wasn't frightened yet.

It was getting dark, though, and there was no moon. I caught her up and walked alongside her, very quietly, only three or four yards away, yet in among the trees of the forest. By then we were out of sight of the parked car and a long way from being in sight of the lights of Theydon. The road was dark, though far from being impenetrably black. I trod on a twig deliberately and made it snap and she turned swiftly and saw me.

She jumped. She looked away immediately and quickened her pace. Of course she didn't have a chance with me, a five-foot woman doesn't with a six-foot man. The fastest she could walk was still only my strolling pace.

There hadn't been a car along the road since I'd been following her. Now one came. I could see its lights welling and dipping a long way off, round the twists in the road. She went to the edge of the pavement and held up her hand the way a hitchhiker does. I stayed where I was to see what would happen. What had I done, after all? Only been there. But the driver didn't stop for her. Of course he didn't, no more than I would have done in his place. We all know the sort of man who stops his car to pick up smartly dressed, pretty hitchhikers at night and we know what he's after.

The next driver didn't stop either. I was a little ahead of her by then, still inside the forest, and in his headlights I saw her face. She *was* pretty, not that that aspect particularly interested me, but I saw that she was pretty and that she belonged to the same type as Carol, a small slender blonde with rather sharp features and curly hair.

The darkness seemed much darker after the car lights had passed. I could tell she was a little less tense now, she probably hadn't seen me for the past five minutes, she might have thought I'd gone. And I was tempted to call it a day, give up after a quarter of an hour, as I usually did when I'd had my fun.

I wish to God I had. I went on with it for the stupidest of reasons. I went on with it because I wanted to go in the same direction as she was going, down into Theydon and catch the tube train from there, rather than go back and hang about waiting for a bus. I could have waited and let her go. I didn't. Out of some sort of perverse need, I kept step with her and then I came out of the forest and got on to the pavement behind her.

I walked along, gaining on her, but quietly. The road dipped, wound a little. I got two or three yards behind her, going very softly, she didn't know I was there, and then I began a soft whistling, a hymn tune it was, the Crimond version of 'The Lord is My Shepherd', What a choice!

She spun round. I thought she was going to say something but I don't think she could. Her voice was strangled by fear. She turned again and began to run. She could run quite fast, that tiny vulnerable blonde girl.

The car lights loomed up over the road ahead. They were full-beam, undipped headlights, blazing blue-white across the surrounding forest, showing up every tree and making long black shadows spring from their trunks. I jumped aside and crouched down in the long grass. She ran into the road, holding up both arms and crying, 'Help me! Help me!'

He stopped. I had a moment's tension when I thought he might get out and come looking for me, but he didn't. He pushed open the passenger door from inside. The girl got in, they waited, sitting there for maybe half a minute, and then the white Ford Capri moved off.

It was a relief to me to see that car disappear over the top of the hill. And I realized, to coin a very appropriate phrase, that I wasn't yet out of the wood. What could be more likely than that the girl and the car driver would either phone or call in at Loughton police station? I knew I'd better get myself down to Theydon as fast as possible.

As it happened I did so without meeting or being passed by another vehicle. I was walking along by the village green when the only cars I saw came along. On the station platform I had to wait for nearly half an hour before a train came, but no policeman came either. I had got away with it again.

In a way. There are worse things than being punished for one's crimes. One of those is not being punished for them. I am suffering for what I did of course by not being allowed – that is, by not allowing myself – to do it again. And I shall never forget that girl's face, so pretty and vulnerable and frightened. It comes to me a lot in dreams.

The first time it appeared to me was in a newspaper photograph, two days after I had frightened her on the Wake road. The newspaper was leading on the story of her death and that was why it used the picture. On the previous morning, when she had been dead twelve hours, her body had been found, stabbed and mutilated, in a field between Epping and Harlow. Police were looking for a man, thought to be the driver of a white Ford Capri.

Her rescuer, her murderer. Then what was I?

Happy Christmas

DAPHNE DU MAURIER

Daphne Du Maurier was born in 1907 and is the author of fifteen novels, plays, biographies and collections of short stories. *Rebecca* was recently adapted for television and is perhaps her best-loved novel. *Jamaica Inn* and *My Cousin Rachel* are other well-known works.

The Lawrence family lived in a large house just outside town. Mr Lawrence was a big heavy man, with a round face and a smile. He motored into town every day to his office, where he had a roll-top desk and three secretaries. During the day he used the telephone, and had a business lunch, and then used the telephone again. He made a lot of money.

Mrs Lawrence had fair hair and china-blue eyes. Mr Lawrence called her Kitten, but she was not helpless. She had a lovely figure and long fingernails, and she played bridge most afternoons. Bob Lawrence was ten. He was like Mr Lawrence, only smaller. He was fond of electric trains, and his father had got some men to fix up a miniature railway in the garden. Marigold Lawrence was seven. She was like her mother, only rounder. She had fifteen dolls. She kept breaking them somehow.

If you met them anywhere you would not recognize the Lawrences as being different from any other family. Perhaps that was the trouble. They were just a bit too much like all the rest. Life was a comfortable and an easy thing, which was, of course, very pleasant.

On Christmas Eve the Lawrence family did much the same as every other family. Mr Lawrence came home early from town so that he could stand around and watch the household get ready for tomorrow. He smiled more than usual and put his hands in his pockets and shouted, 'Look out, you damn fool!' when he tripped over the dog who was hiding behind some evergreen. Mrs Lawrence had cut bridge for once and was threading lanterns across the drawing room. Actually it was the garden boy who threaded the lanterns, but Mrs Lawrence stuck little frills of coloured paper round them and handed them to him, and as she was smoking all the time the smoke got in the garden boy's eyes, but he was too polite to brush it away. Bob Lawrence and Marigold Lawrence kept running round the drawing room and jumping on to the sofas and chairs and calling out, 'What am I going to have tomorrow? Am I going to have a train? Am I going to have a doll?' until Mr Lawrence got fed up and said, 'If you don't stop that row you won't get anything,' but he said it in a way that did not mean much, and the children were not deceived.

It was just before the children's bedtime that Mrs Lawrence was called to the telephone. She said 'Damn!' and some more smoke got into the garden boy's eyes. Mr Lawrence picked up a piece of evergreen and stuck it behind a picture. He whistled cheerfully.

Mrs Lawrence was away five minutes, and when she came back her blue eyes were full of sparks and her hair was rumpled. She looked like a kitten. The kind you pick up and say 'Sweet Puss!' to and then quickly put down again.

'Oh, it's a bit thick, it really is,' she said, and for a moment the children thought she was going to cry.

'What the hell's the matter?' asked Mr Lawrence.

'It's that refugee officer for the district,' said Mrs Lawrence. 'You know – I told you the place was swarming with refugees. Well, like everybody else, I had to put our names down as receivers when the thing started, never thinking seriously that anything would happen. And now it has. We've got to take in a couple, here, tonight.'

Mr Lawrence stopped smiling. 'Look here,' he said, 'the refugee officer can't do that sort of thing to people without proper warning. Why didn't you tell him to go to blazes?'

'I did,' said Mrs Lawrence indignantly, 'and all he could say was that he was very sorry, but it was the same for everybody, and people in every house were having to do it, and he said something about a "compulsory measure" which I did not understand, but it sounded nasty.'

'They can't do it,' said Mr Lawrence, sticking out his jaw. 'I'll get on the phone to someone in authority, I'll see that officer is sacked, I'll go into town myself, I'll . . .'

'Oh, what's the use?' said Mrs Lawrence. 'Don't let's get ourselves all heated over it. You forget it's Christmas Eve and everyone's out of town by now. Anyway, the creatures are on their way, and we can't very well lock the door. I suppose I shall have to break it to the servants.'

'What will the refugees do?' clamoured the children excitedly. 'Will they want to take our things? Will they want our beds?'

'Of course not,' said Mrs Lawrence sharply. 'Don't be such little idiots!'

'Where are we going to put them?' asked Mr Lawrence. 'We shall have every room full as it is with the Dalys and the Collinses coming over tomorrow. You surely don't suggest we put them off now?'

'No fear,' said Mrs Lawrence, her blue eyes sparkling. 'That's one comfort, we can truthfully say the house *is* full. No, the refugees can have the room over the garage. It's been very dry up to now, so the damp won't have got through. There is a bed there that we turned out of the house two months ago – the springs had gone. But there's nothing wrong with it. And I think the servants have an oil stove they don't use.'

Mr Lawrence smiled. 'You've got it all taped, haven't you?' he said. 'No one can get the better of you, Kitten. Oh well, as long as it doesn't hurt us, I don't care.' He swooped down in sudden relief and picked up Marigold. 'Anyway, we won't let it spoil our Christmas, will we, honey?' he said. And he tossed Marigold in the air, and she shrieked with laughter.

'It's not fair,' said Bob Lawrence, his round face flushed. 'Marigold is younger than me and she wants to hang up the same size stocking. I'm eldest, I ought to have the biggest, oughtn't I?'

Mr Lawrence rumpled his son's hair. 'Be a man, Bob,' he said, 'and don't tease your sister. I've got something for you tomorrow better than any toy you'll find in your stocking.'

Bob stopped scowling. 'Is it something for my railway?' he asked eagerly.

Mr Lawrence winked and would not answer.

Bob began to jump up and down on his bed. 'My present's going to be bigger than Marigold's,' he shouted in triumph, 'much, much bigger.'

'It's not, it's not,' cried Marigold tearfully. 'Mine is just as nice, isn't it, Dad?'

Mr Lawrence called to the nurse, 'Come and quieten the kids, will you? I think they're getting too excited.' He laughed and went down the stairs.

Mrs Lawrence met him halfway. 'They've arrived,' she said. Her voice had a warning note.

'Well?' he asked.

She shrugged her shoulders and made a little face. 'Jews,' she said briefly – and went into the nursery.

Mr Lawrence said something, and then he straightened his tie and put on an expression that he considered right for refugees. It was a mixture of sternness and bravado. He went round the drive to the garage and climbed the rickety stairs.

'Ha, good evening!' he said in loud, jovial tones as he entered the room. 'Are you fixed up all right?'

The room was rather dim, for the one electric light bulb had not been dusted for many months and it hung in one corner, away from the bed and the table and the stove. The two refugees stared for a moment without speaking. The woman was sitting at the table, unpacking a basket, from which she brought a loaf of bread and two cups. The man was spreading a blanket over the bed, and when Mr Lawrence spoke he straightened his back and turned towards him.

'We are so grateful,' he said. 'so very grateful.'

Mr Lawrence coughed and half laughed. 'Oh, that's all right,' he said. 'No trouble at all.'

They were Jews and no mistake. The man's nose was enormous, and his skin that typical greasy yellow. The woman had large dark eyes, with shadows beneath them. She looked unhealthy.

'Er – anything else you want?' asked Mr Lawrence.

The woman answered this time. She shook her head. 'We want nothing,' she said. 'We are very tired.'

'Everywhere was full,' said the man. 'No one could take us in. It is most generous of you.'

'Not at all, not at all,' said Mr Lawrence, waving his hand. 'Good thing we had this room empty. You must have had a stiff time where you've been.'

They said nothing to this.

'Well,' said Mr Lawrence, 'if there's nothing more I can do, I'll say goodnight. Don't forget to turn the stove down if it smokes. And – er – if you should need more food or blankets or anything, just give a knock on the back door and ask the servants. Good night.'

'Good night,' they echoed, and then the woman added, 'A Happy Christmas to you.' Mr Lawrence stared. 'Oh yes,' he said. 'Yes, of course. Thanks very much.'

He turned up the collar of his coat as he walked round to the front door. It was cold. There would be a sharp frost. The gong was just sounding for dinner as he went into the hall. The garden boy had finished stringing up the lanterns, and they fluttered from the ceiling with a jaunty air. Mrs Lawrence was mixing a drink at the table by the fire.

'Hurry up,' she called over her shoulder, 'dinner will be spoilt, and if there's anything I loathe it's lukewarm duck.'

'Kids asleep?' asked Mr Lawrence.

'I shouldn't think so,' said Mrs. Lawrence. 'It's difficult to get them to settle on Christmas Eve. I gave them both some chocolate and told them to be quiet. Want a drink?'

Later, when they were undressing for the night, Mr Lawrence poked his head round from the dressing room, a toothbrush in his hand.

'Funny thing,' he said, 'that woman wished me a Happy Christmas. I never knew the Jews kept Christmas before.'

'I don't suppose she knows what it means,' said Mrs Lawrence, and she patted some skin food into her round smooth cheek.

One by one the lights in the house were extinguished. The Lawrence family slept. Outside the sky was bright with stars. And in the room over the garage there was one light burning.

'I say, gosh, just look at this, I've got an airplane as well as a new engine for my railway,' shouted Bob. 'Look, it works like a real one. Look at the propeller.'

'Have I got two things from Dad as well?' asked Marigold,

fumbling feverishly amongst the litter of paper on her bed and she threw aside the large doll she had just unpacked. 'Nurse,' she shrieked, 'where's my other present from Dad?' Her cheeks were hot and flushed.

'Serves you right for being so greedy, mocked Bob. 'Look what I've got.'

'I'll break your silly horrid plane,' said Marigold, and tears began to fall down her cheeks.

'You musn't quarrel on Christmas Day,' said Nurse, and she drew a small box triumphantly from the heap of waste paper. 'Look, Marigold, what's in here?'

Marigold tore aside the paper. Soon she held a glittering necklace in her hands. 'I'm a princess!' she shouted. 'I'm a princess!'

Bob threw her a glance of contempt. 'It's not very big,' he said.

Downstairs Mr and Mrs Lawrence were being served with their morning tea. The electric stove was lit, the curtains drawn, and the room was flooded with sunlight. The letters and the parcels remained unopened, though, for both Mr and Mrs Lawrence listened aghast to the tale that Anna, the servant, had to tell.

'I can't believe it, it's preposterous,' said Mr Lawrence.

'I can. It's just typical of the sort of thing these people do,' said Mrs Lawrence.

'Won't I give that refugee officer hell!' said Mr Lawrence.

'I don't suppose he knew,' said Mrs Lawrence. 'They took jolly good care not to let on that anything might happen. Well, we can't keep them here now, that's certain. There's no one here to look after the woman.'

'We must telephone for an ambulance and have them removed,' said Mr Lawrence. 'I thought the woman had a bad colour. She must be pretty tough to have stood it, all alone.'

'Oh, those sort of people have babies very easily,' said Mrs Lawrence. 'They scarcely feel it. Well, I'm very thankful they were in the garage room and not in the house. They can't have done much damage there.'

'And, Anna,' she called, as the maid was leaving the room, 'be sure and tell Nurse that the children are not to go near the garage until the ambulance has been.'

Then they settled down to the letters and parcels.

'We'll make everyone laugh at the story, anyway,' said Mr Lawrence. 'It will go down well with the turkey and the plum pudding.'

When they had breakfasted and had dressed, and the children had been in to tumble about on the beds and show their presents, Mr and Mrs Lawrence went round to the garage to see what could be done about the refugees. The children were sent up to the nursery to play with their new things, because, after all, what had happened was not very nice, as Nurse agreed with Mrs Lawrence. And besides, you never knew.

When they came to the garage they found a little crowd of servants in the yard talking. There were the cook, and the parlour man, and one of the housemaids, and the chauffeur, and even the garden boy.

'What's going on?' asked Mr Lawrence.

'They've cleared out,' said the chauffeur.

'How do you mean, cleared out?'

'The fellow went off while we were having breakfast and got hold of a taxi,' said the chauffeur. 'He must have gone to the stand at the end of the road. Never a word to any of us.'

'And we heard wheels by the back gate,' chimed in the cook, 'and he and the taxi driver were lifting the woman into the car.'

'The fellow asked for the name of a hospital, and we told him there was a Jewish hospital just before you get into town,' said the chauffeur. 'He said he was very sorry to have given us all this trouble. Cool sort of customer, hadn't turned a hair.'

'And the baby. We saw the baby,' giggled the housemaid, and then she blushed furiously for no reason.

'Yes,' said the cook, 'a proper little Jew, the image of his father.'

And then they all laughed and looked at one another rather foolishly.

'Well,' said Mr Lawrence, 'there's nothing more any of us can do, I suppose.'

The servants melted away. The excitement for the moment was over. There was the Christmas party to prepare for, and what with one thing and another they felt they had been run off their legs already, and it was only ten o'clock.

'We'd better have a look,' said Mr Lawrence jerking his head at the garage. Mrs Lawrence made a face and followed him.

They climbed the rickety stairs to the little dark room in the loft. There was no sign of disorder. The bed had been placed back against the wall, and the blanket was neatly folded at the foot. The chair and table were in the usual place. The window in the room had been opened to let in the fresh morning air. The stove had been turned out. Only one thing showed that the room had been used. On the floor, beside the bed, was a glass of cold water.

Mr Lawrence did not say anything. Mrs Lawrence did not say anything, either. They went back to the house and into the drawing room. Mr Lawrence wandered to the window and looked out across the garden. He could see Bob's miniature railway at the far corner. Mrs Lawrence opened a parcel she had not seen at breakfast. Overhead, shouts and yells told that the children were either enjoying themselves or not.

'What about your golf? Weren't you meeting the others at eleven?' asked Mrs Lawrence.

Mr Lawrence sat down on the window seat. 'I don't feel very keen,' he said.

Mrs Lawrence put back the vanity case she had just drawn from sheet after sheet of tissue paper.

'Funny,' she said, 'I feel sort of flat too, not a bit Christmassy.'

Through the open door they could see the table in the dining room being prepared for lunch. The decorations looked fine, with the little bunches of flowers amidst the silver. Round the centre was a great heap of crackers.

'I really don't know what else we could have done,' said Mrs Lawrence suddenly.

Mr Lawrence did not answer. He arose and began walking up and down the room. Mrs Lawrence straightened the evergreen behind a picture.

'After all, they didn't ask for anything,' said Mrs Lawrence, 'The man would have said,' went on Mrs Lawrence, 'if the woman had been very ill, or the baby. I'm sure they were both all right. They are so tough, that race.'

Mr Lawrence took out a cigar from his waistcoat pocket and put it back again.

'They'll be much better off in the Jewish hospital than they would have been here,' said Mrs Lawrence, ' – proper nursing and everything. We couldn't possibly have coped with it. Besides, going off in a hurry like that, so independent, we did not have a chance to suggest a thing.'

Mr Lawrence picked up a book and then shut it. Mrs Lawrence kept twisting and untwisting the belt on her dress.

'Of course,' she said hurriedly, 'I shall go and enquire how they are and take fruit and things, and perhaps some warm woollies, and ask if there is anything else they want. I'd go this morning, only I have to take the children to church. . . .'

And then the door opened and the children came into the room.

'I've got my new necklace on,' said Marigold. 'Bob hasn't anything new to wear.' She pirouetted round on her toes. 'Hurry up, Mummy, we shall be late, and we shall miss seeing all the people come in.'

'I hope they sing "Hark the Herald Angels",' said Bob. 'We learnt the words in school and I shan't have to look at the book. Why was Jesus born in a stable, Dad?'

'There wasn't room for them at the inn,' said Mr Lawrence.

'Why, were they refugees?' said Marigold.

Nobody answered for a moment, and then Mrs Lawrence got up and tied her hair in front of the looking glass.

'Don't ask such silly questions, darling,' she said.

Mr Lawrence threw open the window. Across the garden came the sound of the church bells. The sun shone on the clean white frost, turning it to silver. Mr Lawrence had a funny, puzzled look on his face.

'I wish . . . ' he began, 'I wish . . . .' But he never finished what he was going to say, because the two cars carrying the Daly family and the Collins family drove in at the gate and up the drive, and the children with shouts of delight were running out on to the steps and calling, 'Happy Christmas, Happy Christmas!'

Other titles to be published by Pandora Press this year:

THE BIGGEST MODERN WOMAN OF THE WORLD

SUSAN SWAN

How to behave in the company of giants: do not ask 'how's the weather up there?' or talk about good things coming in small packages. Such insensitivity from a small person would have upset Anna Swan in her early youth for she was an 18 pound baby at birth and grew into a 7′6″ giantess. But after declaring a life of domesticity to be too small for her, she joined Barnams showplace of freaks in New York and discovered the strength in her size. And so unfolds a dazzling wacky tale of Anna's encounters with tall and small people, with crooks and with friends as she tours America as THE BIGGEST MODERN WOMAN OF THE WORLD and even travels to Britain, where she is summoned to Queen Victoria's court. But this is also a sad tale, of Anna's search for a home in a world in which she doesn't seem to fit.

This is an outstanding first novel from one of Canada's most exciting young talents that will appeal to all lovers of the absurd and all those who enjoyed Angela Carter's *Nights at the Circus*.

£4.95
0 86358 306 7

JESUS AND FAT TUESDAY

and other short stories

COLLEEN J. McELROY

'Colleen McElroy, a marvelous black poet and short story writer. She's just terrific, just a magnificent writer'
John Gardner, *New Orleans Review*

Church ladies, honky tonk piano men, politicos, prostitutes and nurses are the subjects of Colleen McElroy's America – cajun New Orleans, Mid Century St Louis and present day Northern California. Through evocative imagery and strong use of the oral tradition, these powerful, poetic stories conjure up the colour and vivacity of black America.

£4.95
0 86358 310 5

KINDERGARTEN

ELZBIETA ETTINGER

Few novels manage to capture the anguish of the individual struggle for survival as this does. In KINDERGARTEN, Elzbieta Ettinger understands the complexity of human reaction to surviving Naziism as a Jew, as she tells the story of Elli Rostow, a young Polish Jew born into a comfortable, bourgeois family who becomes a relentless fighter in the Warsaw ghetto uprising and in the Polish underground as she struggles to keep herself and Emmi, a young girl found in the ghetto, alive.

This is also an adventure story, filled with intrigue, deception and murder as Elli is forced to lead a double life. She goes secretly in and out of the ghetto in order to help other Jews as she and her lover Adam fight with the Resistance. She lives on forged papers to conceal her Jewish identity, particularly from her German employer and yet she has no choice but to remain silent while all around her Jews are exposed and taken to their deaths.
Elli becomes brave and tough as a result of her experiences. Her very survival is a testament to human perserverence and adaptability when threatened with annihilation.

£4.95
0 86358 311 3

BEAR

MARIAN ENGEL

'Bear like its smelly, shambling, dangerous eponym, turns out to be a quite unscandalous success'

Victoria Glendinning, *The Observer*

'Marian Engel writes with a fine lucidity of mysteries perceived and not glorified'

Jane Miller, *Times Literary Supplement*

'A startling and in many ways a beautiful novel with something of the power and innocence of primal myth'

Christopher Wordsworth, *The Guardian*

When Lou travels to an isolated island in the North of Ontario one summer to catalogue the contents of an estate she is apprehensive to find that the only other occupant is a large brown bear. But as the summer progresses they become friends and eventually lovers as Lou discovers a sensuality and independent strength she has never known before.

£3.95
0 86358 312 1